BACK CREEK

A Novel

LESLIE GOETSCH

bancroft
press

Published by Bancroft Press ("Books that enlighten")
P.O. Box 65360, Baltimore, MD 21209
800-637-7377
410-764-1967 (fax)
www.bancroftpress.com

Cover and interior design: Tammy Sneath Grimes, Crescent Communications
www.tsgcrescent.com • 814.941.7447
Cover photo: K. Rone Baldwin
Author photo: Sherry Insley

ISBN 10 Digit: 1-890862-52-5
ISBN 13 Digit: 978-1-890862-52-7

Printed in the United States of America

First Edition

1 3 5 7 9 10 8 6 4 2

For my Family

Chapter One

I'd stayed up late drinking beer with Cal. As I lay in my grandmother's old pine-spool bed, my head full of cobwebs, I alternately dozed and half-listened to the early morning sounds of Back Creek.

The Creek knew a deep peace that last Sunday morning of May 1975. I could feel it even in my little room on the third floor. Everybody said my great-grandfather had been crazy to build a three-story brick house on low land with a history of flooding, but we Barnetts have never been known for willingly following the advice of others. Personally, I was glad he hadn't listened to the naysayers, because I loved my little room, with its outcropping of small windows facing the Creek. I had the best view in the house—maybe the best view on our side of the Creek. And I loved the Creek.

As I struggled up from the sheets and summer quilt, I heard a gas-powered whine.

I wasn't sure where I'd placed my glasses. It's not like I'm blind without them, but I can see far-away things much better with them on, and I wear them most of the time.

The whine outside grew louder as I leaned over the side of the bed, feeling for my glasses along the edge of the braided rug, just below the ancient dust ruffle. My mess of brown hair fell over my face. Just as my fingertips reached the stiff metal of my wire-rims, my legs kicked up and I landed butt-first on the floor. Sitting up,

I flipped my hair back and pulled the frames over my ears. Somewhere in my fog, I realized that the whine had become a roar.

I bolted to the windows and peered out. The window glass seemed even wavier than usual, and the sun's glare more intense. I turned my head and glimpsed only dead calm directly below. Yet, the sound grew louder.

Jerking the frame open with a paint-ripping pop, I stuck my head out one of the windows to get a better look. Way up, almost to the boat ramp near Dandy Park, I could discern a white outboard boat racing down the Creek. My stomach lurched as I recognized the sleek square bow of a Boston Whaler.

The Creek's mouth faces to the east, cattycornered to where the York River meets the Chesapeake Bay. I watched the boat head toward that opening, churning plenty of white water behind it. Straining my eyes, I could see only a lone figure, standing up at the steering wheel—tallish, with long hair streaming behind him. I brought my head back in from the window, removed my glasses, and rubbed my sun-dotted eyes, trying to imagine what kind of crazy fool would be boating this early, this loud, and this fast on a Sunday morning.

I leaned back out the window to shout a righteous "Slow Down!" So as not to wake my father two stories below, I positioned my hands like a megaphone around my mouth, but I didn't have a chance to get the first word out.

Everything froze in me as I watched the boat veer toward a long-abandoned pier still standing at the mouth of the Creek. When the boat met the pier, it sounded like a bomb exploding. I saw the wood fly—the creosoted planks of the pier, and the white plexiglass of the hull. The boom echoed up and down the Creek.

Within a few minutes, the water's churning white peaks had settled to the silver calm of the morning.

It was as if nothing had happened.

Chapter Two

The Barnetts have lived on Back Creek for generations. It's where all our stories begin. Sometime back in the late 1700's, Elias Barnett, an indentured servant, completed his service suspiciously early, and moved his family to this pine-laden peninsula situated on one of the hundreds of deep creeks in tidewater Virginia. Nothing grew here except debt, so the Barnetts turned to the water to make a living, just like most folks who ventured this far.

Relative success in oystering and crabbing led the Barnetts to higher education, and heading into the twentieth century, family members traded in their water-tied livelihoods for college degrees and business suits. In the late sixties, when more and more newcomers invaded—doctors and lawyers and shipyard vice-presidents who wanted to build their big houses on the water—we were considered an old line family of Back Creek. Our brick monstrosity remained, a tribute to the Barnett inability to follow friendly advice or the latest trends.

I come from a long line of storytellers. My fraternal grandmother, after whom my sister Lillian is named, told her stories as the self-appointed family aggrandizer. She tended to dwell on the triumphs of the Barnetts in local politics, or on their brave wartime exploits.

She also believed that my grandfather, Kenneth Barnett, Sr., held the greatest promise of all the modern-day Barnetts. But the night before he was slated to take up his destiny, to begin an appointed judgeship on the Federal District Court in Richmond ("Next step, the Supreme Court," she said), my grandmother woke up to find him dead of a heart attack, right in the bed beside her. I don't think she ever got over that shock. And, until the day she died, just before I turned five, she was determined that my father would live out *his* father's judicial ambition.

But Daddy, always better at telling stories than living them, is a reluctant and not terribly successful lawyer. He's always enjoyed talking to people about their problems, and knows the law well enough to help them. He just can't, or won't, keep up with all the writing and filing of motions. In addition, he'd rather go into the office late on Monday, and start his weekend early on Friday, or maybe even Thursday.

It was a good thing Daddy had his father's hefty life insurance proceeds to fall back on. He was an only child, and with the income from those proceeds, Daddy didn't have to worry too much about generating income from his law practice. He could keep his family in comfort, at least materially.

I can still see myself, when I was little, curled up in Daddy's lap in the evening's half-light, listening to him talk while he sipped his bourbon and sugar-water. Daddy taught me how to crab and how to steer an outboard. He taught me about the generations of Barnetts and about their lives and deaths on the Creek. Daddy taught me to love Back Creek, and he taught me to love stories.

A lot of people in Back Creek wondered how he ever married Mother, a pretty girl off a small, failing tobacco farm in North Carolina—a girl who had never seen this much water before; who didn't know how to swim, how to steam crabs, or how to dress for a cocktail party at the Yorktown Yacht Club. I'd never allowed myself to wonder how and why they had come together.

Before my older sister Lillian left home, just before graduating from high school, we seemed like a happy family, with Thanksgiving dinners and boat trips to prove it. But after Lillian had her final fight with Daddy and stomped off to New York City, he started spending a lot more time working on his sailboat designs and sleeping in the little den off the study. Mother came home later and later from visiting her sister Grace, whom she'd moved up from North Carolina to live at the Eastern State Hospital, which was much closer to us.

Where was I when all this was going on? I had my nose buried in *Jane Eyre* and *Hamlet* and *The Scarlet Letter*—drama and romance that seemed more real than my family or my life as a high school student. I was also traveling across the Creek whenever I could, to sit on top of the old 30-foot Silverton, permanently docked directly across from our house, and to talk with Cal, who had taken up residence there after returning from Vietnam. I'd come to know Cal, who was 23, through my father, who was also a Civil War fanatic. To me, Cal had always been a good listener and a welcome escape from my side of the Creek.

We never talked much about anything in particular—in fact, I don't remember Cal talking much at all. For me, it was just good to sit above the water, sip a little beer, and look at the Barnett house from a different perspective. I spent a lot of time on Cal's boat that summer.

So when I try to tell the story of the summer of 1975, Daddy, Mother, Lillian, and Cal all figure in. Only by coming to know their stories could I understand my own. Only by diving under the surface of the Creek could I find the bottom and plant my feet in the muck. The story started with the boat plowing into the pier that Sunday morning in May, and the locating of Tommy White's body, which had sunk well below the wreck, a diver's weight-belt tied around his waist.

It was late in the morning before they could actually find and identify his body. The pier was a disaster of splintered wood. The Coast Guard and the York County Police arrived on the scene within 30 minutes or so, but not before a crowd of bathrobed Back Creek dwellers made their way outside to solemnly watch and whisper. After they were shooed away, the Coast Guard sorted through the wreckage and located Tommy's body on the bottom, wrapped around a piling just at the edge of the channel.

Later, I told the Coast Guard what I had seen before the boat hit the pier. After hearing the part about the pilot's long hair, the police thought a woman might have been at the helm, and began a frantic reassembling of the search party. But then someone remembered that Tommy had been sporting a ponytail since his unexpected return from New York City in late March. That explanation seemed to satisfy everyone.

My father retrieved Mrs. White, Tommy's widowed mother, who had moved from her bungalow in Back Creek to a condo in Hampton, Virginia once Tommy had left and the developers had swooped in. Everyone agreed that Daddy should be the one to break the news to her and to bring her back. He had seen to Mr. White's will, and to the selling of their place, and, naturally enough, Mrs. White leaned on him.

The Coast Guard labeled Tommy's death a boating accident. That Sunday afternoon, as I explained carefully what I had seen from my window, I could sense no one wanted to admit the obvious—that he had deliberately steered the boat, at high speed, directly into the pier.

At first, this bothered me—not that they didn't want to believe my story, but that everyone seemed satisfied with theirs. I didn't protest. I knew their story about an "accident" would be more of a comfort to Mrs. White, who spent the afternoon on our stiff living room sofa, silently leaking tears and grasping onto my father's arm.

So I did what else I could that morning to be useful—I brewed coffee, took the Coast Guard officer up to my room to show him the view, retrieved a bottle of Jack Daniel's at my father's behest, and made apologies for my absent mother, who was visiting my Aunt Grace at the psychiatric hospital up the road.

The Coast Guard and County Police finished their reports and paperwork some time after lunch, and the neighbors, who had drifted in with the tide of official cars, returned to their homes. As my father spoke to Mrs. White in his low, lilting tone, the late sun lighting up the room, I cleaned up. The poor woman was still wearing her aqua housecoat and a fringe of pink curlers she hadn't had time to remove. Twilight was arriving by the time he could finally take her home, a little drunk from the whiskey he had persuaded her to drink to "help her sleep." I listened as the tires of our decrepit station wagon rolled along the gravel of our driveway.

After piling the last of the coffee cups in the sink, I tiptoed over to the kitchen's bay window and looked hard to find the tiny light inside Cal's boat. He was probably up reading some Civil War journal—when I rowed over to visit, I often would find him immersed in a soldier's story. As I gazed out on the silver water that stretched between us, I wondered where he'd been during all the excitement. He must have seen what had happened, just as I had. But Cal had pretty much avoided excitement of any kind since returning from the war three or so years ago.

I switched off the light in the kitchen and felt fatigue wash over me. I knew Daddy would soon return, and probably Mother, too, unless she stayed over, as she sometimes did, in Williamsburg. Daddy would settle into his deck chair with a nightcap. He would come inside eventually, but long after I had headed off to bed.

In the mist of my sleep, I would hear the comforting sounds of the screen door creaking softly and then the scratch of the little latch fitting into the lock. In my dreams, I would hear the floorboards give a little as Daddy tiptoed to his bedroom in the den. His shoes would hit the floor, and the bedsprings would protest a little at his weight.

My mother would return to the house unannounced and unnoticed, closing her bedroom door softly behind her. The house would grow silent, except for the lapping of the water against the muddy bank, and the banging of a rope on the empty flagpole across the Creek.

But my dreams that night, the last Sunday of May 1975, were filled with rushing water and the disturbing feeling that something big lay just beneath it.

Chapter Three

People on the Creek come together in hard times, and funerals tend to bring out the best in everyone, especially the women. I sensed this at an early age. Old Barnetts always seemed to be dying—aunts and great-uncles and once, a young cousin killed in the Vietnam War. Any kind of funeral is quite an event on the Creek, but a patriotic funeral, complete with a seven hunting-gun salute—now, that is something memorable.

For funerals, we always dressed up in our somber best and stood together as a family in the second pew at Dandy Baptist Church—Daddy in his immaculate pinstripe suit, Mother in her navy poplin suit, my sister Lillian in whatever struck her fancy, and me in "something appropriate" purchased for and worn only at funerals. I'm sure we made a nice picture, and often wished that photographers were present at funerals, as they were at weddings, to capture the dressed-up occasion for the sake of family togetherness and posterity.

To attend Tommy's funeral that Wednesday morning, I had to take the day off from school and miss the final assembly. But school was already beginning to seem a distant past. The summer loomed somewhere in the not too distant future, as did the red brick of the University of Virginia, which I was destined to attend. Charlottesville, with its mountains and manicured lawns, had seemed a promising new landscape in the winter of my senior year, an appealing escape from the redneck football players and idiot cheerleaders who filled the high school halls. And with everyone in my family off in their own directions, it would give me a place of my own. But now, with the coming of summer, the inevitable prelude to fall, it felt too far away, too different.

Somehow, for me, solving the puzzle of Tommy's fatal incident was becoming much more interesting and real. On Tuesday, between exams, I'd ducked into the library to look up Tommy White, class of 1970, in the York High School yearbook. He stared up at me with a shy smile, his chin pushed out over a crooked bow tie. Next to his picture was printed a terse summary of his high school activities: *JV Track Team, 9th, 10th; French Club, 10th, 11th; Thespian Club, Secretary/Treasurer, 12th.*

Because it was a small school, all seniors were given a full page in the yearbook, to do with as they pleased. Tommy called his "Dreams and Wishes," and thanked his mother for "all her help"—not too many clues to be found there.

I flipped through the book, and though I came across no more pictures of Tommy, there were plenty of my sister Lillian, also class of 1970. Her long blond hair and doubtful smile were hallmarks of her popularity. Lillian Barnett and Tommy White, on opposite ends of the alphabet, were, apparently, at opposite ends of the high school social scale, too. But this was information I already knew. I would have to look to other sources to find out Tommy's story.

Upon her return early Monday morning from visiting Aunt Grace, Mother had closeted herself in her bedroom, emerging only to make a few phone calls, to consult with Bernice, our maid, and to instruct me on the necessity of finding something "appropriate" to wear to graduation Friday night.

This, of course, was completely unnecessary, because I planned to avoid the entire graduation hoopla, including the class party and especially the actual ceremony under the lights of the York High football field. It's not like anyone would miss me or that I would miss anyone else.

I wish I could say that I'd been swept along by the hurricane that was Lillian's high school presence, or that general knowledge pegged the Barnetts as thinking they were too good for anyone else. But the truth is that I passed through high school like a shadow, doing what I had to, getting good grades, avoiding the popular crowd, or any crowd at all. High school wasn't of great interest to me: I was far more absorbed by the fiction I read than the fiction I lived.

I had not revealed my plan to skip the graduation ceremony to either of my parents. I nodded my head at Mother's suggestions, knowing that when push came to shove and the time grew near, they would both feel relief when I persuaded them not to go. I would celebrate the end of my high school career the way I wanted to—sitting with Cal on the front of his boat, sipping on pony bottles of Rolling Rock, and watching the stars brighten in the sky.

We hadn't heard from Lillian, who was still in New York, for maybe six months. If I'd thought to call her and tell her about Tommy's death, my yearbook research convinced me she wouldn't care—in her brief communications, Lillian had long ago declared a disinterest in Back Creek developments. So just the three of us would be attending the funeral.

I got ready by sneaking down at night to inspect the shattered pier and the pieces of the Boston Whaler that remained. I waited until I heard the chink of Daddy's glass in the sink and the soft swish of my mother's bedroom door closing. Then I pulled on my old Keds, laces long gone, and walked quickly, placing my feet down carefully so as not to disturb the gravel driveway until I came to the overgrown trail leading along the bank to the end of the peninsula. The moon was my only illumination as I stood in the silver dark, observing the uneven white plexiglass pieces amidst the splintered planks from the pier.

At the accident site, I didn't touch anything, and, for some reason—maybe because it lay on county-owned shore and was, therefore, the county's responsibility—no one else did. I tried to figure out the story behind the story, but it remained a jumble.

~~~

The day of the funeral, which was held on the first of June, a blindingly bright sun pulled me out of a stream of complicated, water-filled dreams. It couldn't have been much past five in the morning, but I am, and have always been, an early riser. Throwing off the covers, I listened to the customary early morning Creek sounds—the hollow metal ring of the rope hitting the flag pole, the gulls putting up plaintive cries, the heartbeat rhythm of a waterman's boat engine chugging in the distance.

For my morning ritual—checking out Cal's boat across the Creek—I pulled on a pair of cutoffs and creaked across the floor-boards. The white Silverton rested next to the pier. No sign of life was visible, but I knew Cal was inside and that he would not join the parade of solemn cars when they headed up Route 17 to the cemetery today. Since I'd known him, Cal pretty much ignored everything having to do with church and crowds.

As I peered out one of the little dormer windows, just as I had four days earlier, I heard some rustling noises downstairs— unheard of in our house before eight o'clock. I abandoned my post and tiptoed down the back staircase to the kitchen, which, besides my bedroom, was my favorite room in the house. It was a big old country kitchen, with nicked pine planks for flooring and stained pine for walls. An original wood stove took up much of one corner. Probably new technology in its day, the stove now functioned only as a temporary point of deposit for dirty dishes and unread newspapers. There wasn't much cabinet or counter space. The original Barnetts, largely uninvolved in actual food preparation, were served their meals in the now unused dining room, on the imported Spode china, still displayed in the tall mahogany cabinet.

When we ate together as a family, it was always in the kitchen, seated around the big oak table in the center of the room. A large pantry stood off to the side of the stove. My father continually stocked it with cans of beans, Spam, and spaghetti sauce, "in case we're ever attacked." I couldn't believe the Communists would be much interested in Back Creek. I steered clear of the Spam.

Windows completed the boundary between the pantry and the screen door opening out to the deck. Through those windows, you could identify the snake tail of the Creek's beginnings, which wound around to Dandy Park—the boat ramp, and the only asphalt way off the peninsula. Looking left, you could see the widening span of water opening out to the York River. And, if you strained your eyes a little more, you could even make out the turbulent area where the York met the Bay.

Of course, if you gazed straight across, you would be looking at Cal's boat, which remained in its place at John Whythe's marina. This morning, my eyes followed just that path. Without my glasses, I could only see a big blur of white, so I walked closer to the window, actually pressing my nose against the glass. As I concentrated, a soft chink of china cup against china plate surprised me from behind and I nearly jumped out of my skin. When I jerked my head around, there was Mother, dressed in her suit, hair done up in a neat bun, and navy pump heels resting uneasily against the floor.

"For mercy's sake, Grace, what are you doing up at this hour? And where are your glasses?"

As I faced her, the warmth of the morning sun on my back, I had the distinct feeling that something unusual was up, despite the standard query about my glasses.

"I left them upstairs. I heard a noise. I was about to get ready for the funeral—you know, Tommy White's funeral." I watched her finger the delicate cup handle. "That's what you're dressed for, right?" I threw a glance at the battered coffee pot plugged in next to the stove. She ignored my question.

"Go ahead," she said. "Get yourself a cup." Whether I should be allowed to drink coffee had been a topic of longtime family debate, with Mother insisting it would stunt my growth. At seventeen, I said, could I really expect to grow any more? Anyhow, because I was the tallest female Barnett around, maybe I should stop growing. We'd gotten tired of talking about it, and I usually made sure to drink my morning coffee early, before anyone saw me. Ironically, she didn't bother me too much about cigarettes. Growing up on a tobacco farm must have colored her judgment. I was the only one in the family who didn't smoke like a chimney. When I was ten, one inhaling adventure left me green and throwing up, and that was enough for me.

"I know you drink coffee in the morning." A pause. "And I know about the beer-drinking across the Creek." She lifted her cup and gazed back out the window.

So I made my way across the kitchen, grabbed a mug from the sink, and rinsed it out. Pouring in the brown steaming rush, I repeated my question.

"I've been up since three," she said dreamily. "I just can't seem to get out the door." She came back to the kitchen. "Grace, stop blowing on that mug. It's not polite."

"The funeral's not until eleven," I said. I glanced up over the edge of the mug.

"Oh, now, I really intended to get to that funeral. I've known Addie White for so many years, and her boy's accident is such a tragedy. But . . ." She worked to place the coffee cup precisely in the saucer.

"But *what?*" I asked.

"But it's your Aunt Grace." She punctuated the sentence with a final clink of cup into saucer. "She wants to go back to the farm in North Carolina. I told you the cousins have up and moved to Greensboro, and there's no one to take care of the farm, which they've been unable to sell. So I was thinking that maybe it's time for me to straighten things out down there, pretty it up so somebody'll buy it. And I thought I'd take Grace down with me.

Maybe she'll find some peace there." Mother stood and began brushing invisible crumbs from her jacket.

My mother's sister, Grace, for whom I was named, had been "staying" at Eastern State Hospital, the "loony bin," as the locals called it, for the last several years. For reasons not explained to me, my mother had taken responsibility for her and, with my father's permission and financial support, rescued her from the shrinking family tobacco farm in North Carolina. Mother was a little vague on the reasons for the rescue, and I'd gone to visit Aunt Grace only once.

She was an artist of sorts, and hadn't seemed crazy when I talked with her. But the wild red and purple landscapes that covered the walls of her tiny white room had given me nightmares for several nights. After that, Mother alone visited her sister every Sunday, and sometimes stayed over until Monday morning. My mother called my Aunt Grace *her* "saving grace"—whatever that meant.

My mother had left home before, for several days at a time—once, for as long as a week—but she'd always returned. We just told people she was visiting relatives or, more recently, seeing Lillian up in New York. The truth was, I didn't know for sure where she went, and I came to understand my father didn't, either. I just made myself believe that all mothers left home occasionally to take care of crazy sisters.

I watched while my mother patted her hair and put on her lipstick, peering into a tiny drugstore compact. Two of her pretty, rose-colored suitcases (one more than usual) stood waiting by the staircase. As I watched, Mother left with a click of her heels on the pine floor and a brush of her lips against my cheek. I hadn't heard the gravel-crunching wheels of the taxi she had called.

But there sat the china cup, uncleared from the table, still bearing faded lipstick marks on the rim.

I wandered over to the big window. All I could see was the usual—Mr. Whythe raising his controversially large flag in front of his marina; the crabbing boats puttering from pot to pot; and watermen shaking out the chicken wire to release the struggling crabs. I could see Cal emerging from his boat, getting ready to continue scraping the hull of the three-masted sailboat he was being paid to restore for some Richmond banker.

As always, Creek life continued, even with loss and leaving. So I would continue, too, putting away for now the powerful hurt in my heart always produced by my mother's goings and comings.

Chapter Four

Daddy and I stood in the parking lot of the small church. Someone had just finished mowing the neatly squared lawn; small green clumps of wet grass littered the walkway.

I smoothed Mother's black linen skirt, which I had selected from her closet—it was slightly short for me and a little tight, but it was funeral dark. Daddy stood ramrod straight. He looked handsome and almost dashing as he offered his arm to Mrs. White. A quick shot of whiskey with his coffee had given him "backbone," he said. I could feel the sweat trickling down my legs and wondered how he could always look so cool.

A big crowd was waiting in front of the tiny church. Almost the entire Back Creek community had turned out, including a bunch of Tommy's high school classmates. No one seemed quite sure how to act. We'd gone to funerals of young men killed while fighting for their country, and knew the flag folding and other protocols that went along with a military ceremony. But this was something different—there just wasn't much to say about a boating death on the Creek involving someone who'd been away such a long time. So, once we filtered into the church and crowded ourselves into pews, white-haired Reverend Burke offered a few words of comfort.

I only half listened to the old reverend. Frankly, I had trouble taking my last image of Tommy and connecting it with God and salvation. Mrs. White, gripping a soggy handkerchief as if she would never let it go, was sitting quietly now, stifling sobs that made me feel embarrassed for watching her. I turned my eyes away, searching the crowd to see who was there, to wonder who had talked to Tommy last, and to think about the absent Cal.

He hadn't even gone to his own father's funeral, though he'd gotten leave from the Army to fly home from the hospital. My father had told me this. Daddy also said that Cal was getting full disability from the Army, though he was as fine physically as I was. When I asked Daddy what he meant, he dramatically held his finger up to his head, and waved it in a big circle around his ear.

Cal and I never talked about such things—about things that had happened to us, or about things that *hadn't* happened to us. We'd talk about the Creek, or about what we'd like to do someday, like traveling the Inland Waterway (that was Cal) or writing down all the Creek stories (that was me). Sometimes, we didn't talk at all; we'd just "sit and be," as he liked to say. I tried to imagine him at the funeral, tried to see his bony frame towering at the back, his streaked blond hair combed and pulled tight with a rubber band, his fingers fiddling with an unfamiliar collar.

Thinking about his fine, straight blondness made me push back the mop around my face, which was even more of a mess than usual because of the humidity. I realized I'd never seen Cal in anything but old khakis and t-shirts, and so my image of him faded into the side-burned faces of the boys around me, trying hard to appear grown-up but managing only to look worn and confused, like old men.

My eyes scanned the jam-packed pews, my head turning to glance at the back of the church, where the door had been left open to let in some air. As shafts of light filtered in from out-side, I caught a glimpse of something white. Daddy elbowed me gently and called my attention to the praying that was going on. I sat forward on the hard pew and folded my hands together. My senses were full of the sweet smells of talcum and lilies-of-the-valley, which nearly masked the church smell of mildew and workingman's sweat.

I stole a glance at my father. His eyes were shut tight and his hands folded together—he seemed to be praying earnestly. Maybe he was praying my mother would come back soon, or maybe he was praying for the weather to be fine for the regatta next weekend. I could never tell what my father was thinking—what daughter really can? As Reverend Burke encouraged us to confess our sins, I thought about our ride to the church that morning, and Daddy's coaching on how to respond to inquiries about my mother.

"Now, people are going to ask you about your mother," he instructed me, gesturing with the unlit cigar he'd taken to holding all the time. "Just tell them one of her people in North Carolina took sick and she had to go down there and take care of 'em." He nodded thoughtfully. "People are just curious. If you give them a believable answer, they'll be satisfied."

"But isn't that where she really went?" I said, trying to unstick myself from the vinyl seat. "That's exactly what she told me."

"Now, Grace, stop worrying about your mother. She'll be fine—she always does whatever the hell she thinks she needs to do, then comes on home, where she belongs. Why she had to go running off right now, of all times, I don't know. You'd think she'd have the common decency to get herself to this funeral. This is something tragic."

We were among the last to leave the church. Daddy insisted on helping Mrs. White up the aisle. She had seemed to be in a stupor, watching the casket as the funeral home men wheeled it out. I kept glancing at the dazed mourners making their way out of the church, and looked for that splash of white again, curious to know who would dare to wear white to a funeral, to stand out that way at such a time.

I could feel the humidity steaming up my glasses and longed to get back to the Creek and away from all this sweet-smelling heat.

Still holding on to Daddy's arm, Mrs. White walked with dignity up that long aisle to finally slide into the old black limousine. Just before she disappeared into the car, she patted Daddy's arm, like he was a little boy.

He smiled at her and passed her a handkerchief—he's the only man I've ever known to insist on having a starched handkerchief with him at all times. We climbed into our broiling station wagon and pulled out behind the limousine. For some bizarre reason, Mrs. White held Daddy's handkerchief out the window as the line headed slowly toward the cemetery. People must have thought some movie star was waving—or surrendering. We followed the white flag, our windows rolled down and hot air streaming in. I closed my eyes and concentrated on catching the air.

The Newport News Memorial Park cemetery was doing a booming business, what with the war and so many thousands of military people living on the Peninsula. It was beautiful, with tall trees and a little duck pond. The green tent for Tommy's graveside rose conspicuously in a newer section of the cemetery. Everyone was either seated on the wobbly folding chairs under the tent, or milling around the periphery. Daddy and I walked across the already browning grass. Hoofing after Daddy was a challenge in my platform sandals.

We stood under the edge of the tent, our feet just touching the plastic green carpet covering the ground inside. I avoided looking at the carnation-covered mahogany casket in front of me. Instead, I scanned the crowd once more, finding only dark suits and dark dresses. Reverend Burke continued his preaching while the ladies discreetly fanned themselves. I glanced beyond the tent, my eyes roaming first over the glistening stone monuments in the new section—familiar names rose up in bold letters from all sides. My gaze then traveled beyond the ring of "Dearly Beloveds," and back to the edge of the cemetery, where the grass grew longer and the trees offered shade to the living.

Then I saw it again—the white blur I had spied in the

church—standing out against the young pine grove hiding the highway. I took off my glasses, wiped them on my skirt, and put them back on. The white was still there. We were called to bow our heads in prayer, but ignoring Daddy's elbowing, I focused my eyes as hard as I could. With a realization that came so fast and furious it almost hurt, I knew, just from the defiant slouch and the blond cascade, that the figure in white was Lillian, watching the funeral from a distance.

With my heart and brain racing each other, I bowed my head, just as Reverend Burke had instructed, but I concentrated on what to do next. Should I tell Daddy? *Could* I tell Daddy? What was she doing here, anyway? What if he and Lillian made a scene right here at Tommy White's funeral? They had made quite a scene five years ago, when Lillian left town. Then again, maybe his feelings had mellowed. And maybe she was sorry she'd left. I glanced up at his bowed head, his eyes tightly closed, his lips moving in silent prayer. Out of those lips had come some pretty harsh words, all directed at Lillian.

I said "amen" and raised my head. The white figure was still there. *What would Mother do?* I asked myself. I tried to imagine her standing next to us. I tried to imagine tapping her gently on the shoulder, pointing to that figure in white. My imaginary mother opened her mouth as if to speak, then faded into the crowd, leaving me to figure out what to do on my own.

Fear suddenly overcame my ability to reason—fear I wouldn't reach Lillian before she disappeared again. I couldn't lose two people in one morning, so, as Daddy, dabbing his neck with a handkerchief, made his way over to Mrs. White, I moved around him and ran toward Lillian, as best you can run in platform shoes on uneven ground.

Her face and figure became distinct as I approached, shouting "Lillian!" That was all I could think to say. She came toward me, her ankle-length dress flowing with her movement. Anyone driving by might have mistaken her for a wingless angel or a ghost. Even in her tent-like muslin dress—my memories had her dressed in tight jeans and halter tops, much to Daddy's and Mother's mutual disapproval—Lillian was still Lillian. The flawless features, the wide blue eyes fringed by startling black eyelashes, the shining golden halo you couldn't help but want to stroke—the impact of her physical beauty hadn't changed.

What was different was her aura—the way she held herself, as if she knew she merely had to wait a little and everyone would soon be tripping over themselves to help her. She flashed her siren smile and held out her ivory hands, and we collided, hugging. My sweaty fingers tangled in the fine silk of her hair as she gently pushed herself back from me. She held onto my shoulders and examined me. I guess I shouldn't have been surprised, but she now had to look up to see me.

"Well, Grace, I think you've grown!" She stared at me thoughtfully, then crossed her arms. "I drove down this morning and came straight to the funeral." She looked toward the crowd of mourners, gathered in little groups, preparing to head back to the long line of cars waiting along the road. Her gaze passed over the tent, with only the flower-covered coffin awaiting final deposit in the soil. For a moment, there was only the sound of cars rushing by on the other side of the trees, cars filled with people going to lunch, or shopping, or maybe playing hooky from work or school—people whose lives were no different than they had been a minute ago.

"How long has it been? Three years? Four?" Lillian's voice took on a less dreamy tone as she turned to face me.

"It's nearly five years," I said. "I remember because it was right at the end of seventh grade. But who told you about Tommy? I didn't know you even—"

"Where's Daddy? And Mother?" Lillian said.

"Well, Daddy's back there." I pointed toward the crowd walking away from the tent, Mrs. White still holding onto Daddy's handkerchief. She started to walk alone, hunched over, while a group of mourners, my father included, swarmed around her, like ants fighting over a discarded morsel.

"He's tending to everyone, like always. Mother . . ." I paused, not sure what to say. "She headed out again this morning, taking care of Aunt Grace, she says." My voice sounded funny.

"I guess some things don't change much," said Lillian. "I would've thought he'd make sure she came to this—looks like the whole Creek is here . . ." Waving her hand at the tent, she began walking toward an asphalt path that curved away from the line of cars. I followed behind, feeling hulking and huge.

"I'm sure she'll be back soon, like always." I repeated those words, finding them a temporary comfort. "So," I asked, "are you going to stay at the house a while?" I made my way over the uneven turf. Lillian seemed to glide over the same lumpy ground, the gauzy material billowing around her like a robe. Her pace increased as we neared the single car parked along the path—a beat-up red convertible.

The top was down, revealing a disaster of suitcases, Coke bottles, and cigarette butts. Lillian opened the door and slid herself into the cracked leather seat, then lifted her face up to me.

"Now, Grace, I'm going to drive around for a while—do a little sight-seeing—so you can prepare Daddy. Tell him I came home for the funeral. Tell him I ran into Tommy in New York and we were kind of friends. Someone was going through his stuff after the accident, found my number, called me, and told me what happened. Good thing, too, since my own family couldn't manage to let me know." She turned the ignition and a startling hum went up from the engine.

It was the same old thing, and I wasn't about to argue with her. Lillian hadn't called us since last Christmas, and I had a feeling she only called then to try to borrow some money. But there was never any use trying to defend yourself around Lillian.

"But what should I tell Daddy?" I said, raising my voice over the engine.

Lillian grabbed a pair of Yoko Ono sunglasses perched on the rearview mirror. "Say I've come back. That's all. Just get him a little used to the idea, okay?" She shoved the sunglasses over her eyes and worked on lighting a cigarette. The acrid tobacco smell wound around my head.

"Oh, and Grace, before you tell him, pour him a big one. And have one waiting for me, too. Now, go. I'll see you soon." I jumped back as she raced through the gears and skittered off, scattering gravel behind her. I watched her turn out of the cemetery and onto the highway, joining the ranks of the people who had somewhere to go.

I noticed the dust gathered on my sweaty skin, and felt the dribbles of perspiration making their way down my sides and legs. I thought hard about what I should say to Daddy. It was bad enough to have to be the messenger about Mother's departure that morning. He usually pretended he was merely inconvenienced by her absences, asking about where his black socks would be and who could get him some coffee.

But I had sneaked a glance at him as he sat on the deck that morning, still in his ratty old bathrobe, holding the mug of coffee I'd brought him. For the first time, I'd noticed some gray in his black hair. He was staring into space, his brows furrowed, like someone who'd misplaced something and was trying hard to remember where he'd put it.

The sound of engines firing up from the parked car-line called me back to the present. I walked at a faster pace toward our station wagon, still unoccupied and waiting at the back of the line. In desperation, I darted behind a shoulder-high headstone, unbuckled my shoes, pulled off my pantyhose, and started back across the cemetery in bare feet. The dry grass prickled, but I was definitely steadier and faster this way. When I reached our station wagon, the other cars were slowly peeling off onto the concrete trail. Daddy was helping Mrs. White back into the limousine. He noticed me, waving his hand and pointing to the driver's seat, indicating I should drive myself home. I got behind the wheel and grabbed the keys from under the mat, where they were always kept.

Pulling behind the rest of the cars in line, I was relieved to have the drive home to myself. It would give me some time to decide what to say to Daddy about Lillian's return.

25

Chapter Five

Having taken my time getting home, I half-hoped to find Daddy and Lillian already there, working out a truce, duking it out, or even getting drunk together. As I'd driven along Route 17, digging my heel into the rubber mat and pushing the accelerator down with the toes of my bare feet, I'd even imagined that Mother had come back and all three were happily together again.

But I returned to an empty driveway and a tomb-like house. I sat alone in the kitchen, watching a moth throw itself at the Tiffany lamp hanging over the table. I twirled my eyeglasses, trying not to see what I knew would be the true picture. If they actually all made it home at the same time, an even deeper silence would soon follow. I decided to head upstairs to make my usual escape into the moors of *Wuthering Heights*, to find relief in the much graver and more eloquent dramas of Emily Bronte's imagination.

I reached under my bed to retrieve the worn paperback, rescuing not only *Wuthering Heights*, but my other favorite escape, *Jane Eyre*. As I propped myself up on the bed and got ready to lose myself in the passions of Cathy and Heathcliff, I could almost hear my mother admonishing me, "Grace, why don't you pull your nose out of those books? Get out there. Listen to some real people tell some true stories for a change." And then I could see her shake her head and hurry off to her hair appointment or her sculpting class at the Community Center.

I sat up and focused. Surely, if I just thought hard enough, I would hear her sandals *clack-clack-clacking* down the hall. I concentrated with all my might. But I heard only the vacant sounds of the breeze against the pines and the outraged quacking of a mallard protecting his property. A little disappointed, and maybe a little relieved, I hunkered down in my unmade bed and buried myself in my books.

When I detected a high-pitched whine coming from somewhere outside, things were still happy at Wuthering Heights. Sliding off the bed and over to the window to check out the source of the noise, I had a breath-sucking sense of déjà vu. I looked up and down the Creek in a panic, but all I saw was Cal sanding away on the sailboat, perched on the main mast like a wiry monkey. The water looked like black silk—not the tiniest of wakes marred the surface. The whine grew louder, and I suddenly realized it was coming from the opposite direction—the driveway. Someone was coming home.

I flew down the steps and yanked open the front door, which we never used—it always stuck because of the humidity. The thumping percussion from some soul song heralded the arrival of Lillian's little red convertible.

"I was about to give up on you!" I shouted from the top of the wooden front steps. Lillian swerved onto the edge of the gravel and turned off the car, around which dust was still swirling. I stepped gingerly across the driveway—my feet were not yet summer tough.

Lillian got out of the car, catching a piece of her dress in the door. "Shit," she muttered and pulled the material out from the door, leaving a big grease spot on the white gauzy material.

Standing there in her bare feet, she didn't look so New York to me. In all the wind-blowing, her hair had lost its sleekness. She reached back into the car and, from a large leather bag, removed a mashed pack of Salems—Mother's brand. When she lit a cigarette, I noticed the match's tiny flare shaking. I first thought it was a breeze, but everything was dead quiet. She took a big drag, exhaled, and leaned back against the side of the little car.

"It all looks the same," she finally announced, flicking ashes onto the oyster shells lining the driveway. Though I stood beside her, she was not talking to me, but to some invisible body out near the water, and maybe to the Creek itself. I tried to catch her expression, but all I could see was the bright reflection of water and tall rushes in her mirrored sunglasses.

Everything else might be the same. Yet, something about Lillian was different—something I hadn't seen at the cemetery. I recalled an old image of her, leaning back against a car—it was the spring, before she left the house for what I thought was good. Lillian was laughing, all hard smiles for the football hero who had driven her home. Her hair was longer. I remembered watching from the kitchen window as her white teeth flashed in the twilight and the boy, with what he must have imagined to be a smooth move, leaned over to kiss her. But Lillian kept on laughing and moved aside just as he neared her. Ulysses himself couldn't have resisted her.

But this Lillian looked older—and tired. I waited beside her, digging my toes into the dirt at the driveway's edge. As I squinted in the setting light, I saw a heron standing tall and calm in the inlet just behind the car. I tried to feel like that heron looked: distant, regal, and in control. But I couldn't stop the rising tide of emotion I felt standing next to Lillian.

When we were younger, I had been Lillian's deputy, her attendant in every fairytale fantasy—even, on occasion, her partner in crime. As we grew older, I was just the little sister who took phone messages for her and, when she needed, to cover for her with Mother and Daddy.

While she lived here, she dominated our house and commanded our attention. After she left, no one spoke of her—and, if someone did, Daddy would kill any further mention of her with a single look. She became a ghost, with only her abandoned room to suggest she had ever existed in the Barnett house. I didn't know what to do with, or how to talk to, this living, breathing Lillian standing right beside me.

To steady myself, I studied the inside of her car—a jumble of camera bags; a huge, battered and taped-together suitcase; one high-heeled shoe; a crumpled grocery bag; and a few other items smushed together. The car interior told me she must have left New York in a hurry, yet it failed to answer my biggest question: how long did she plan to stay with us?

"Man, nothing changes around here, does it?" Lillian had a way of disturbing people, of shaking them up. I used to think she had to be pretty smart to know how to get to everyone. But after all this time and distance, I saw there was no such strategy—it was just some instinctive defense she put up.

"Oh, I don't know," I said, watching the heron stretch his graceful wings and take off from the marsh. "Some things change. You've been away a while." Lillian hadn't been around to watch Daddy, at night, shut himself up in his office, choosing for company his sailboat designs and a bottle of Jack Daniel's. Nor had she been around to hear Mother tiptoeing in late on Sunday nights, then shutting her bedroom door behind her.

Lillian exhaled a final plume of smoke, tossed the butt to the ground, and smashed it into the dirt with her heel. "You're right. I *have* been away—a million miles away! And things do change. You're right about that, too. When I left here, you were just a kid, and now you're practically all grown up. Tell me, how have *I* changed, Grace?" Lillian took off her sunglasses and curved her lips into a smile.

She looked tired and older, but I couldn't tell her that. Besides, I knew little of Lillian lately. Mostly, I had imagined her life in the big city. And my version of Lillian in New York made life at Wuthering Heights seem tame. "You know, Daddy should be home any minute," I said, changing the subject. "Maybe we should unpack and get you set up in a room, and figure out what we should say . . ." Nervously, I looked up the driveway.

"I was hoping he'd already come home and you'd straightened everything out. But you're right, again. And listen, I'm pretty wiped out, what with the driving and the funeral . . . and all. I'm going to need your help, especially now that Mother's not here. I hadn't planned—I know you can help me . . . It's one reason I came back."

As I considered what in the world Lillian could need help with, and why she might need help from someone else—especially me—she began reaching into the car and grabbing bags.

"Grace, come on, give me a hand with this stuff. Let's go fix up my old room. Can you find some sheets and towels?"

The sun was just a pink streak behind us as Lillian handed me a dusty leather camera case. When I nearly dropped the bag, and looked in her direction, I saw tears, and her free hand wiping them fiercely. Clearly, she hadn't wanted me to see her cry. "It's kind of nice to be back," she said.

Lillian's bedroom, or former bedroom, was down the hall on the second floor, almost right under my little room. It had become the repository of boxes full of Barnett memorabilia. In the wake of one of Mother's vague ventures to "take care of things in North Carolina," Daddy had gone on a generation-recording binge, collecting and cataloguing Barnett family documents and pictures.

The results of his long-abandoned efforts lay marked inside dozens of shoe boxes and liquor boxes, now stacked amidst the Indian print bedspreads and Rolling Stones posters. After she walked out, Daddy made no secret that he considered Lillian's room to be empty space, and proceeded to fill it up as fast as he could. After one glance at the mess, which even loyal Bernice refused to go near, we turned and headed down the hall, to Mother's room.

"I'll just stay in here until Mother gets back," Lillian said. "I can't deal with all that mess right now." Lillian dropped her bags to the floor and collapsed onto the delicately quilted bedspread. The room had the sweet gardenia smell of Mother, and, for a minute, I just stood there, inhaling her essence. I could see my flushed face in the small square mirror on her dresser, flanked by tiny amber bottles standing at attention on a lacy dresser scarf. Next to the dresser stood the double bed, rescued from some Barnett attic. Her flower-patterned spread lay neat and tight, the pillows plumped and piled against the headboard—until Lillian sprawled across the bed.

We both found our eyes caught by the unframed charcoal sketch hanging on the wall across from the bed. The precise lines and shadows presented a large spreading oak tree in an empty field. The leaves, the roots, and the scars of time were painstakingly etched in the drawing. Somehow, the fineness of the lines only added to the depths of the shadows. The effect was a deep sense of desolation—certainly not what I wanted to wake up to every morning. I turned toward Lillian. We nodded in agreement, then burst into laughter.

"It's got to go!" she declared. And so I carefully took the sketch down and placed it against the wall, tree-side in.

"Maybe I can hang some of my pictures up there. They can't be as depressing as that thing!" Lillian struggled up from the pillows and reached for one of the canvas bags she had tossed to the side of the bed. As she fished around in the bag, she said, "I think I threw some decent shots of Soho in here. That's where I lived for a while, you know."

The hint that she might hang around a while threw me into silent piddling—finding towels, clearing closet space, playing hostess. After raiding her closet earlier that morning for the now very wrinkled black skirt, I already knew Mother had left a good deal of space there.

Lillian pulled out a series of black and white photographs and examined them, lips pursed and eyes narrowed. "Not too bad, if I do say so myself," she said, handing me the photos. As I sorted through the shots—of uniformed schoolchildren crossing the street from a bus stop; of an old woman inspecting an apple at a fruit stand; of a tall woman with model-like good looks, head shaved, striding down the street holding hands with a heavy-set man—the city came alive. I could almost hear the cars honking, the taxi drivers shouting. The pictures had a three-dimensional quality to them.

"Tell me about New York," I burst out. "It must be so different, so . . ." Words failed me; I knew only the slow rhythm of the Creek, and nothing about the fast beat and hum of the big city.

Lillian settled back against the pillows. She smoothed over her wrinkled cotton dress and, glancing at the black and white pile I had neatly stacked beside her, folded her hands across her stomach. "Oh, Grace," she said, "it *is* a different world up there. I couldn't have possibly known what I was getting into. I left here in a state and just found myself on a Greyhound, with 'New York City' on the little sign in front. All I could think was 'I'm getting away from him. I'm getting out of Back Creek for good!'" She paused. "Do you think that's what Mother thinks—when *she* leaves?"

Lillian's question, coming completely out of the blue, pulled my eyes over to the framed snapshots lining Mother's nightstand. There was one of the three of us, seated in our green wooden canoe and brandishing paddles. I must have been about four years old then—you can hardly recognize my face because of the life jacket riding up around my neck. Kneeling in front and behind me, Mother and Lillian wore the same brilliant smile for the camera, undoubtedly perfected for my father during his photography phase. I turned my eyes back to the real Lillian, who was wearing a different kind of smile as she remembered her first days in New York.

"So I arrive in New York and get off the bus—I have a couple of names that some art teacher gave me, but I have no idea how to find any of them, or even how to ask how to get there. The first thing I see is a bum in a top hat wheeling a shopping cart and singing 'Someone to Watch Over Me,' and I know I'm not in

Back Creek any more. The place is all concrete, all cars and bodies and horns honking. Everything is moving—fast. I had never realized just how slow everything moves down here."

I seated myself on the edge of the bed, still holding onto the hand towels—white, with the fancy script monogram—I had found in Mother's bathroom closet. Lillian continued her story, which assumed a rehearsed feel as she went along.

"It took me a while to get used to things in the city. I stayed pretty mad at Daddy for a long time. I moved from place to place. One guy I met along the way encouraged me to use the camera and to take pictures, so that's what I found myself doing. When I left for New York, I'd thrown that camera Daddy liked so much for a while into one of my bags, though I didn't know why at first. But later, I figured out I was supposed to take it. To me, the city looked clearer through the lens. So I kept taking pictures."

She stopped abruptly and rolled across the bed, digging through another of her bags, and pulling out a large yellowed envelope. "Here's some more stuff. You can look at it—I've got to go to the bathroom." She threw a stack of black and whites at me and pushed herself off the bed.

Carefully shuffling through the pictures, I noted the variety of perspectives and the different faces. But I almost dropped them all when the shot of Tommy White popped up. I held the picture close to my face and studied it. He was sitting at a café table, framed by two poles holding up an awning. He wore jeans and a t-shirt, and sat with his legs crossed, left arm resting on the table. His right arm was lifted in a wave. All you could see of his face was a toothy smile. He looked happy—a lot happier than he had in his yearbook picture.

I waved the picture at her as she emerged from the bathroom. "Lillian, what's—" I started, but she was already talking.

"This one guy had a crappy old studio apartment near the river. I used to look down at that dirty water, with all that stuff floating in it, and I'd think about the Creek and about you all sometimes."

"Lillian—"

"I'd remember the boat rides and crabbing parties—all the things we did on the water when we were little and they seemed happy. Up there, the water is filthy, it stinks, and it's plain nasty. Nothing like the water here."

She stopped abruptly, glancing at what I held in my hand and cocking her head to one side. "Oh, so you found that one. Yeah, that was in the spring. He wanted me to take a picture of him he could send to his mother." Lillian grabbed it from my hand. "I guess I'll give it to her when I see her next," she said, stuffing it into a pocket. She held up her hand, saying, "Listen . . . do you hear that?" I did hear it—the creak of the deck steps and the slap of the kitchen screen door. Tommy disappeared again, temporarily.

Daddy was home.

Chapter Six

❧

My eyes met Lillian's as we listened to his settling-in noises—the refrigerator door opening, then shutting; shoes tossed
down on the pine floor; water running for an instant; a muttered,
"Now where is she?"; and then, finally, a bellowing question,
"Grace?"

I jumped off the bed, shouting, "I'm right here, Daddy!" and
grabbed Lillian's hand to pull her with me. She hung back at first,
but I held on, and both of us walked out to greet Daddy.

Daddy was already talking when he saw us. "Grace, whose car
is that out front?" I squeezed Lillian's hand harder and dragged
her into the hallway between the kitchen and the den.

"Daddy," I said, "I've got someone . . ." I looked at Lillian and
added, "I've got a surprise for you." And defying the Barnett
family distaste for surprises, I thrust Lillian into the kitchen and
announced, "Look who's here!"

An ice tray slipped out of Daddy's hand, ice cubes tumbling
onto the floor. Daddy's expression of irritation was immediately
replaced by a look of horror as he processed the image of his eldest
daughter, whom he was seeing for the first time in five years. He
probably thought she was a ghost.

And Lillian did look like a ghost. With that white gauzy material floating around her body and a sudden, anemic pale, she could
have passed for one of those dead Barnett relatives we sometimes
listened for in the middle of the night. She and Daddy faced each

other while I automatically knelt to pick up the melting cubes surrounding our feet. I ducked and waited for the shouting to begin. But all I heard was what passed for silence on a Creek summer evening: the drone of insects and the swishing sound of water against the shore. I deposited what I could into the sink. Daddy and Lillian just stood there, their blue eyes like mirrors. Everyone always said how much Lillian took after the Barnett side. Watching the two of them standing there took me back six years, to when I was twelve and had watched another such scene.

It was in the fall, when the Creek reflected the oranges and browns of the few hardwood trees brave enough to grow near the shore. I had the cold I always get when the seasons change, and I was upstairs, holed up in my room, re-reading *The Diary of Anne Frank*. My fever and the book gave me terrible feelings of desolation and actual, physical cold, though it was probably just as warm then as this summer day. I could hear the sounds of my mother talking with Bernice, and I knew Lillian would soon be home from school. But I found a strange comfort in the isolation and the feeling of abandonment, so I remained upstairs, burrowed under my quilt.

Then I heard the kitchen door slam and Daddy's unexpected holler, "Rosemary! Do you know what that daughter of yours has been doing?" I tossed the blanket aside and tiptoed into the hallway, where I could hear better. I felt a little light-headed, so I knelt by the banister.

I knew I was not the daughter he meant. Lillian was always doing something to aggravate my father, from wearing "lewd" halter tops without a bra (he couldn't bring himself to say the word) to shaking the walls with her soul music. She came home late, and, once, not at all. She went out with boys whose families my father did not know. She made her own plans and informed my parents of them only when she felt like it. She came home drunk and woke up, hung over, late on Sunday mornings. Sometimes she missed church. I figured she did all this just to annoy

Daddy—and it worked. Daddy thoroughly and constantly disapproved of Lillian during her adolescence.

I'd thought she was brave and strong to do what she felt, or seemed to feel. But with 20-20 hindsight, I wonder if Lillian just didn't know what she wanted and took the path of rebellion, which was a pretty popular route then. I wonder if she might just have been avoiding herself. Maybe all our behavior boils down to that. At twelve, I was of course fascinated by her behavior, but not at all tempted to follow her lead. But I had to know what was going on then, so I held onto the banister and listened hard.

"Now, Ken," said Mother, "why don't you fix yourself a drink? I'll take Bernice home, and we'll talk about it when I get back." I could imagine my mother's graceful hands lightly touching his shoulder and checking his bluster—they were still touching each other then. "I'm sure Bernice doesn't want to hear about this. She's done raising her teenagers." Mother was rustling around in the kitchen, putting glasses or plates or something heavy away in cabinets. I heard Bernice's deliberate tread and knew she was standing by the door, swapping the slippers she spent the day working in for the old brown loafers she wore to and from our house.

"That's right, Mr. Barnett," Bernice's reassuring voice called out. "You just gotta let them go and do. Then they come back to you and do like they're supposed to." I'd never met any of Bernice's five children, but she talked about them often—I knew where they worked and the names of their spouses. My ears picked up the jingle of keys, the click of my mother's high heels, and the sound of the car's engine. My father, left alone in the kitchen, was popping the top on a Budweiser.

I started down the steps, thinking I could get him calmed down by the time Lillian came home or Mother returned. My bare toes felt cold against the polished floor of the front hall. Daddy was standing by the kitchen's bay window, sipping on his beer. I slid toward him, ready to call out to him. If I could just get him to tell me the story about Lillian he wanted to tell my mother, maybe he would see her behavior wasn't so bad, maybe even see it was funny, and then everyone would come home and we could have a fun dinner together. But the second I got close to him, we both jumped at the slam of a car door and a furious rush of steps coming up the deck behind the house.

And there was Lillian, mad as a hornet. I slid into the corner by the wood stove, trying to make myself invisible. She paid no attention to me—she had eyes only for Daddy, and a few choice words.

"What the hell are you doing sending the police after me?" Despite her heaving chest, her voice was even and calm.

Daddy stood right across from her, took another sip of his beer, and then placed the can on the window sill. He crossed his arms, cocked his head, and looked down through his bifocals. Now I really panicked. If he had screamed and shouted, I wouldn't have worried. But slow, deliberate head-cocking meant Daddy was really serious. County lawyers knew they'd lost their cases whenever Daddy looked through his bifocals.

"I asked Larry to run by and pick you up before you made even more of a spectacle of yourself. I'd like to know what you were doing, hanging out with all those dope-smokers and drop-outs."

Lillian faced him squarely, crossing her arms in an unconsciously identical manner. "Bullshit. I was at a concert." She flipped back her hair.

"Oh, a concert, huh? More like a goddamn orgy." Daddy uncrossed his arms and put his hands in his pockets, a posture he took only when addressing a jury or a trespasser.

Lillian threw back her head and laughed, her hair falling down her back in a cascade of deep yellow. "Now what would you know about a 'goddamn orgy'?" She turned away from him and began walking toward the screen door.

"What the hell do you mean by that?" Daddy's voice took on a low, growling tone. Lillian was the master at pushing his buttons.

Just as she reached the front door, she turned back around. "I'm out of here. Don't wait up." Daddy removed his hands from his pockets and stood facing her. With their reserved fury, the two were mirror images of one another. Then Lillian flounced out the door, which curtly slapped shut.

Daddy reached out his arms—for a minute, I thought he was reaching for Lillian, trying to hold her shadow back. But he leaned forward and grabbed his beer can instead. I emerged from the corner I had backed myself into, and watched as Daddy took his beer and his angry thoughts out to the deck, where he stayed most of the night.

Something between Daddy and Lillian changed that night. She'd walked out, and though she eventually came back—that night or early the next morning—some rule of order had been broken.

And something was changing now, mutating right in front of my eyes. I stood close to them this time. As they faced each other again, the mutual fury was gone, replaced by a wariness and something like fatigue. I watched and waited and listened, but all I heard were the sounds of the Creek. The humidity of the dark June night was all around us, coming through the open windows with the confusing smell of new grass and old marsh.

Daddy found his voice first.

"Well, the prodigal daughter returns," he said, as if reading a headline from the *Daily Press*. "I guess we better kill the fatted calf and welcome her home." He moved slightly—and I realized he was drunk.

"Yes, I'm back, Daddy. Let's not make a big thing of this. Let's try to stay out of a fight, at least until tomorrow. I'm too tired." For the first time, I noticed dark shadows under her eyes, disrupting the fine porcelain quality of her skin.

So Daddy and Lillian stood facing each other again, only this time they looked like two punch-drunk fighters at the end of a round. Where were the fireworks I was waiting for? I remained between them. Daddy turned to me and I got ready for the sarcastic, dismissive comment.

"Grace, did your mother call?"

"Well, no, Daddy. I didn't know you expected her to. She hasn't been gone that long . . ." I lifted up my head and looked at him. He was still holding the dripping ice tray, which deposited tears of warming water on his pants. His white shirt, gray around the collar, had taken on a wrinkled state. His face looked unexpectedly wrinkled, too. Then there was that slight, unsure weaving, which had continued throughout what I guess you could call our conversation. Where had my always neat, always correctly-dressed father disappeared to? Would no one stay the same today?

I took the ice tray from his hand and placed it in the sink. This small action seemed to unfreeze everyone. Daddy began brushing off his pants with a determined gesture, and Lillian, her hand in a pocket, pulled out a cigarette and a nearly empty book of matches. I turned on the water in the sink and began rinsing the pile of dirty glasses accumulated there.

"It's been a long day," Daddy said. It came out like an apology.

"It *has* been a long day," said Lillian, actually agreeing with Daddy about something.

"Grace, I'm going to have one last cigarette and then turn in." Lillian made her way barefoot across the kitchen floor. The screen door squeaked shut with barely a protest.

As if given a cue, Daddy stopped brushing his pants and began to set himself in motion, picking up the discards of the day—his suit coat, a striped silk tie, a church program. He rummaged through the stack of papers on the wood stove, pulling out that day's *Daily Press*, which was still folded neatly.

"Addie White asked me to check on the obituary and the articles about Tommy's accident, so I'd better see what the old *Daily Press* had to say." He stopped in his tracks long before he got anywhere near the paper, and rubbed his eyes. "Then again, maybe I'd better get to bed. Grace, you'd better get to bed, too.

Looks like we're in for some busyness." He staggered out of the kitchen with the day's debris folded over his arm, leaving me to put things right in the kitchen. The unexpected quiet, in the wake of so much expected noise, made me uneasy. So I put the last glass back on the shelf, shut off the light, and retreated to the refuge of my room.

I found *Wuthering Heights* on the floor, precisely where I'd tossed it—a century must have passed since I'd last read it. After these last few days on the Creek, the moors seemed a pretty predictable place. I slipped off my shorts, shook out my ponytail, and turned out the little reading lamp by the bed. Now, in complete darkness, I took up my place by the dormer window.

As I did almost every night, I focused my eyes across the Creek, searching for Cal's boat. Sure enough, I spotted the tiny light from his cabin and knew he was reading. I knew he would read until the morning light began to filter across the misty water.

Cal had always had trouble sleeping, but the problem worsened after his return from Vietnam. This revelation, offered in a late night conversation, was about the only time he had ever mentioned Vietnam to me. As I knelt at my window, training my eyes on that small brightness in the vacuum of the night, I felt like things were as they should be—even after all the tidal wave changes of the day.

As I lay in bed, I considered the new puzzle of Lillian's return. I knew the only place I could properly sort this out was across the Creek, sitting on the bow of Cal's boat. So I decided to skip out of school early tomorrow. Because the last day before summer break was largely devoted to locker-cleaning and yearbook-signing, no one would take much note of my cutting out, and I would get over to see Cal early.

Comforted, I drew up my thin summer quilt and fell asleep inhaling the Creek's potent promise of summer.

Chapter Seven

❧

As I walked the York High halls that Thursday morning, grasping only a thin notebook with lots of pages torn out, all I could think about was getting over to Cal's boat. I felt a shifting current taking hold of me. The best things about school—the unselfconscious, self-avowed nerds who made me laugh in the cafeteria; Mrs. Richardson, my ninth grade English teacher; the library I loved—were now so much debris on the shore. I made a powerful effort to stay afloat as I moved through the building; collecting grades, cleaning out my locker, smiling.

I knew I'd never really been a part of things here—not like Lillian, who had plowed through York High School at high speed, churning up a lot of white. But that was my choice. I had just drifted along the best I could, friendly with everyone, close to no one. It was the only strategy I could come up with. I was never comfortable trying to worry about all the things everyone else seemed to be concerned with: who was dating whom, how short a skirt you could get away with, and how to buy beer with a fake ID.

I had never felt like a teenager, and folks noticed. My mother once said to me, "Grace, you were born an old woman." I like to think she meant I was born wise, but she might also have meant how impatient I was with my own generation. What went on in this school building had seemed not very real, and certainly not very important, in my eyes. What interested me was the Creek, the life it reflected, and the life that hid under its surface. This choice had never concerned me, but my near-absence from school came sharply home to me that morning, as the happy, excited noises of kids ready for summer clanged in my ears.

Shutting my locker—number 366—for the last time amidst the party-like atmosphere in the halls, I felt a surge of energy. So I tossed my notebook in the overflowing trash can at the end of the hall and walked out the building, passing the noisy masses as they headed for graduation rehearsal in the gym. For the first time, I did something entirely against the rules.

My inability to take the bus home required a long walk back to the Creek, so I headed over to Cal's side, planning to borrow his canoe to get back home later. I walked briskly along the back roads in the early morning heat, passing the rust-ridden house trailers with old Dodges and Fords stationed permanently in their front yards.

Pungent green weeds and black and orange day lilies grew between the drainage ditches and the hot asphalt. My pace slowed as the sun beat down on me—I had to wipe off my glasses once or twice. But even with the heat, my determination never flagged. Before ten o'clock, I was heading into Mr. Whythe's potholed driveway.

John Whythe owned the marina directly across the Creek from my family's property. The Whythes had lived on the Creek as long as the Barnetts, but had not chosen higher education as their means to advancement. Instead, they preferred to live off their waterfront property and their dubious connections to a first family of Virginia—the Wythes.

Mr. Whythe and my father grew up together, competing against one another on the county baseball field. Now, they occasionally shouted at each other across the Creek, and one night, in a fit of Jack Daniel's-inspired glee, Daddy fired off his cast iron cannon, a replica from the Civil War, in the general direction of the marina.

John Whythe retaliated by erecting the largest American flag in the Tidewater area, which flapped incessantly and sounded like a hurricane at night. To Daddy, the flag served as a constant source of irritation.

I could hear the flag even now as I made my way down the dusty driveway toward the piers. When I was younger, the marina had been a fascinating garden of metal and wood—mysteriously shaped engine parts strewn around the yard, and entire sailboat hulls propped up on sawhorses, waiting for scraping and a faster life on the water. The smells of motor oil, turpentine, and tar permeated every inch of the marina—they somehow seemed natural on this side of the Creek.

Daddy used to bring me across with him to gas up our little outboard. I would clamber onto the pier and direct myself to the shed that passed for a tiny store, which was filled with rubber fishing lures, dusty flashlights, and bloodworms and squid for bait. Mr. Whythe's mother, the only Mrs. Whythe in existence, would hand me a piece of hard candy from a glass jar beside the cash register. I'd return to find Daddy and John Whythe arguing the merits of state oystering restrictions or county zoning laws, or gossiping about the watermen they both knew so well. I was left to wander the yard and throw bread crumbs at the flock of mean white geese Mrs. Whythe used as an alarm system.

Though it was only across the Creek, the marina seemed like another world to me. When we got back to our side, I would marvel that it was really so close. Even now, as I approached the little dock where Cal lived in his immobile Silverton cruiser, I looked across the Creek at our house, hidden among the tall pines, and knew that being over here would give me a completely different perspective.

I drew in the sharp odor of heated-up tar and the rhythmic *scratch-scratch* of Cal sanding the old sailboat. He'd finished and launched others. But this boat was special—a huge three-masted job rescued from a boatyard on the Outer Banks. The owner, a rich banker from Richmond, wanted it hand-stripped to its original boards. He didn't care how long it took, or how much it cost, so long as it was done right.

Cal was certainly the right man for the job. To most people, he appeared to be in a fog. But around boats, he was all careful attention. And though he didn't have much tolerance for anything related to real life, especially calendars and appointments, he had the patience of Job when it came to salvaging a boat. It was a good thing this boat's owner was in no hurry. By the time Cal had the boat looking like he wanted, the man would be in a nursing home.

Cal kept at it, even in all this heat. I loved watching his muscled arms moving the sandpaper in ever-closing circles, the once graceful hull awkwardly propped up on land, out of time and out of place.

Cal's attention was so devoted to a spot of stubborn white paint that he didn't see or sense me as I drew up behind him. His bare browned back glistened with sweat, and his blond ponytail reached limply below his shoulders. Cal's constant companion, a transistor radio, lay on the ground near his feet, jangling out what sounded like high-pitched Jimi Hendrix. Cal nodded his head and sanded in time to the beat. I half-expected him to stop and perform a little air-guitar, which he was prone to do at odd moments. Cal did most anything at odd moments. Experience told me I should shout my arrival. He did not take well to surprises.

"Hey, Cal!" I tried to shout over the noise. I was drowned out by Mr. Whythe, who was firing up a lawn mower to take care of his two acres of crabgrass behind the house. No answer.

"Hey, Cal!" I shouted louder this time. Again, no response. Finally, I reached out and touched his shoulder. Cal whirled around, hands poised to rip someone apart. His sandpaper went flying and the radio received a swift silencing kick. Except for the dull background of the lawnmower, a sharp quiet settled. I stood there, feeling pinpricks of sudden adrenalin across my arms and a weakness in my knees. Cal scared the shit out of me sometimes.

"Jesus, Grace!" he muttered, sounding like an evangelist minister. "What the hell are you doing here this time of day?"

"I ditched the last day of school," I said, gathering myself. "I came to talk, not to attack."

"Well, jeez-*us*. How about letting a body know you're standing there! . . . Oh, come on, let's go get a cold one and sit on the pier. I was about to take a break anyway. Man, when that sun comes up over your back . . . I should just quit for the day." The eight-hour workday was not a regular part of Cal's life—probably the other reason he was still working on this particular boat.

Cal retrieved two beer cans from the styrofoam cooler that was his other constant companion. He might not have a clean shirt, but Cal always had a cooler full of ice and beer. I was unaccustomed to drinking beer before eleven o'clock in the morning, but in the spirit of the day, I took a big gulp. The two of us sat on the pier, our feet dangling over the water and our eyes squinting out at the gleaming Chesapeake, just beyond the mouth of the Creek. To the left, across the slow moving Creek, stood the shaded brick of Barnett's folly.

"Whooee, it's hot!" Cal generally liked to cool off by downing a few cold ones, which I could see he had in mind to do now. He was glad my visit gave him the excuse, but I could tell he was also glad to see me.

I was probably the only person who ever came to visit him. Both his mother and father were dead and gone, and he had no brothers or sisters. Even his arthritic aunt, and her donations of hamburger casseroles and banana bread, had stopped coming his way. Daddy was just about the only other person Cal enjoyed talking to, at least during his non-working hours. Especially in the summer months, Cal would arrive at our place, and he and Daddy would retreat to the deck, sip whiskey, and argue the fine points of Civil War battles and generals. I loved falling asleep to the low rumble of their voices drifting up to my open windows.

But today I was here for a purpose—this was no idle visit. I wanted to tell Cal all that had happened yesterday. I didn't want to get his opinion—I knew he would never give me one—but to hear myself tell the story of yesterday's developments, because I knew he would listen. And I must have dimly sensed that sharing my story might be the first step to understanding and healing.

As Cal popped open his second beer, I set my nearly full can on the pier and began my account of the day, beginning with my mother's taxi-ride from home. Our conversations always began this way, with me just jumping in. Being with Cal was about the only time I didn't wait to follow someone's lead.

"So your mother headed out," Cal interrupted almost immediately. He smashed his empty beer can on the pier. "And missed that funeral?" He might not participate in local events, but Cal always knew what was going on around Back Creek.

"She said she was going down to North Carolina to take care of the farm and her sister."

Cal wrestled around in the ice for another beer. "Don't you believe her?" he said.

"I don't know if I believe her or not. She seemed different this time. I don't get why she had to go now, with the accident and everything. You'd think she'd be front and center, directing the casserole-making. But that's not all." My legs swung faster as I prepared to deliver the big bomb.

Then, as I waved my arm at the dark brick across the water, I told him about the dramatic return of Lillian.

Cal stopped mid-sip.

"Lillian? Your sister Lillian?" Shading his eyes, he stared at the house, as if he could see her.

"The very same. Isn't it weird she came back the same day my mother left? She's been up in New York for five years now. Did you know her in high school?"

Cal turned his face back to me, creasing up his eyebrows in the bright sun. "Everybody knew Lillian," he said. Cal was often cryptic, but never ironic, and his comment confused me for a minute. But then he handed me my now warm beer.

"You'd better drink up. Sounds like some pretty crazy things goin' on over there. That Lillian is a wild one, if memory serves."

I took the beer and ran my hands up and down the wet can. "Maybe I should just stay on this side of the Creek," I said. Cal returned his attention to the Bay, and I was left to guess whether he was pretending not to hear me or was thinking about what I had said. "By the way, what do you mean?" I asked. "You were pretty wild in high school, and look at you now." Cal just took another gulp. "Anyway, she says she's back for a visit. I think it might be a long stay. But I can't figure out why. She hates it here. At least that's what she's always said . . ."

"Does she still look good?" Cal asked, almost surprising me.

No one could mention Lillian without talking about her beauty—even Cal, apparently.

"She's still got the hair everybody used to talk about, and that perfect skin. But if you're so interested, you ought to come over and see for yourself." I took a swig of beer, trying not to squinch up my face at its now metallic taste.

"So," I continued, "as soon as my mother finds out Lillian's home and remembers how helpless Daddy can be without her, maybe she'll come back . . ." We didn't even have a phone number for Mother this time. At least when she went to Williamsburg, we could call the hospital—if we needed to, which we never did.

Cal rose to his feet, joints popping and beginning to stretch. He pointed toward a small crab boat shaking out a final pot.

"I'd better empty out John's pots this afternoon—they've been sitting in there since yesterday, and old Wainwright isn't above stealing other people's crabs." He reached over me and took hold of his cooler. Our conversations often ended this way, with Cal simply moving on to something else. Usually it was okay. But this time I wasn't quite finished.

"Hey, I have an idea," I burst out. "Why don't you bring those crabs over tonight? We'll cook and pick 'em—you, me, Daddy, and Lillian." I stopped short and looked down at my hands, cradling the beer can. I had to make sure it was indeed still me, sitting there on that pier, planning dinner for Cal and the family.

He considered the idea. "Well, okay, I guess." He started to walk down the short pier, the cooler bumping against his legs. I rose quickly and felt a wave of dizziness.

When he turned back to face me, I figured he'd reconsidered. "But I don't know what time I'll get over—I still have some sanding to do."

"That's okay," I shouted back. I thought about how I'd better find the steamer pot, get out the recipe books, and figure out how to do all the things Mother usually did. "Hey, Cal, can I borrow your canoe to get home?" I asked.

"You mean you don't want to cool off by swimming across?" he said with a laugh, standing at his boat's cabin door.

Swimming across the Creek was a kind of private joke between Cal and me. The older I'd gotten, the less I wanted to find out what was beneath that inky surface. Memories of stringy weeds and a mucky bottom kept me from wading out—even when the tide was low. Cal, as far as I knew, didn't like to take showers, much less dive into the water. Though he lived on the Creek, I'd never seen him so much as put a toe in it.

I looked down into the murky black below me, and could make out only the ghostly shapes of jellyfish. At first, I noticed only one or two, but then, as I looked closer, I could see dozens—so many that they almost drifted into each other. "No thanks!" I hollered and began to untie the rope holding the battered metal canoe to the pier.

Taking up the paddle he kept under the seat, I turned to wave at Cal. He raised his beer can and shouted over the sound of the rumbling lawnmower, "See you tonight—and we'll pick some crabs!"

I waved at him as the canoe floated away from the pier. But

he'd already ducked into his old Silverton, probably to catch a nap before he went back to work or to empty crab pots. Cal sure had his own lifestyle.

I envied him for that.

Chapter Eight

As I clumped up the back steps to our deck, Lillian lay sprawled in a redwood lounge, a glass of something reddish in one hand, a cigarette in the other. She wore one of Mother's silk bathrobes, looking like a balloon pulled back to earth and uncomfortable with gravity, but definitely landed. She set the glass down on the deck and struggled up to a sitting position, shading her eyes against the sun, now directly overhead in noontime intensity.

"Crabs? Tonight?" she asked. "Whose idea was that? God, I can't remember the last time I picked crabs."

"Lillian, you've been away too long. Haven't you missed it? I was just over talking with Cal. He lives across the Creek, in that old boat. See it?" I pointed to the Silverton. Lillian squinted in the general direction. "Anyway, he told me he was going to empty some pots this afternoon, so I said, why not bring them over here tonight and we'd cook 'em up and eat 'em."

Lillian ignored my social initiative, instead zeroing in on my choice of companions. "Cal?! He's way too old for you—he's my age. And didn't he get drafted?" She returned to her cigarette.

"We're just friends. I go over there and we talk sometimes. It's no big deal. He lives over there"—I made another panoramic gesture toward John Whythe's place—"and he works on sailboats. We're just friends," I repeated.

"Grace, you need to find . . . someone your own age. You need to get out."

Without knowing it, Lillian took on Mother's tone and words. She stubbed out her cigarette on the deck, sighed, and shifted her attention once more toward the shining water.

"You know, I've been sitting here and thinking all morning. Over there must be right where he came down the Creek." Her fingers drew a trail in the air, beginning with the distant Dandy boat ramp to the far right, continuing right in front of our house, and finishing with a final gesture toward the disaster zone—with the telltale yellow tape—near the mouth of the Creek. "I've been trying to visualize how it must have happened—how he must have looked."

It took me a few moments to realize she was talking about Tommy. I hadn't yet told her what I'd seen that morning. We'd been too busy talking about her.

"You know, I saw the whole thing," I said. "The boat came barreling down the water. He was standing straight up at the wheel, all this long hair flying back. I didn't know who it was until after they found him." I debated telling her about the diver's weight belt. I was pretty sure that wasn't public information—I'd overheard the Coast Guard people quietly talking about it that afternoon. They hadn't let anyone come near the accident site once the divers started searching for his body. I looked at Lillian, ready to give up this information, but something in her face kept me quiet.

Lillian shook her head and clucked her tongue. "Well, he must've forgotten about that pier being there. He'd been away from the water a long time. You know," she said, holding up an almost empty glass, "he called himself Thomas when I knew him in New York," as if that explained everything. Lillian worked much better with the tangible.

"It's too hot out here," she said. "Let's go inside. I'll fix us a nice cool drink—I found some strawberries and Daddy's rum." She stretched out her arms and insisted I pull her up.

I reached down and extracted her from the lounge chair, a bit surprised by her heaviness. As we crossed the deck toward the kitchen door, Lillian murmured, "'Saving Grace'—isn't that what Mother always used to say?"

"I think she was talking about her sister. If you remember, she named me Rosemary Grace—to remind me that *her* name always came first." Yet, right from the beginning, I was called Grace, and Grace I stayed.

"Well, you look like a saving grace to me. I'm still worn out from yesterday. I was kind of worried about what Daddy would say about . . . everything. But he was pretty quiet—not what I expected. Something must have happened to him while I was gone. Did you see him leave this morning?"

"No, I had to catch the bus before anyone was awake. I still go to school, you know. This was my last day." Lillian looked as if she was headed back to the bedroom. I grabbed onto her hand. "Come help me get us ready for the crabs!" I said. Small gestures were all I knew.

So the two of us entered the kitchen. Daddy had apparently headed out early for his Thursday morning Rotary Club breakfast at Pop's Diner, after which he'd attend to endless paperwork in his air-conditioned office in the Yorktown Municipal Building. Nothing short of an atomic bomb would interrupt his routine, even cataclysmic events involving his immediate family.

Bernice only came in on Tuesdays, although she would come out and cook dinner whenever Mother couldn't seem to make it back from her visits. Bernice never "cooked" much more than Peerce's Take-Out Barbecue, which we kept frozen in huge vats, ready for emergencies. Daddy couldn't seem to think about things like dinner and regularly feeding himself. He relied on Mother or, in her absence, Bernice. And with Bernice's annual month-long vacation coming up, he'd have to rely on me until Mother returned.

But tonight I had a crab feast to prepare—the first time in my life I would take full responsibility for a real meal. This was a significant occasion—the first time Lillian and Daddy and I would sit down at a table together in over five years. And while I drank a fair amount with Cal, this would mark the first time I'd actually eaten a meal with him.

I moved around the kitchen with a new energy, searching for the black enamelware steamer, the crab mallets, and the red-checked tablecloth with which we always covered the picnic table. I began to lose the emptiness I'd been feeling since listening to those taxi tires crunch up the driveway early yesterday morning. In fact, as I worked through Mother's organized pantry, index cards listing the ingredients on each shelf, I wrestled with a rising anger. I don't get mad that often, and I hardly ever cry, but I felt angry with Mother—angry that she would run away and make us all miss our chance to be a family again, even if it was only for a single meal.

I rattled dishes and pawed through drawers while Lillian blended and sipped various combinations of ice, fruit, and rum. We talked in dreamy ways about things we'd done as children. "Remember the time we all went clamming and got stuck for hours on that tiny island?" "Remember when Mother made a sculpture out of oyster shells and marsh grass we collected?" "Remember the time Daddy taught us how to start the outboard?"

If you'd been a fly on the wall, listening, you would have thought we'd been the world's closest family. It's funny how Sunday morning boat trips, dashing along the white-tipped waves and feeling the spray hit your face, can make you feel everything is just fine with the world.

As the clouds turned into long silver and pink streaks, and pine shadows stretched out over the Creek, our memory trail reached Lillian's adolescence, and we finally grew silent. Lillian had abandoned the blender and was fingering a beer can.

"Well, it wasn't all boat trips and picnics, was it?" she said.

"No, but there were some fun times," I replied, preferring to hang onto the nice pictures we had painted in our conversation. I was admiring my domesticity. Everything was ready for crabs—butter melted, mallets lined up, and the table set and even decorated with a few of the early wild roses that grew (with stubborn abandon) beside the deck's pilings. I'd readied coleslaw, corn muffins, and sliced tomatoes—all by myself, wearing Mother's apron and feeling in charge.

"But all the time we thought we were having fun," said Lillian, "maybe it was because somebody was trying too hard."

"I don't know what you mean," I said. "If it seemed fun at the time, then it must have been fun." I placed the silverware around the table, positioning each fork and knife with a studied deliberation.

"Maybe it was all fake—somebody's idea of how it ought to be. Have you ever thought about that?" Lillian rose up from the table and set her nearly full beer can in the sink.

"What do you mean?" I repeated, sounding stupid to myself. Visions of closed doors started to crowd out the nice pictures.

"Aw, Grace, it's hard for you to know. But Mother and Daddy were never a close couple. They stopped trying even before I left. Mother was always coming and going, doing whatever she does up in Williamsburg, and Daddy was forever holed up with whatever he does in that office. Both of them were trying to get somewhere else, but both were still stuck on Back Creek."

Lillian moved to the window to watch the striped sail of a Catamaran move slowly up the Creek—pleasure sailors returning at the end of the day. The setting light, soft on her face, erased the city hardness—and her alcoholic haze. I moved to lower the blinds. It had never occurred to me that Mother and Daddy might want to do anything besides live together on Back Creek.

"Wait," she said, touching my arm gently. "It's too beautiful, too peaceful to block out yet. In the city, I used to look out over the water in the late afternoons. All I'd see were big ugly barges, patches of oil, and God knows what else floating down the river. I'd close my eyes and try to see the Creek again, but I just couldn't pull the picture up in my mind. So I'd block it all out with the blinds."

She was still standing by the window, draped in Mother's silk robe. I untied my apron strings. "We'd better get dressed for dinner," I said softly. "Daddy'll be home any time now." I glanced again at Lillian. "And," I added, hoping she caught my drift, "I think we should be dressed."

When she turned around suddenly, I thought at first she was about to take issue with my suggestion, but she didn't speak, only reached out and gathered my hands into hers. Her touch and her tone kept me silent.

"Grace, last night and today—they're the calm before the storm. So I'm glad we had some time alone together to talk about old times . . ." She let go of my hands and turned back toward the window. "Daddy's going to have to know why I came back and why I'll probably stay a while. I'd figured Mother would be here. I could tell her, and she'd tell Daddy . . . So much for *that* plan."

Her hands were cool and smooth, her fingers long and graceful. Even while I was listening hard to what she was saying, I couldn't help but compare our hands. Mine were big-knuckled, muscular, brown, like a farmer's. Lillian's looked like an artist's. I pulled mine away.

"What are you trying to tell me?" I asked. The sun was getting to be just a blur on the horizon—we'd have to turn on a light soon. I pushed my glasses back on my nose, trying to see clearer in the gathering darkness. Filtering in through the open windows were the sounds of a boat engine sputtering down the Creek after a day of fishing. I leaned forward, waiting.

But, perverse as always, Lillian gave me a short laugh, shaking back her hair. "Aw, shit, I guess we take everything too damn seriously around here. Whatever's going to happen will happen, whether we like it or not. Don't worry, Grace. I'll put on something nice for your crab feast. Hell, I'll even put on a nice attitude." She began to walk past me, heading for Mother's bedroom. Before she left the kitchen, she returned to her momentary seriousness. "It'll be better," she said, "if we all get along for real this time."

I watched her retreating figure and had a sudden desire to run upstairs and bury myself in *Wuthering Heights*, where people seemed less complicated. I examined my afternoon's handiwork again. It now seemed ridiculous to think that luring Daddy and Lillian to a special meal together would solve everything between them. I picked up a stained wooden crab mallet and banged it softly against the cheery tablecloth. The jangle of the phone broke the heavy silence.

The phone rarely rang in our house, at least in the five years since Lillian left. So when it did ring, it had a panicky, emergency feel to it. At the sound of the second insistent ring, I threw aside the mallet and grabbed the white plastic receiver, my heart beating fast. I yelled, "What's the matter?" before I remembered to say "hello."

"Good Lord, Grace. Were you waiting there by the phone? You scared me!" Mother's voice came over the line.

I was struck mute again. She sounded far away.

"Grace? Are you there?" Pause. "Grace? That *is* you, isn't it? Are you alone? Is something wrong?"

"It's me!" was all I could muster, sounding like a three-year-old child. I stretched the white cord around me as I turned toward the window to stare out at the Creek. I could hear the sound of the shower running.

"Well, good. I was wondering if I'd gotten the wrong number. I called to let you know I arrived at the farm yesterday, and it looks like I'll need to be here a while." Another pause. From outside came the sounds of a little outboard—it must be Cal, coming over with the crabs. And then I heard the sound of crunching gravel— Daddy finally making his way home. A random thought came to me: if I could only keep Mother on the phone long enough, the four of us would be together again.

"I'm calling to let you know I'm okay. And to ask you to take care of things . . . because your father's going to need your help."

I felt my head start to swim. I'm not saying I thought I would faint, but as I held the receiver and watched the last sun rays dance on the Creek, a far away buzz started in my head and kept getting closer and louder. It was as if I'd been underwater too long and the pressure in my ears was building. I knew I had to either give up and sink peacefully to the bottom, or break the surface and take a breath. I could hear my heart pumping away, louder than the outboard outside, louder than even Daddy's approaching car. It was probably only a few seconds before I responded, but it seemed like hours.

"Mother, explain to me . . . why did you—things are going on here you need to know about. Lillian came back ..."

"Lillian!" she said, her voice sharp. "Is she all right? What does she want?" I could hear her take a draw on a cigarette and exhale loudly.

"I don't know. Everything's happened so fast. I'll get her for you . . . and Daddy's home—you can talk to him, too. Can you hold on a minute?" I held onto the receiver tightly, closing my eyes now, listening for her assurance that she would, indeed, hold on. I heard her sigh and take another draw. She was calming down, getting her thoughts together, measuring how much information to give out.

"Grace, I'm going to have to go. The phone lines aren't working at the farm, and I've had to walk all the way down to the next place to call you with coins in a pay phone. I'll call again soon. There are things I just have to get done here and I don't know when I'll be back . . . I don't know what to do about Lillian—never did, I guess. You'll have to find out what she wants. I have to go. Just tell everyone I'm all right. Bye now."

Then came the real buzz of the abandoned phone line. The sounds outside began to take over, and I knew that the three of them—Daddy, Cal, Lillian—would be together in that room with me soon. I carefully placed the receiver back in its cradle and thought about the conversation.

I'd failed to keep Mother on the line, and I failed to get her full story. I should have felt like crying or just running upstairs and hiding myself in my books again. But the buzz in my ears was gone now. In its place were the voices of Cal and Daddy, joking about something as they made their way up to the deck together, and Lillian singing "Natural Woman" in Mother's bedroom. I felt my anger rise again. I decided I wouldn't sink peacefully to the bottom, but kick my way to the surface.

Just then, the kitchen door popped open and Cal burst in, straddling a big wooden basket of crabs. "Amazin' Grace! Look at this haul! Let's get these suckers cookin'! Time's a-wastin'." He shoved the basket toward me and I waved it away at first. But his obvious pleasure in the catch was too much to resist, and I pointed toward the kitchen and the steamer, gleaming on the stove.

"Okay! Okay!" I said. "Let's get dinner going!" I moved toward Cal with my arms outstretched to take the basket.

With a deep breath and a laugh, I broke the surface.

By the time we all sat down to the steaming pile of crabs, the moon had risen. Daddy and Cal were in a fine, well-oiled state. I could tell Daddy had worked himself up into a storytelling mood, which was his best stage of drinking. His eyes took on a faraway glow and his cheeks a revealing ruddiness.

Daddy knew all of Back Creek's stories, and on nights like this, when the Jack Daniel's flowed and the moon was properly aligned, he would bring the stories to the table like a gift. Tonight, as Daddy meticulously picked a heap of crabmeat, I could see he was also picking through his story collection and, when the time was right, would bring forth a healthy harvest.

Lillian and Cal sat opposite each other, across the headlines of the newspaper spread over the table. They had greeted each other warily and awkwardly, like seventh graders at a school dance. I was sure Cal hadn't intentionally encountered a female besides me since coming home, and I couldn't help but feel a little pain when I noticed how he all but gawked at Lillian. He even ran his hands through his stringy hair, pulling it back tight in a ponytail, and tucked the ends of his t-shirt into his cut-off jungle fatigues. Lillian always made people feel like they should straighten their collars, pat back their hair, and check to see if their shoes were tied.

In the shower, she had somehow energized herself, and she sat cross-legged in her chair, her long white fingers delicately searching the bits of shell. She wasn't talking much, just glancing from Daddy to Cal as their argument about the Battle of the Peninsula moved back and forth.

I couldn't imagine what she was thinking. Cracking open claws with my mallet, I took up my usual observation post. The four of us seemed like strangers seated next to each other in a family-style restaurant. It wasn't what I had pictured, but at least we were all breaking bread at the same table.

I wondered at Daddy's calm. I didn't see him address her directly, but he was acting as if Lillian was there by his invitation—as if Cal and I were his guests, too. Clearly, he had chosen the path of least resistance, as far as Lillian's return went. Or was he so worn down by the last five years that he lacked the energy to react? I decided to tell him about Mother's call later, when he might remember what I told him.

It wasn't long before the newspaper covering the table was piled high with wreckage. Over everything hung the vinegary odor of the crabs, made heavier by the dark humidity seeping through the windows. As we pushed back our plates and wiped off our hands, there was a moment of silent appreciation for the carnage that had just taken place.

"'Feast for the gods,' your grandfather always used to say," Daddy declared.

Lillian stood up and touched her stomach gently. "I think maybe I overdid it," she said. I stood up, too, and took her by the hand.

"You just need to move around," I suggested. "Nothing a little plate-clearing won't cure." Still holding her middle, Lillian made a pretense of gathering up some paper towels while Cal piled up the plates and Daddy rescued his glass. He held the highball up to the light and squinted at the amber inch still remaining.

"You know, your mother had the same reaction the first time she ate crabs, except she was grabbing her stomach before ever taking a bite!" Daddy hugged the glass to his chest and leaned back in his chair. Lillian and I stopped our clearing to listen. We'd heard the story before, but Daddy's storytelling voice drew us in. Even Cal sat forward in his chair and propped his elbows on the table.

"We met for the first time on the train—I was coming home from Charlottesville, and she was heading back to North Carolina from that art school in Richmond. She carried this huge canvas, with the back facing out—a naked woman had been sketched on the front. 'A nude study,' I think was the artsy-fartsy term. But I told your mother, then and later, how could you notice any other woman—even a naked one—when she was around? On the train, I acted like I was interested in her sketching.

"I was pretty impetuous in those days. And probably a little full of myself, too. I asked her to get off the train with me in Newport News, and tell her folks she'd be home a little later than planned. And by God, that's just what she did.

"So we traveled to Back Creek together. Coming from a tobacco farm in the middle of North Carolina, she'd never seen so much water. And she sure as hell had never seen people eat things that came in hard shells and looked like monsters. When my mother—I swear she did it just to test Rosemary—put that plate of crabs, red and steaming, in front of your mother—well, Rosemary just grabbed her mouth with one hand, her stomach with the other, and ran out of the room.

"I laughed till I cried. Your mother laughed, too, when she returned to the table. And she did try one. I taught her how to open it, how to get rid of the bad parts, and how good that sweet white meat is, once you work your way to it."

He stopped talking long enough to drain his whiskey glass, then looked out the dark window. "But you know, she never did take to eating crabs, though she learned well enough how to catch and cook 'em. And my mother never did take to her. But that wasn't the only time I'd disappointed my mother with my choices. Hell, I've made a lifetime of it." I'd never heard Daddy finish the story this way.

Out of the corner of my eye, I noticed Lillian leaning over the table. She was twisting up her mouth and tightly pressing her lips. Her eyes narrowed and she grimaced. I thought maybe Daddy's story had gotten her in the mood to cry. Maybe she was realizing that, for whatever reason, Daddy was reaching out to her the only way he knew—by acting like things were normal, by carrying on with the everyday, by telling the same stories. But as I watched her grasp the edge of the table, lean over, and moan, I realized that wasn't it.

"I think . . . I need to go to the hospital," she groaned. It took me and everyone else, even Lillian, a minute to realize the source of this sound. Cal was the first to react, bouncing up and knocking over a chair as he backed away from the table. Daddy remained in his seat, stirring like he was waking up from a dream. Still clutching at the table's edge, Lillian accidentally pulled a pile of newspapers to the floor. Crab shells tumbled across the rug and beer cans dribbled foamy drops onto the table's pine surface.

I looked at Cal. He dug his hands into his pants pockets, as if he might find an answer there. "Why don't you give me your keys?" he said to me. "I'll drive her to the emergency room." My eyes met his and I found a steadiness.

"No, I'll take her. Can you stay here with Daddy? I'll call when

I get there. Okay?" Cal and I were acting like an old married couple, taking shifts with the children.

I put the plates I was holding back onto the table and gently placed my arms around Lillian's waist. I walked with her to the door and down the steps and got her seated in the old station wagon. As I leaned over to close the car door, I patted her shoulder and offered her some comforting words. "It's just the crabs—they didn't agree with you," I said. "We'll get you all fixed up."

But Lillian again moaned and muttered through clenched teeth, "No, Grace, it's the baby. I can tell."

Baby? I stopped dead in my patting. "What baby?" I managed. Lillian returned to her moaning and doubling over. With a realization that came so fast and hard that I knocked my head on the car as I jerked back, I pulled together all the differences I'd seen and sensed in her—differences I'd chalked up to time away and to city living: the flowing white dress, the bathrobe, her heaviness, her fatigue, her lethargy. I stepped away from the car, feeling the sharp sting of the gravel on my bare feet.

Lillian reached out and, nearly falling out of the car, grabbed my hand. "Grace, there's no time to explain. You've got to get me to the hospital. Now. I don't care what you have to tell Daddy. Just get me there!" She let go of me and resumed her fetal-like position.

I flew back into the house, my feet somehow toughened by my panic. Daddy and Cal hadn't moved from their positions. Looking at Daddy's flabbergasted expression, I knew I couldn't tell him what Lillian had just told me—he might disappear into that study of his and never come out again. Instead, I shouted at them as I raced around, locating my shoes, keys, and wallet, "Lillian's in a lot of pain. I'll call you from the hospital."

Moving suddenly, Cal grabbed my arm as I blew past him. "Call us when you know something. And drive careful." As I headed out the door, I could only toss him a nod over my shoulder.

Then I ran back down the steps and into the night.

Chapter Nine

And so I spent my graduation night in a gown—only it was a hospital gown, which the hospital people required me to wear over my cut-offs and t-shirt. This I realized when I woke up Friday morning in an uncomfortable, very green plastic chair.

At first, I was relieved that I'd been able to avoid the entire school ceremony by spending part of the night the way I'd wanted to—with Cal. Then the memory of everything else came crashing in and graduation, and, for that matter, high school itself, seemed a million years ago. I opened my eyes to the antiseptic white of a hospital room. I had laced my arm through the metal bars of the bed and was holding onto Lillian's arm.

Pale light filtered through the thick Venetian blinds and I couldn't help but marvel that Lillian could look so angelic and untroubled. Her hair made a golden frame for her face. Her hands, clasped together, rested on her stomach, a small lump under the sheets. I thought of Jane Eyre sleeping with her dying friend Helen Burns, and reached out to touch Lillian's shoulder. Lillian, still very much alive, unsettled herself and turned over, presenting her back to me as she continued to sleep.

I focused my eyes on the shaded window, glimpsing a rising pinkish sun. I thought about the bits and pieces of last night—the confusion of racing for the emergency room while comforting Lillian, having to nearly carry her through the hospital sliding doors, the doctors and nurses surrounding her like so many moths, and all the medical people disappearing through some large white doors with tiny, tiny windows.

I was left in the ridiculously cheerful waiting room—me and some rednecks sharing a pizza and waiting to hear about a friend who'd been in a motorcycle accident. The possibilities of life and death hung in that silly-looking room, with its sunflower posters and harsh light.

For the second time in a week, I was almost paralyzed thinking about how quickly people come and go—Tommy's fatal accident, my mother's leaving the day of the funeral, Lillian's coming home—and now this, a pregnant and very sick Lillian. Everything had happened so fast, and none of it made any sense.

Yet I knew I had been thrust into the middle of this mess, and I was beginning to sense that I would have to be the one to put the pieces together. These were not the romantic tragedies and comedies of fictional characters. This was the even stranger fiction of real people, and I would not be allowed to just sit back and experience it vicariously. I would have to live it right along with them.

At the sound of the door opening, I rubbed my face and yawned, just as a linebacker of a nurse barreled into the room. I knew I looked bad, and wished I at least had a toothbrush to get rid of the stale beer and crab taste in my mouth. The nurse, whose hard yellow tag read "Barbara," created quite a commotion, raising the blinds and lowering the metal bar on the bed. As Barbara began smoothing the sheets, Lillian stirred, turning her head to find my eyes. "Grace," she whispered in a hoarse voice, "is everything okay? Is the baby okay?"

Barbara, who overflowed the metal stool next to the bed, grabbed onto Lillian's wrist. "Oh sure, honey," she said, ignoring my presence and taking it upon herself to reassure Lillian. "You're gonna be just fine, and your baby's just fine. You just had some spasms, according to the chart. Lots of women have that problem with their first pregnancies—I assume this is your first. You're just going to have to take it easy while you're growing this baby."

She paused as she watched tiny hands move around a Timex planted like a mole on her wrist. "Now, sugarpie, we didn't notice any ring, and we were wondering if there's someone else"—she glanced at me—"like, well, the father, who ought to be contacted." She mechanically replaced Lillian's arm and scribbled something on a chart retrieved from the table next to the bed.

It was good to see the old spark of righteous indignation take over in Lillian—I could see it in her eyes. I sat up and pushed my hair out of my eyes. Before Lillian could let go of what was clearly forming in her mind, I burst in, "Oh no, that's okay. We're all . . . just fine, like you said, and we'll be checking out this morning. I think the doctor said that was okay."

Barbara pondered this, studying the chart before her, and said to me, "Before she can be discharged, one of those doctors will have to put his signature on this chart. I'd better catch somebody while they're still on the floor—you know, they all play golf on Fridays, and they'd sooner leave a patient in for another day than miss their tee-times." In her noiseless white shoes, she walked off, catching the door silently with her butt.

"That old bitch," Lillian began as she struggled up out of the sheets. "I'd like to contact *her*." She grabbed onto the bed's arm and lifted herself into a sitting position. "How is it her fucking business who to contact? Man, I wish I had a cigarette," Lillian muttered, working to tie up the back of her gown and search for clothes.

I moved across the room to bring her the small pile I'd neatly folded last night. As I handed it to her, I guessed it wasn't a good time to seek more particulars about the baby—like the identity of the father. I found it impossible to believe that Lillian could be so careless, so ignorant. It was a mystery even more perplexing than Tommy's death.

Lillian took her clothes with one hand and then sank back onto the flat pillows. Her free hand moved toward her eyes, wiping sudden tears. I'm not a crier, but those tears set my eyes burning. Lillian looked at the shirt and shorts. "You folded my clothes," she said. "I don't even do that for myself."

I waited by the bed. This was yet another Lillian I didn't know. I felt more comfortable with the angry one who had just made her presence known. Back up to a half-sitting position, she hugged the clothes to her chest, bowing her head over them. Then she raised her head and shook back her hair. "Did Daddy ever show up?" she asked.

I began folding a blanket crumpled at the end of the bed. "I called him as soon as they took you back, to let him know we got here and you were okay. That was close to two a.m. and . . . well, you know Daddy . . . he was just about passed out by then. Actually, Cal answered the phone. He stayed to take care of Daddy."

"Take care of Daddy?" she snorted, straightening herself up and removing her hospital gown. "Talk about the blind leading the blind. Anyway, I knew he wouldn't come." She jerked on her white dress over her bare shoulders and bare breasts—white on white. I averted my eyes and listened to the *creak-creak* of a cart with one bad wheel traveling down the hall. It made me think of the empty rope banging against the flagpole at night, across the Creek at John Whythe's.

"Lillian, *is* there someone we should contact?" I asked timidly.

"Not you, too!" she screamed. "Let me tell you just one thing, Grace. I'm the one stuck with this baby. It's mine—all mine. There are a lot of guys who could be the father, but just one woman's the mother. So don't bother trying to figure out that part of the story. Help me roll up these sleeves."

"But Lillian, what are you going to tell Daddy? What are you going to do?"

"Well, Grace, if I had all that figured out, I guess I wouldn't be asking you to help me, now would I? He was going to find out one way or another. Maybe he'll be too hung over to get upset."

"But I still don't get why you went to the funeral even before you came home. Why didn't you call ahead of time or something?"

Lillian eased herself into a standing position, combing out her hair with her fingers, then pulling it back in a knot at the back of her neck. Without the golden frame, her face looked pale and tired. She seemed to consider something, or maybe she was just concentrating on her hair. Finally, just as I heard the quick swish-swish of white shoes outside, Lillian spoke.

"Look, Grace, I know I owe you all an explanation. As I said, I was hoping to get Mother to do my explaining, but she flew the coop." I opened my mouth to tell her about Mother's strange phone call—I hadn't found the right moment at dinner. She held up her hand.

"I'm just trying to figure out what to do—what's best, you know. Coming back to the Creek is as far as I've gotten. I told you, Tommy and I were friends in the city. I thought I should come—to say goodbye. I never did when he left New York." She stopped just as Barbara pushed her way through the door, waving a piece of paper victoriously.

"I found one of the doctors to sign your papers, Missy. You can go home this morning." She stopped and looked Lillian up and down. "Oh, I see you're already dressed."

The chameleon Lillian suddenly changed her tune. "I didn't want to trouble you, because I knew you were helping me out, rushing around to get those papers signed. Now, I was wondering if you could do me one more little favor. You don't happen to have a cigarette on you, do you? For the ride home?" She smiled her old siren smile.

Barbara seemed to be at a loss. "Well, now, honey, you shouldn't be smoking, with the baby and all." She pursed her lips. "But you have had a bad night, and I can see how you might want to calm your nerves. Let me see now . . ." She first searched one white polyester pocket, then another, finally producing a wrinkled pack of Marlboros. Lillian gratefully took one cigarette and smiled again.

"A match?" she asked, holding up the cigarette.

Barbara rustled around again in one of her large pockets to produce a pack of matches. "Bill's Seafood" was advertised on the cover. She efficiently removed the top paper from the clipboard and spoke as she began to fold it in three sections.

"You all live on that creek where that boy had that bad accident, don't you? I declare, I've never heard of such a thing. I was just coming on duty—I have to work most weekends. You know, they brought him in, or what they could find of him. Of course, I couldn't see much, but . . ."

"Stop!" said Lillian, covering her ears. Both Barbara and I stared at her in surprise. Lillian raised herself up from the hospital bed and took the paper from the nurse's hands. "Grace, take me home. Right now."

Barbara was almost thrown into shocked silence, but she managed to react quickly enough to shout some doctor's orders at us as we left. "The doctor says to rest, that you shouldn't go up and down stairs, make an appointment for next week, and . . . don't smoke so much. It makes the babies small."

As we walked to the car, Lillian hung onto my arm. We found our old station wagon, parked at a crazy angle in the emergency room parking lot. The sunlight blinded us, and I could already feel the heat waves rising up from the asphalt. Helping Lillian into the front seat, I suddenly wanted more than anything to be back on the Creek, sitting on Cal's boat and looking over at our house, a comfortable distance from Lillian and Daddy.

Lillian slammed the door behind her as I made my way to the driver's side. She rolled down the window and flicked ashes out of it, seeming to study intently the windshield in front of her. "Take me home, Grace," she repeated.

The car started on the first turn of the key.

Chapter Ten

W hen we arrived home from the hospital, Lillian brushed past me and walked up the stairs to the bathroom. In her oversized white oxford blouse, she looked like a sad ghost, discouraged from haunting the lower regions. I paused in the front hall and listened hard for the sounds of other spirits—like Mother and Daddy. I even thought Cal might be hanging around. But I heard nothing except the gulls crying as some waterman dumped his bait.

I tiptoed down the hall to Mother's room. As I opened the door, I saw myself in the large mirror over her dresser and wondered for a moment what she might be doing at exactly that second. Maybe she was looking in a mirror, just as I was, wondering who was staring back at her, just as I was.

I took off my glasses and compared the features I observed in the mirror with the features captured in the silver filigree frame immediately below it. Only the hazel eyes and thick lashes connected us. My lips had none of the fullness of hers, reddened with lipstick and pulled back artfully in a smile. I dismissed the unruly mess of brown hair surrounding my face, which was no match for her neatly-styled blondness. I knew, without consulting the picture, that I was bigger, and had longer legs and wider feet. I knew my nails lacked her polish.

I wondered if she looked different on the farm down in North Carolina. I tried to imagine my mother in overalls, tying up her hair in a red bandana. I kept getting down to her feet and seeing her navy pumps, the kind she wore to nice luncheons.

As I ran my fingers around the frame, it occurred to me that she didn't fit on the Creek. She was always wearing not quite the right thing—a linen skirt when everyone else had their cotton shorts on, or her pink suit when all the other ladies wore sundresses. I opened the door to her carefully arranged closet, the summer clothes up front, the winter things pushed to the back. There was a lot of empty space in there now. Again, I thought how different this latest leaving felt.

A sharp creak from above—Lillian getting out of the shower, I guessed. I shut the closet door quickly, as if something might escape. I returned to the mirror, put my glasses back on, and attempted to pull my hair back with a rubber band I found in a pocket. I stuck my tongue out at my reflection and went in search of Daddy.

Walking into his office uninvited went against all my training as a Barnett. Respect for the property of others was an inviolable tenet. As long as I could remember, Daddy's office was off limits, especially to children with sticky hands and a knack for mess-making.

Bernice once ventured in to straighten up his papers and to dust. With pressed patience, Daddy explained to her that the mess was exactly as he wanted it to be, and that the dust was necessary to his "work." I was standing nearby when he offered this explanation, and I could see that it was on the tip of Bernice's tongue to ask, "What work?" but she, being the soul of tolerance and glad to have one less room to worry about, just said, "Yes sir," and never went near the office again.

As far as I knew, Mother never showed the least bit of interest in going in there, either, referring to the room as "Ken's room," and avoiding the entire hallway, with its collection of Barnett family photographs in sepia and dark frames. I studied these pictures sometimes, when nobody was home; the eyes seemed to follow me if I looked at them long enough. Once, when Daddy had left the door slightly open, I peeked into the office. But the sight of piles of paper and dirty whiskey glasses was enough to satisfy my curiosity.

So it was with great reluctance that I knocked softly on the office door and called out for him. Somehow, I began imagining that Daddy had had a heart attack, or fallen, or was stuck in there, helpless. Or, possibly, he was sleeping it off. Even that was better than imagining he just didn't care about Lillian or me. I called out again, a little louder. No response. So I pushed open the door and tiptoed in.

It was a small room, made even smaller by the collection of heavy mahogany furniture that lined its walls: one highboy, two dressers, and two mismatched nightstands. The office was the final resting place for some deceased cousin's odds and ends. I couldn't imagine Daddy had any use for the furniture, until I opened one dresser drawer and found piles of drawings—designs of sailboat hulls in all sorts of sizes. In the center of the room stood a card table, covered with more drawings and some balsa wood models of sailboats.

I knew Daddy was interested in sailboat design. Until Lillian departed the family, he would talk ad nauseam about the physics of sailing—at the dinner table to us and over cocktails to everyone else. He never showed much interest in actually sailing; he just seemed to like the idea of making the ride as fast and smooth as possible. We didn't own a sailboat or even the little sunfish I had learned to sail one summer.

But running my fingers along the dusty, painstakingly measured sketches and the delicately carved balsa, I knew for the first time that my father, who seemed so stuck in the past, had some dreams for the future. I was touching them.

Suspecting an indiscernible order to the chaos, I made sure I disturbed nothing. It was clear he had not been in here last night or this morning, so I left the room, closing the door softly but tightly behind me. I continued my search. He must be somewhere on the property—he would never just up and leave, like Mother.

The house continued to drip in silence—Lillian must have fallen asleep. I padded through the kitchen and out onto the deck to find some comfort in the sights and sounds of the Creek at morning. I felt dog-tired and dirty, but a few deep breaths and the sight of that calm water lifted my spirits. A long sleek sailboat, sails still stowed under a tarp, motored its way out to the Bay while two crab boats gracefully danced around their pots. A blue-gray heron stroked across the sky, and gulls cried out their songs. Looking down at the tiny stretch of low-tide shore below me, I saw fiddler crabs emerging cautiously from their holes, ready to chance a little more time in the rising sun.

Who could believe that Tommy's explosive accident, not even a week old, had disrupted these sights? Standing on the deck, watching the water flow out toward the York River and the Bay, I was reminded of the larger forces that are always at work. Life didn't stop long for much of anything.

Across the Creek, even as early as it was, I noticed activity. My eyes instantly went for Cal's boat, but it rested undisturbed—tied, as always, to the pier. No, this commotion was coming from over by Cal's project, the sailboat he was refinishing. At first, I had trouble recognizing Cal. He had a shirt on and someone was with him. I retreated into the house to grab the binoculars Daddy kept handy in the china closet by the door. Focusing the lenses, I could hardly believe my eyes. Beside Cal was Daddy, running his hands up and down that old hull.

I knew for a fact that Daddy had not voluntarily crossed the Creek in years—not since he'd had a run-in with Mr. Whythe over his crab pots. Back then, Daddy had ventured over in the little outboard to deliver the pots he'd accidentally run over days before. Some words passed—loud enough for the entire Creek to hear that Daddy was a "menace on the water" and that John Whythe "owed back taxes." Ultimately, Daddy paid for the pots and Mr.

Whythe began sticking to his own water when depositing his crab pots. It made for a good story, but Daddy stuck by his final words as he navigated back to our side. "I will never darken that side of the Creek again!" So he hadn't—until now, apparently.

I propped my elbows up on the railing and watched them talking, gesturing with their hands, laughing together. The binoculars gave me the funny sensation that I was standing right in front of them, and that they merely had to turn around to catch me spying on them. I guessed that Cal and Daddy had taken my "all's well" phone call to heart, because neither seemed at all concerned about our absence, nor about our possible presence.

More difficult to figure out was how Cal had gotten Daddy away from his pencils and blue-lined paper to put his eyes and hands on a real sailboat across the Creek, or how Daddy had gotten Cal to talk about his project. I couldn't help but feel a little sting of jealousy—Cal always abandoned his work as soon as I came along, even when I asked to see the boat and his progress.

But the two of them seemed to be having a grand old time. I watched them walk and gesture along the hull of the sailboat, which rested on sturdy sawhorses. It was strange, watching them so intimately from such a distance. Even with the heat beginning to radiate up from the deck boards, I couldn't seem to remove my elbows from the railing and put down the binoculars. I would have stayed there all day, I suppose, until Daddy suddenly turned and pointed at the house—and at me, it appeared. I lowered the lenses and quickly backed into the house, replacing the binoculars in the china cabinet and running up to my room to get cleaned up.

As I exited the shower, a towel wrapped around me, I peeked in on Lillian, who was curled up in the bed in her old room, boxes pushed aside. She slept peacefully, her head balanced on a pile of pillows and her long fingers crisscrossed over her stomach. I retreated to my room and, still damp from the shower, curled up in the unmade bed, sinking into sleep almost immediately.

I awoke to the smothering heat of late afternoon and the distant sound of voices. At first, I had the crazy idea that the murmurings were coming from old Barnetts lining the hallway outside my room, dismally staring from their faded frames. Too many Victorian novels filled my head with suspicions about these figures from the past and their desires to pop into the present. I started up from my bed, drawing the towel tightly around me, and peered through the crack in the door. No Barnett ghost greeted me, but I did hear louder voices coming from downstairs.

It was Daddy and Lillian. I couldn't hear the words—I could just sense the rise and fall of the volume. Filled with a sudden sense of dread, I crept out and crouched by the banister. With one of those déjà vu feelings I'd read about, I was transported back five years, to the day Lillian left, when I had stood just below, frozen in the front hallway, and listened to them hurl words at each other in the kitchen.

I had been up early that day, picking blackberries from the huge brambly bushes hidden in the woods along the driveway. Picking blackberries was a tricky business because those luscious treasures were guarded jealously by sharp and plentiful thorns. But I was pretty adept in my picking and I returned to the house with a bucketful of fresh ripe berries. My fingers were purple and my legs itched from dozens of mosquito bites, but it was worth it because the blackberries surely would make everyone happy and maybe create a temporary lull in our war-like atmosphere.

Remembering my berry-picking made me realize I was always trying to make peace through gifts—drawings I made, unusual shells I found on the shore, even a heron's feather. I guess I didn't know how else to respond to the tension I felt in the house.

That morning—a Saturday morning close to the end of my

seventh grade year—I entered the house swinging my bucket, relieved and happy to be barefoot and messy in a summer-like sun. I was headed for the kitchen when I heard the voices. It seemed much too early for that kind of noise. Mother and Daddy hadn't yet retreated to separate bedrooms. Nor had they begun their practice of sleeping late on the weekends. Lillian never rose much before noon any day she was allowed to, and when she did get up, she usually wasn't around long.

So when I heard voices, I was at first surprised, then kind of happy because I could present my triumph right away. I set the bucket down in the mud room just outside the kitchen and tried to rub some of the dirt off my legs, in case Mother was in the kitchen. But as I balanced first on one foot, then the other, and listened harder, I realized that the voices belonged to Daddy and Lillian. And they were mad—too mad to be calmed by a bowl of blackberries. I was about to enter the kitchen when my father's language froze me in my steps.

"Whore. That's the only word for you now—whore. How could you do this?"

"Please!"

"Doesn't family mean anything to you? Don't you have any respect for your mother and me, or yourself?" His voice had none of the careful, deliberate tone he almost always used with us. I had never heard my father use a word like "whore" before.

"Oh, that's great, that's just great," said Lillian. "I come to you for help, and all I get is a bunch of shit about the family."

"Come to me for—"

"Believe me, if I didn't think you were my last resort . . ." It was harder to gauge Lillian's voice—she always sounded like she wanted to fight.

"Come to me for help? Oh, that's rich. You got caught, Lillian—once and for all."

There was a pause. I picked at a scab on my elbow, thinking. Lillian was always getting caught doing things she wasn't supposed to be doing (as my parents took pains to point out to me), but this had to be something worse than usual—something really bad. Daddy rarely got involved in Lillian's behavior, except to comment editorially on it. He left reaction to my mother, who usually gave Lillian a "serious talk" and pronounced her "reformed."

Whatever Lillian had done this time, it must have been something that people could really talk about. By his own admission, Daddy's main criterion for judging our behavior was its impact on the family's reputation. When Yorktown Battlefield Rangers caught Lillian drinking with a bunch of boys, Daddy went after her. At the time, he was thinking of running for County Council and didn't need any midnight calls from journalists to wreck his electoral chances. I remembered his exact words that night because Lillian repeated them so often. Listening hard, I rubbed some spit on the bleeding scab and tried to sink into the wall.

A chair scraped the pine floors. Then came a drum roll of sharp clicks—Lillian's boot heels as she paced around the kitchen. "I'm going then! And I'm not coming back! I'll take care of this myself!" The shattering of glass punctuated her speech. I shrank from the sound.

"Then go! You'll end up back here and you'll marry the boy who's responsible." Daddy's voice had a controlled fury I had never heard before.

"What makes you think I know who it is?" she flung back.

Heavy steps entered the front hall. I held my breath and watched as he stomped past my hiding place and into his office. Right after the door closed firmly behind him, I heard the kitchen screen door snap shut and a clatter of footsteps move down the deck steps. Lillian fired up the engine of her little Volkswagen. As the noise of tires spinning and gravel flying grew more and more distant, I knew Lillian was gone and I sank to the floor, grasping my knees. Words I had read somewhere, "A bang and a whimper," floated around in my head, and I stayed in that position for the longest time.

~~~~~~

But today the voices were lower, calmer. There was no glass breaking, no chair scraping. Just a background murmur in ebbs and flows, like the Creek washing the shore at night. I braced myself for a sudden eruption, but the talk sounded almost domestic, and I wondered if I really knew either of these people—these people supposed to be my family. Maybe five years *was* long enough to change someone—maybe even two someones.

As I stood there by the banister, I could feel the soft early evening light start to descend over the Creek. I loved the peace that time of the day always brings, when you've finished doing all you can do that day and can look forward to a drink out on the deck, contemplating the water. The voices ceased and I waited to hear some angry stomping or doors slamming. Instead, I heard ice rattling in glasses and Lillian call out, "Let me get my cigarettes," just before the kitchen screen door squeaked open and almost closed.

The sudden clatter of the phone made me jump. It must have rung four times before I figured out I was the only one around to get it. So I dashed downstairs, wrapped in my towel, to answer it. That heavy black telephone had sat in the front hall as long as I could remember. Daddy never thought about replacing things, even when they didn't work too well.

Lillian and I had long ago discovered we could pull the phone into the coat closet if we wanted privacy. So far, this had not been an issue for me, but Lillian had spent hours in the darkness of that coat closet, sneaking cigarettes and conversations. I grasped the telephone now and, guessing it might be Mother again, squeezed myself into the closet. The combined odor of mothballs and ancient furs smothered me.

"Hello?" My voice came out muffled, as if I were far away.

"Grace? Is that you? I can hardly hear you. Are you all right?"

Mother's voice came over the line clearly. I could almost see her long manicured nails wrapped around the receiver at the other end. In spite of the mothballs, I could almost smell her gardenia scent.

"Mother! When are you coming back?" The words burst out of me. I realized I sounded like a five-year-old child with a cranky babysitter.

"Well, Grace, I'm getting along all right here, but I think it's going to take a while longer to straighten everything out. I called to see how you all are doing."

I assumed she meant Daddy.

"Daddy's okay. I can get him for you, if you just—"

"No, no, don't bother. I can talk to you. Is Lillian still there? Is she in trouble?"

I felt my breath falling out of me. How could I begin to explain the situation? "She came back because . . . because she needs help, I guess. I should let her tell you. I can get her, if you'll hold on."

"You just tell me what's going on. And fast, because I can't stay on the line long—I've had to walk down to the next place again. The phone lines still aren't up at the farm. I tell you, it's been something else, trying to get things working down here. Now, what did you want to tell me about Lillian?"

So I told her. I told her how Lillian had come back during the funeral. I told her how sick she had gotten at dinner.

And I told her about the baby.

I tried to see Mother's face as she silently took in the news. I tried to see the smooth skin on her forehead wrinkle just a bit. I tried to see if the hazel eyes would fill with tears. I closed my eyes in the darkness of the closet, but I couldn't form any mental picture of her.

"I had a feeling," she said.

She had a feeling? Lillian and Mother hadn't talked in months, as far as I knew. But maybe I didn't know everything. I uttered the only thing I could get out of my mouth.

"How?"

"Look, Grace, you're going to need to watch her—and your father."

"Watch her? Take care of Daddy? And Lillian? But I'm supposed to be leaving soon—" I stopped short. I believe it was the first time I'd ever said anything out loud about leaving the Creek. The words sounded hollow, even to me.

Mother's coolness returned. "Grace, you listen to me. You've never worried about being in the crowd, or dating, or wearing the right things. You've had your nose in some book or been perched on that pier across the Creek. And you've always been true to yourself and to everyone else. You'll do whatever you need to do, and you'll still have your chance to leave, when you want to . . ." Hot tears squeezed out of my eyes and mingled with sweat. "I waited too long to leave, and I can't come back now. You'll have to take care of things."

"But, Mother," I pleaded. "I don't know what to do. When are you coming back? You *are* coming back, aren't you?"

"Grace, I've got to go. I'll call again. You'll know what to do. You're stronger than you know. Goodbye now."

A distant click preceded silence again. I pushed my way up in the close space, my arm heavy with the receiver. I felt weighed down by Mother's words. What did she mean—*I was stronger than I knew?* I should have heard the sadness in her voice, realized her pain and indecision, and decided she might not be as strong as she thought she was. But, thinking I'd lost her, I was too busy feeling sorry for myself.

As I removed my sweaty, towel-wrapped self from the dark closet, emotion overwhelmed me. Slowly, I went up the stairs to my room. I got back into the shower, where the hot water could stream over me, where I could cry without anyone knowing. Even blinded by tears, I could see that Mother wasn't coming back, and all of us would have to find a way to live with that reality.

Chapter Eleven

🕊

After putting on some clothes, I surprised Daddy and Lillian out on the deck. For a second, they looked almost as if they were conspiring, and I felt like I was intruding. I shouted, in what sounded to me like an unnaturally loud voice, "Hey, I was looking for you guys!" Both turned in a single motion to look at me. I felt like I was on the other end of a zoom lens, where the figure suddenly looks miles away, despite standing right in front of you.

"Daddy," I burst out, as if I'd suddenly remembered. "I just got off the phone with Mother." For a second, his face shrunk back from my words, as if I'd slapped him. When the old creases took up their usual places, I realized he was drunk. "She's okay," I added. Daddy turned his face back toward the Creek and sipped at his glass, bobbing his head in response. I wanted to shake him. *Why was he drinking this way?*

"Grace," asked Lillian, "did you tell her I was here? When's she coming back?" She put out a hand and rested it on the arm of Daddy's chair. "Daddy and I talked and everything's okay. I'm going to stay here and help take care of things, at least until the baby comes." I suppressed a snort. It was becoming clear to me that Lillian couldn't take care of herself, let alone "things." Lillian took another sip of her beer. "Anyway, I'm sure Mother'll be back soon," she decided.

I looked at the two of them as if I were seeing them for the first time. This was not the proper father I had observed from a distance until last weekend, and this was not the wild, fascinating sister I had created in my mind. I planted my feet firmly on the sturdy deck planks and looked down at both of them, stretched out in the creaky redwood lounges. Like the beaches after a severe storm, the images I had clung to were being washed away by the events of this week.

"She's not coming back," I said. Daddy sat up and looked at me, his arm reaching down in slow motion to place his glass on the deck. "At least, not for a while, as far as I could tell," I said, backing off. "And she knows about you," I shot at Lillian.

Lillian sat up now, sending cigarette ashes and splashes of beer all over herself. "What did she say? What do you mean she's not coming back? She always comes back." Lillian sounded like a kindergarten child left at her classroom door on the first day of school. She stopped abruptly and shook off the ashes.

"Well, not this time." I was amazed the words came out of my mouth so clearly.

I heard the ice cubes rattle as Daddy lifted up his glass. For a moment, the only other sounds were the lapping of the water against the pier and one lone gull crying overhead. I walked to the deck railing, hung my elbows over, and wished desperately I could dematerialize myself like they did in *Star Trek* and reappear across the Creek, sitting on Cal's boat.

"You know, your mother was something else when I met her," Daddy said softly. Lillian looked at me, lifting her eyebrows. I waved her off—I'd heard this preamble plenty of times before. It meant Daddy would soon head off to his room, although I'd never heard him begin this story so early in the day. I watched Daddy's eyes take on a distant look, as if he was struggling to see something just ahead. Actually, he was trying to hold onto something far behind him.

"We met by pure chance," he continued, "on the train, when she was traveling back from that so-called art school. I was heading back home from Richmond, where my mother had sent me to buy a suit. Walking back from the club car, I saw her, just sitting there with a canvas practically bigger than she was, propped up in the seat next to her. The train was jerking along and, when I stopped to talk to her, I almost fell right into her lap. I can still remember what I said: 'I don't know why you bother painting on that piece of canvas when you're the greatest work of art I've ever seen.'

"Well, she was right off the farm, all done up in drugstore lip-stick and hand-me-down heels, studying in Richmond thanks to a beauty pageant scholarship. What did she know? I must have been the first man to talk to her like that, because she looked around like someone ought to arrest me. All that made me more determined to get her to come home with me for the weekend."

He paused and took a big swallow, finishing off the now watery liquor in his glass. Most families in Back Creek were sitting down to a nice, home-cooked meal, saying a blessing, and digging in together. But here we sat in our uneasy household, brought together by Mother's absence.

"I remember she had a blue linen dress on—all wrinkled up from travel. She'd spent an entire week sewing it from a fashion magazine brought home from the doctor's office in Durham, I found out later. The belt was a little too wide, the hemline a little too short, and the shoes were the wrong color. Even *I* could see that. But that's what made it all so charming. Rosemary always did have a way of dressing that made even the wrong things look right."

Just like Lillian, I thought. Daddy paused to sip his drink. Lillian lit up another cigarette, and I watched the red ashes glow.

"Well, we got along just fine on that train ride, and I persuaded her to get off in Newport News—turns out she really didn't want to go back to North Carolina right away. So she came and stayed with us here, like a foster child. I tried to teach her how to swim, but she preferred going out in the little outboard, over to York-town Beach, where we'd be alone in that crowd of people. At night, we'd sneak out to the cottage my uncle used to keep down there on the Point. We ignored my mother's eyebrow-raising. We played together for a week.

"We were like kids. I don't think she'd ever just played before. From the time she was little, she'd always had to work on that hopeless old tobacco farm. But she learned how to play the week she spent here. We fished and crabbed and drank a lot of beer. At the end of the week, we had to get back to real life. I was clerking for a lawyer my father knew up in Charlottesville, and she went back up to Richmond. We promised all those things you promise when you're young and you go your separate ways."

Full darkness had settled in around us—I could barely see the outline of Daddy's figure, lying on that lounge chair. No one had moved to turn on any lights; only John Whythe's cross-Creek floodlight reached over to illuminate us. The air was heavy and loud with insects' droning. Lillian creaked around in her chair—since coming back from the hospital, she'd had trouble getting comfortable almost everywhere. She never could listen as long and hard as I could, anyway. But she stayed quiet, just lighting up one cigarette after another.

I could feel my stomach rumbling and turned to go in and find some dinner. I knew that this was as far as this story went. But just as my thoughts ventured over to what might be canned and waiting in the pantry, Daddy cleared his throat and began again.

"Well, we did write, just like we promised, once a week the rest of that summer. But then fall started up and I was back to law school, and pretty soon, with the parties and the football games and the classes, I forgot about our week at the Creek together. So when my mother sent me a note on one of her fancy mono-grammed cards and asked, in her way, about Rosemary, I wrote back that I hadn't heard from her, and that there were plenty of good-looking girls right down the road at Sweetbriar. She breathed a sigh of relief when she got that letter. Some farm girl out of North Carolina wasn't her idea of a future daughter-in-law.

"But I got another short letter right after that. The handwriting was small and neat. Rosemary said she needed to see me. There was a 'problem.' Well, I couldn't imagine what kind of problem there could be. We'd had fun—she'd gotten to do things she'd never done in little Hendersonville, North Carolina. She'd gotten free from the farm, at least for a week.

"After thinking about it, I figured I owed her a conversation, so I wrote back and agreed to meet her in Richmond, in a little coffee shop right near the art school. I still remember—it was a glorious fall day. The leaves were just starting to turn, and the air was crisp. As soon as I got off the train, I bought myself a cigar and walked down the street, puffing away. I felt like a real man, taking care of his 'problem,' then heading back to important things in Charlottesville.

"She was waiting for me in a booth—way in the back. I can still remember what she wore—a maroon skirt and sweater, and those same high heels I'd first seen her in. She was nervous, sipping coffee and holding a lit cigarette. She looked skinnier and paler than she had at Back Creek. Her hair was pulled up in some kind of bun and she had glasses on—I'd never seen her wear glasses before. I wondered for a minute if maybe I'd been a big blur to her that entire week.

"When I arrived, she jumped up and shook hands with me— everything felt awkward. I looked around to make sure I didn't know anyone in the coffee shop. The place was empty except for some tired waitress reading a newspaper in the front. I realized it was the middle of the afternoon on a beautiful fall day—who would be dining in a dark coffee shop?

"So we sat across from each other for what seemed like a long time. The waitress eventually came up and poured me some coffee, warmed up Rosemary's cup, and disappeared into the back. I stirred the coffee and checked my watch. Rosemary sat with her hands folded, studying me. Finally, she took off her glasses and reached over to grab my hand.

"'Ken,' she said. Except she still hadn't managed to get rid of that Tobacco Road accent, so it came out 'Kin.' I looked hard at her and wondered if I'd be able to make the four o'clock train back to Charlottesville. There was a little cocktail party a professor was throwing and I was counting on being there.

"'Ken,' she repeated. 'I have something to tell you. It's hard for me to say, but you need to know.' She paused. 'Because it's your problem, too.' She ducked her head and whispered. I had to lean over the table to hear her words. I wondered if she needed money—maybe she'd lost some of her scholarship. I could help her out there, I decided. My mother would probably agree to give me some extra money. I took hold of her hand.

"'I don't know how to say it, except right out.' I nodded my head. Her fingers wound around mine. 'I'm expecting.'"

My head spun, and I didn't need to look to know that Lillian was sitting up in her chair. I let go of the door handle.

"For a moment, I really did wonder what she was expecting. In my family, we'd always said, 'She's in a family way,' usually in a whisper. We didn't choose to recognize that people had babies because that would mean acknowledging that people did the things that led to babies. So when Rosemary told me she was expecting, I had no immediate idea what she was saying. I must have been sitting there with my mouth wide open, because she finally leaned over and looked me in the eyes—she did have beautiful eyes. 'I'm going to have a baby,' she said clearly this time. 'Your baby.'"

Daddy paused again to drain his glass and hug it to his chest. I never really thought about it much, but if I had, I would have assumed, just like in the novels, that fate and true love had brought my parents together. Who doesn't want to find her beginnings in a romance? But now I knew the truth, and I knew why he didn't fly off the handle when Lillian retreated home this time. After all, she must have brought them together once. And, I guess, she'd pulled them apart, too. But before I could work out the equation,

Daddy continued his own story. It was like some kind of confession.

"I stayed in Richmond with Rosemary the rest of that day and night. She lived in a crummy little walk-up, next to the colored section of town. The room was furnished with someone's cast-off sofa and table. She made me go up the fire escape because the landlady was pretty nosy, and religious to boot. Rosemary didn't feel too good. Her being pregnant never sat too easy with her.

"We went to dinner at some barbeque place and she couldn't eat anything but crackers. As the evening went on and I watched her, I realized there was only one thing I could do. By about nine o'clock that night, we had agreed to marry—we'd make it romantic by eloping. We'd surprise everyone, and then settle down to the good life of Back Creek. We talked about it all night long.

"And so the next day we ran off to a Justice of the Peace— found his address in the yellow pages at a phone booth. I was still wearing the clothes I'd worn to class the day before. Rosemary took time to put on some lipstick, and *bang*! I was a married man. I suppose we both looked bright-faced and happy. The clerk even offered to take our picture, but Rosemary said no, she'd rather remember how we looked. We treated ourselves to a hot dog and Coke at a lunch counter down the street."

Lillian suddenly spoke up. "What the hell are you talking about? On Mother's dresser, there's a picture of your wedding—Mother in a white dress, you in a tux, posed and smiling."

Daddy's voice lost its cadence—it almost sounded like he was sobering up.

"Once we came back to Back Creek, my mother was fit to be tied. She insisted on holding a real wedding, as soon as your mother could look like a bride. We'd been married over a year when the wedding took place. By then, she'd already lost the baby."

It took me a minute to fully grasp what he was saying. And, judging by the way Lillian got up and disappeared inside, I knew she grasped it, too. She didn't need or want to hear about dead babies. Okay, so a mistake had brought Mother and Daddy together. But what had kept them together—at least until now?

Chapter Twelve

Even the Creek's recent explosion of jellyfish couldn't keep me from heading over to visit Cal that night. To get there, I took the long way around the peninsula, down the graveled driveway, left onto Dandy Road to old Poquoson Road, around the shallow marsh of the Creek where the weekenders brought their boats to launch, and, finally, turned into John Whythe's potholed driveway.

On the narrow country roads, I dodged the occasional pick-up lights, earning a host of mosquito bites for my efforts. I found Cal sitting on top of his boat's cabin, studying maps (Civil War battlefields, I figured) with a flashlight, and sipping rum. For the thousandth time, I wondered if he ever slept. I made my presence known this time and, sure enough, Cal almost seemed to expect me. "Amazin' Grace!" he greeted me, making room.

I tried to adjust my eyes to the dim light. At one time, before the arrival of industry, the Creek must have been a place of total blackness at night. But in 1975, thanks to the scallop factory, the refinery, and every little dock along the way to the Bay, lights stayed on until the morning sun took over the watch against thieves.

Here, on Cal's boat, we were shadowy images, our outlines made visible by the token security light next to the boat. Cal's long hair hung loose around his shoulders, silvery in the light's faded glow. His face was a blur, except for his eyes. And his chest was bare. I had to resist an urge to trace his shoulder blades with my hand.

Sitting there next to him, feeling his closeness, I wondered in a distracted way what I looked like to him. I ran my fingers through my hair to try to tame it, wishing I'd taken the time to comb it before coming over. I removed my glasses, drew up my knees, and focused on what I had come over to tell him.

Cal never asked me what was wrong or urged me to talk. Anybody else would have mistaken his patience for a lack of interest. That night, it didn't take me long to begin. Once I put my thoughts about Cal's shoulders somewhere far away, I told him what I had heard just hours before—the story Daddy had told me and Lillian. It was the only way I could make sense of it for myself.

I could feel the flow of my words in rhythm with the gentle rocking of the boat. It was late, the tide was coming in, and a fading piece of moon peered out at us from behind some grayish streaks of clouds. I saw Cal's shoulders rise with his breathing. He was still listening, still awake, though I'm sure I was talking more to myself than to him, making Daddy's story part of my story.

Cal surprised me by prodding, "So, it was a shotgun wedding, without the shotgun. Plenty of folks do that."

It must have been four o'clock in the morning, but the night's inkiness still covered everything. I'd been talking so fast, and the picture unrolled itself so quickly in my mind, that I'd hardly been aware of Cal. I was facing out to the water, like I was talking to the fish or the tide. His words brought me to a pause and I stretched my legs out, rubbing my cramped muscles.

With a suddenness that nearly knocked me off the boat, Cal let go of his cup, swung his arms, beat his chest, and ended his quiet presence. He cried a high-pitched jungle noise—it reached across to the other side of the Creek, then echoed back.

The adrenaline of panic pricked my arms and legs and my heart beat up and out my throat. I scrambled to my knees and grabbed his thrashing arm. "What the hell's wrong with you?" I whispered, as if my low voice could counteract his yell. My legs fell out from under me and I started slipping down the side of the cabin, the worn soles of my tennis shoes squeaking along the smooth wood.

Cal grabbed me under my arms and lifted me back onto the top of the boat, swinging my feet over to settle next to his. As scared and breathless as I was, I couldn't help but notice how easily he'd lifted me. For a minute, I'd felt weightless, as if I were floating. But then my feet snapped back down on the deck with a sharp clap and I sank to my knees, panting.

"I was scaring away the ghosts," he said. He stood over top of me, his gaze focused on the faint rays of light creeping from behind the horizon.

"Ghosts?" I said, looking up at him. His long hair fell in a halo around his face.

He knelt down and reached out to hold onto my arm. Now I could see into his eyes. "Something weird happened to me while you were talking, telling that story. Something sort of cosmic." His grip tightened and hurt me a little. But I just kept still.

"You sure can tell a story, Grace. While you were telling about old Ken, I sort of lifted off this old boat, got on the train with him, and sat in that diner with him. And then I found myself back in a shitty old farmhouse in Poquoson, looking at my father."

The comment seemed to take a toll on him. In fact, it was the longest I'd ever heard him speak at one time. As I sat there, hoping he wouldn't let go of me, I reminded myself that when I visited Cal, I always did most of the talking. While he didn't seem to mind, it made me sad. And so I did something I'd never done, or even thought to do before—I asked Cal about his life. "Tell me about your father," I said.

Cal plopped his behind down hard on the deck, spread out his long wiry legs, with their many scars and nicks, and flexed his toes toward the water. But he said nothing.

I figured that, if I was ever to prod him, now was the time. "Come on, Cal," I said. "I talk and talk, and you hardly ever say anything."

"Well, I don't have nice stories to tell about school and weddings. My father was a mean sumbitch and everyone knew it. I just had to make the best of a bad situation. When I was your age, we'd about gotten around to not talking at all. The only way we could live in the same house was not to be there at the same time. I didn't mind that much—I was playing football, partying. It was my last year in high school and I knew I would leave soon.

"My mother was gone by then, and I never could blame her for leaving us. She drove off early one morning, just before Easter that year—never heard from her after that. Later, after I got out of the hospital, I got word she'd died." Cal trailed off.

I'd never heard Cal mention one syllable about a hospital before—I just knew about it from my father's vague comments. There must have been something potent in that fading shell of a moon. I wrapped my arms around my knees and listened hard.

Cal took up his thread again. "I didn't know what I would do when I got out of high school, but I knew it would be something far away from that sad piece of land he called a farm. His daddy owned that land before him, and *his* daddy before that. But my father drank too much and got in too many fights to ever keep up with the farm. Mostly, he kept me working it—after school and on the weekends. I kept it up best I could. They foreclosed on it after I left." I could discern his features clearly now. The early light gave everything a fuzzy glow.

"So one day in late spring, almost summer, I cut school and came home early. I was looking for some money—to buy a pack of smokes—when I found my draft notice, scrunched up in an out-of-the-way place. I'd turned eighteen that winter. Since I hadn't received anything, I thought maybe I'd gotten out of the draft. I looked at the notice, and my number was pretty high.

"Then I heard his truck pull up and he came in, drunk again. I shoved the paper at him and yelled, 'What are you doing messing with my mail?' For one second, he looked scared. Then he said, 'You think the government's gonna miss you? You gotta stay here, take care of this place for me.'

"I looked at his ugly face, and I got so mad I couldn't see anything for a minute. Then I felt his blood on my knuckles and watched him fall to the floor, bleeding real bad. He didn't move and I got scared. But I felt good . . . because I'd been wanting to do that ever since I could remember. I threw some things in a paper bag and left.

"Then I did the craziest thing I could imagine. I drove over to the recruiting station in Yorktown and I enlisted—I fucking enlisted."

Once Cal finished, his breath came as fast and heavy as his words. Sneaking glances at his face, I fought an impulse to reach out to touch his cheek or stroke his hair, to tell him the scene was already played out, and that the worst of it was long past. I shifted myself, so I was sitting right next to him, practically touching him. Together, we watched the water reflect the colors of the dawn. We sat and waited, just like the rest of the world.

Then, without any warning, Cal grabbed me around the shoulders and kissed me. I mean, a real kiss—like the one I'd been waiting for—the kind I knew the kids in the cars at the York High School parking lots couldn't give—the kind of kiss Heathcliff must have given Catherine. It melted me. I was the bespectacled, bushy-haired Grace no more—only some watery vestige of her remained on top of that old boat. It was my first kiss, not counting the pecks relatives give and one wet smack some kid had given me on a dare in sixth grade.

Cal must have felt me melt away, because he held me tight around the shoulders and sat me up. I felt the hard wood beneath my tailbone. The pieces of me flowed quickly back together as I realized the fatigue and chill that the late night, now morning, produced. The initial shock of Cal's lips began to wear off, and more mundane worries set in—should I kiss him back? And would he like it?

But there wasn't much time to entertain such thoughts. Just as I put my hand on Cal's arm and lifted my face back up to his, he rose silently and pointed over across the Creek. I followed his hand and saw the lights on at our house, sending out vague, shimmery beams across the water. "You'd better get back home," he said, "before they miss you." He hoisted himself off the top of the cabin and onto the pier, landing softly on his bare feet. I just sat there, unwilling to remember who they were or why they might miss me.

"Grace!" Cal rattled the tow rope hooked to his canoe. "Come on, now. It's time to get on your horse and ride it . . ."

His nonsense roused me from my stupor. How could Cal be so serious and deep one moment and talk such stupid stuff the next? Like they said, he must be crazy. Rubbing my sore behind, I rose up from the cabin and slid down onto the pier. I felt as stiff as one of those pier boards. By the time my tennis shoes plopped onto the splintery boards, part of Cal had disappeared into a big wooden storage box nailed to the pier. I had to feel my way over to him—the early dawn light made it hard for me to see. In fact, everything that night seemed a little foggy.

Cal popped out of the box, brandishing a small paddle. "Here, take this," he said. "Just paddle on across in my canoe. You can sneak back into the house and be back in bed before they even get up. Bring the canoe back when you can."

"You sound like you know all about this sneaking-in business," I said. About the length of my arm, that paddle looked like rodents had been gnawing away on it.

Cal shook his head, his blond hair floating around his head. "Naw, I haven't had to do any sneaking in or out for a long time. I've just been here, big as life, if anyone wanted me."

I turned to step into the canoe, which was tied to one of the pilings on the other side of the pier. I folded my knees under me, as Daddy had taught me, and held out the paddle, pondering how much help it'd actually be. I had to lean over the side of the canoe to break the dark surface of the water. Glancing over the low side of the canoe, I saw the iridescent shapes of the jellyfish somewhere below the surface.

Cal untied the canoe's tether and steadied the little boat with his toes. I fought to keep my attention on the canoe and not him. There was so much I wanted to ask him, and so much I wanted him to tell me. Mostly, I wanted him to touch me again. But I knew Cal well enough to know that to ask, to demand, to reach for him, would drive him back into that little cabin, where he would stay.

As I prepared to push off, Cal spoke in a low, urgent voice, suddenly sounding like the Cal who'd told me the story of his father. "Grace," he said, "all I know about the sneaking-in business is that some people are real good at it and others can't do it to save their lives. So you be careful, okay?"

Before I could puzzle out a response, he pushed the front of the canoe and I was floating out into the black- and silver-striped Creek. As I dipped the tiny paddle into the water in a comforting rhythm, moving the light aluminum across the Creek's flatness, I thought about how this was the closest Cal had come to advice and understanding. He was probably right about that sneaking-in stuff, too.

When I finally reached the marshy edge that marked the boundary of our property, I held the paddle up and braced for the canoe to hit the soft mud. Strings of jellyfish dripped from the paddle, so I quickly banged it on the side of the canoe, hearing, rather than seeing, the disembodied globs fall back into the water. I knew they could still land a powerful punch, and I had no intention of getting stung.

I dragged the canoe into the tall grass, determined to return it that night. Then I did just what Cal suggested: tiptoed into the house and made my way up the stairs to my room. It would not be difficult to fake sleep if and when Daddy ever roused himself and decided to check on me. Of course, I'd only worry about that when the dull rumble of his snoring ceased. I didn't know about Lillian, but I noticed her door closed up tight when I passed by.

So I'd come full circle. My absence had again gone unnoticed.

Chapter Thirteen

Only the heat of the noonday sun could get me out of my bed. My tiny third-floor room was not intended for daytime occupation during the summer and, truth be told, I rarely needed to be reminded of that fact. I was usually up and out early, but not that morning.

I woke up with the foggy sense that something had happened, but just what it was, I couldn't say. When I tried to organize myself—throw off the sheets, brush back my hair, put my glasses on to see the world more clearly—I couldn't find my wire-frames. With that realization, the early morning events quickly came back to me. I could even visualize where my glasses lay, tucked under the windshield of the old Silverton. They'd be safe, but until I could retrieve them, it might be tough to explain to Daddy and Lillian why I wasn't wearing them.

So far, not a peep out of them and no signs of concern or even interest. But, to them, I couldn't be Grace without my glasses. Without them, I looked different; I even felt different—older, maybe more confident, even pretty. I do have pretty eyes. Like my mother's, they're hazel, flecked with bits of yellow and deep brown, and surrounded by dark, thick lashes.

As I remembered Cal's kiss, I felt an unexpected happiness, the first clear, pure feeling I'd had since Tommy's accident.

The sound of Lillian's voice turned me away from the mirror and set me to finding some clean shorts and pulling my hair back into a ponytail.

"Grace, Grace! Are you up yet?! Listen, I've talked Daddy into playing hooky from the office and taking us for a boat ride—just like old times, you know! Come on down here and let's fix a picnic lunch. We all could use a little fun for a change." Her words floated up from the bottom of the stairs. Closing the door carefully, I bounded down, nearly knocking her over on the small landing, where the steps took a right turn.

She grabbed my shoulder and held me at arm's length for a minute. "Where're your glasses?" she asked, scrunching up her face, eyeing me. For a minute, I thought she might know I'd been up to something last night. But then, she let go and laughed. "You look older, you know. Why don't you leave them off, anyway, and show the world that brown-eyed girl?" We ran down the rest of the steps, just like we were little girls again.

"Daddy's out messing with *Pappy*'s poor old motor." Out the big bay window, Lillian motioned toward a tiny figure hunched over the motor box of our old wooden boat.

Pappy had been a great boat in its day. On it, the Barnetts had made many a Bay pleasure cruise, and once even ventured up to Baltimore on a weekend. Daddy inherited the boat from an uncle and, at one time, had cared for it diligently. But since Lillian's leaving and Daddy's retreat into sailboat design, the *Pappy* had fallen on hard times. It remained tied to our pier, paint cracking in the summer heat, placidly riding the tides. Once a year or so, Daddy paid somebody from the marina to clean the hull and run the engine, but *Pappy* remained stationary, a disintegrating reminder of how we used to be.

From the kitchen, I could barely see Daddy working on that motor box. As Lillian and I delved into the pantry, we heard a huge roar and couldn't help but clap our hands, knowing that Daddy had somehow resurrected our boat.

The intense rumbling that continued from the pier inspired us to quickly throw a bunch of food into a paper bag—bread, peanut butter, Bernice's strawberry preserves from 1972, and the surprise treasure of an unopened bag of potato chips. We headed out at a fast trot, before Daddy changed his mind. Once I reached the pier, I shifted my bag to one arm and motioned for Lillian to hurry up.

With her newly added weight, she'd begun to waddle a bit, though most people wouldn't have noticed. She was wearing an old button-down shirt of Daddy's over some cut-off Army-Navy Store fatigues. Her legs were still shockingly white, despite after-noons spent lounging on our deck at home. I wondered if living in New York had stripped her of her ability to tan.

She had pinned up her hair into a bun and, as she came up beside me, I felt a sudden urge to pull out her bobby pins and free up that golden waterfall. I reached for her head and Lillian swat-ted my hand away. "Cut it out," she demanded. "What the hell's wrong with you?" We had to smile at each other—similar scenes had often played out on past boat trips. We reached the boat and carefully stepped down onto the rear deck, holding hands to steady each other.

Daddy had come alive, opening up the cabin, fiddling with the steering wheel, and brushing off the old deck chairs resting below deck. Watching him move around the boat in his old Topsiders and khaki shorts, I realized that he, too, looked like his skin hadn't seen the sun in months. He had been spending most weekends holed up in his study or in his office. But he started to look like his old self as he emerged from the bunks below brandishing a bunch of old towels and shouting, "Whooey! Smell these towels! Get them out on the pier and into the sun!" I obliged, and together the three of us straightened out the abandoned debris of our last family outing and prepared to head out to the Bay.

I stood in position at the bow, ready to release *Pappy*'s tethers from the pilings and watching across the Creek for some sign of Cal. Surely, he must have heard all our noise. But I could see no evidence of life—the old Silverton bobbed silently in the tiny waves we were creating. A light breeze blew against my face, stirring up my hair. Gripping the ropes tightly, I feared that last night I had just been imagining someone else's story. I tried to replay the night in my head, but Daddy's shouting brought me back to the present and I concentrated on taking the right rope off at the right time.

I heard the *thunk* of the stern ropes as Lillian tossed them onto the rear deck, and suddenly she was there, beside me on the bow. After I removed the last rope and the boat eased its way out of the pilings, we climbed high atop the cabin. Holding our faces to the sun and grasping the edge of the cabin roof, we lay back against the warm wood. Though my eyes were closed against the sun's brightness, I could see Daddy sitting at the wheel, chewing on an unlit cigar, squinting out to the Bay, smiling his captain's smile. I grabbed Lillian's hand and we were transported forward to the head waters of the York—and backward in time.

Old *Pappy* took on a new life as we crashed through the small tidal waves, sending up silvery sprays that got our legs wet and sent us screaming to dry safety in the stern. We had to shade our eyes against the sparkling light that danced all around us. Daddy yelled out landmarks to us: "Look now! Over on the shore, there's old Uncle Jim's place . . . There, on that point, is where we used to go oystering . . ." His voice competed with the roar of the engine and our own pointing and remembering.

But we were silent as we passed by the pile of white plexiglass and broken pier boards, still surrounded by yellow police tape. I knew the three of us were thinking our own thoughts about the accident, and I realized I had almost forgotten about poor Tommy. I sneaked a glance at Lillian as we rumbled by the remains, but she turned her head to face out toward the Bay. I couldn't help but wonder if we'd forget Mother, too, during this summer of losing and finding people. The shock of last night's phone call was already wearing off. I turned to ask Lillian my big question, but she was now covering her eyes with sunglasses and locating a seat facing the sun.

We left the no-wake Creek and headed for the mouth of the York, picking up speed. Watching the water churn behind us, I thought about all those times we had ventured out as a family on this old crate. There were rituals tied to the boat trips, from Mother's careful packing of the wicker picnic basket—always ham salad sandwiches, potato salad (her mother's recipe, made the day before), and oatmeal raisin cookies—to Daddy's ceremonial anchor dropping.

Though Lillian must have been nearly a teenager by then, and I still in elementary school, we had both been eager crew members and, later, island-bound explorers. While Mother took up her position in an ancient deck chair by the cabin, coating herself in baby oil and disappearing behind sunglasses, Lillian, Daddy, and I became pirates or whalers or Confederate Navy officers—whatever struck our fancy.

Daddy barked orders or pleaded for mercy as his two-member crew alternated between submissive obedience and rank mutiny. I followed Lillian's lead, scrambling up by the anchor or hiding down in the hold—whatever her imagination determined. We were cohorts on those sun-drenched trips, partners in crime and joint saviors of the world—at least until Daddy threw in the anchor and we waded onto the shore of some island or the Yorktown Beach to eat our picnic lunch.

I glanced at Lillian, now seated in Mother's old chair, salvaged from the cabin. The early excitement of again being on the water was gone, replaced by the calm contentment found in moving ahead steadily. Sun glinted off her hair, the tight bun replaced by a careless pony tail. She propped her feet onto the railing, her red toenails standing out against the bright white of the boat and her skin.

As she held her face up to the sun, she reminded me of the zinnias Mother used to grow in a tiny cultivated square by the pier. Those rust-red and purple flowers, with their upturned petals and leaves, basked in the baking sun all summer. Mother could never bring herself to cut them because, as she would say, they looked so happy just where they were. Lillian did too, sitting in Mother's spot by the cabin.

We continued toward the channel, waving at the few pleasure boaters escaping the office. Once we reached the York River and the mouth of the Bay, we didn't know where Daddy would take us; he was familiar with every nook and cranny of the York and had traveled the Bay more times than I could say. Sometimes, he would hone in on an island among the many little land masses marking the way out, or take a conventional turn and travel down to the York River Bridge, a metal drawbridge that, from below, looked like some kind of huge space contraption. Daddy was the one who decided where we would end up—we were just along for the ride.

He seemed headed for the Bay today, veering a sharp left and picking up speed. Lillian and I held onto the railing and laughed as we crashed along, our landlocked worries disintegrated by the warm sun.

"Land ho!" Daddy hollered, throwing his cigar out the cabin window. In the near distance, we spied a small island, covered in sand and scrubby pines.

"Grab the wheel, Grace!" Before I could protest, Daddy left the cabin and threaded his way toward the anchor at the bow. I jumped into the cabin and gingerly steadied the thin metal steering wheel, trying to follow Daddy's wild hand directions as we moved out of the channel to a place where we could anchor without running aground.

After Daddy spent several minutes excavating the rusted chain from its resting place and giving directions to me, the inexperienced captain, the anchor finally landed with a splash. Daddy gave me the signal to turn off the engine. This was an act of pure faith because we were never quite sure if the engine would start up again, and especially today.

However, unlike other trips when Daddy would leave the engine sputtering while Mother unloaded lunch and we slipped on our bathing suits, today he dramatically drew his hand across his throat and I turned the key. Suddenly, there was only the sound of the wind and the water against the wood.

Lillian appeared beside me as we watched Daddy sit down on the bow, his legs dangling over the water. In former times, Daddy hardly took any interest in anything outside the boat once we reached his destination—it was always Mother, Lillian, and I who went swimming or wading out to land. Daddy just seemed satisfied with having gotten us wherever he intended us to go. Once there, he would retire with a beer or Bloody Mary and, eventually, fall asleep in his captain's chair. I tried to follow his gaze off the bow today. He was watching a three-masted sailboat far off in the distance. It looked like a ghost ship on the horizon—you could see the three sails but nothing else.

"Daddy, come on back here. Let's eat," said Lillian, who took command by rummaging through our brown bag of supplies. He turned briefly, waved her off, and continued his watching. I was looking in the opposite direction, out the back, at the small island.

"Lillian, let's go exploring, just like we used to!" I grabbed her arm. "Come on, we can eat later. Last one in is a rotten egg!" Lillian gave one last poke through the bag, grabbed a handful of potato chips, and followed me to the back of the boat. We gingerly let ourselves down into the water.

The chill surprised us, and we both sent out high-pitched little-girl screams as we jumped up and down, feeling the mud between our bare toes. We bounced toward the island, adjusting to the watery walking and the water's early June temperature. Glancing back, I saw Daddy move back from the bow, reach around in the cooler, and pop the top of a Budweiser. He settled himself into one of the deck chairs facing the island. Then, just like the old days, when he would assure Mother he was "watching" us, he promptly fell asleep.

We continued our trek toward the tiny hump of land. Lillian glided along at a fast pace and I had to work to keep up with her. The mud turned to sand below our feet and finally we were on the island, ready to explore.

And there were lots of things to find—oyster shells washed a shocking white, dried sea grass twisted like a nest, stray feathers pinned to the ground, and in the mesh of debris trapped on the shore, a waterman's glove bobbing in a shallow tide. Lillian screamed when she saw it—it did look like a hand separated from its owner.

Despite Lillian's squeamishness, we collected the glove as well as the feathers and the shells, placing them in an old burlap sack we'd dragged through the water for just this purpose. As we walked along the shore, the wind came up and blew our clothes and hair around us, making me feel as if I should anchor myself to one of the scrubby pines that struggled up through the sand behind us.

"This makes me think of Mother," Lillian shouted as she bent over to retrieve a long piece of driftwood polished smooth by the water. I had been thinking the same thing, remembering the "treasures" Mother would help us find when we went exploring. While Lillian and I strolled along the shore, tossing pebbles and shells out into the water, Mother would walk slowly and deliberately, selecting debris and explaining its beauty.

Heaving the sack onto the tiny beach and plopping herself down, Lillian pulled out a package from her shirt pocket and fished out a cigarette.

"You know, you shouldn't smoke. It's not good for the . . ." My voice trailed off as I sat down beside her in the sand. I don't know what stopped me—the idea of giving advice to Lillian, or the word "baby."

She put an unlit cigarette between her lips and circled her stomach with her hands. "I don't have any matches, anyway," she said. She propped her knees up and moved her toes against the sand, making small ridges. We sat, surrounded by the sound of wind running through the spiky sea grass and the water lapping against the shore. With the sun baking my legs and face, I began thinking about the night before, and leaned over to trace an elaborate C-A-L in the sand, intertwining the design with an equally elaborate G-R-A-C-E. I'm no artist, so no one else would have known what I was doing. With each stroke in the sand, I could more clearly see Cal's face as he grabbed and kissed me. The memory made me feel warmer.

Suddenly, Lillian rose, spraying sand over my artwork and bringing me back to the island. She stepped out into the water and tossed her cigarette out into the tiny, gentle waves.

"Food for the fishes!" she shouted, the wind grabbing the words from her mouth. I scrambled to my feet and joined her at the water's edge, letting the water meet my toes.

"Isn't that some line from Shakespeare?" she said.

I shook my head. "Not that I know of. But there is that line from *Hamlet*, 'Sweets to the sweet.' I remember. We read it last year in junior English. It comes while they're all standing around Ophelia's grave—you remember, she kills herself, Hamlet jumps into the grave, and . . ."

Lillian waved off my *Hamlet* story. She'd never been too interested in books, especially ones she had to read in school. In fact, she'd never been too interested in school at all, except as a place to socialize. When we were little, Mother called Lillian her "little glow-worm" and me her "little bookworm."

As we continued our stroll around the tiny island, *Pappy* waited for us, bobbing patiently against the taut anchor rope. I could barely see Daddy's figure slumped in the deck chair. He never thought to use suntan lotion—by the time we got back, he'd be burned to a crisp. I thought of returning briefly to wake him up, but Lillian was walking purposefully now and I worked to keep up with her. We came round to the tangle of grass and driftwood we'd started from, and I stopped to look at the Bay's gray and blue horizon, trying to imagine just how far it might take us if we had the gumption to follow it.

"Grace," said Lillian. She turned me around to face her, grabbing onto both my forearms so I dropped the sack.

"What did you see that morning—the morning Tommy White ran into the pier?" She looked intently into my eyes.

I stuttered in surprise. "I . . . I saw the boat coming down the Creek—I heard the engine first. It was going really fast and I was confused. It was early. I'd barely gotten my glasses on and the sun was glaring and I could—"

"Forget all that," she said impatiently, tightening her grip on my arms. "What did you see?"

I twisted out of her grasp and retrieved the burlap sack. "I saw Tommy, up in front of the wheel. He was standing straight up—just what they tell you never to do in a boat. And his long hair was flying behind him."

"What did his face look like?" Lillian leaned in on me.

"I couldn't see his face. I was too far away."

"But you must have seen something—something that could give you a clue . . ."

"A clue to what?" I'd never mentioned my suspicions to anyone, because everyone seemed satisfied his death was nothing more than an accident. "What do you mean? He was standing straight up, driving faster than anyone should, heading out of the Creek like a bat out of hell. Then he swerved. I don't know why. Maybe the steering wheel went bad. Maybe he misjudged the turn . . ."

She stepped back and turned toward the water, wrapping her arms around her shoulders. Her hair had come loose in the wind—it blew wildly around her face. She moved to the water's edge, and I watched the little waves lap over her ankles. I joined her. But before I could ask her what I really wanted to know, she spoke without looking at me.

"I saw a lot of Tommy in New York last winter. I just wanted to know what he looked like, driving that boat. I just wanted to see him . . ." She resumed, sounding as if she was talking to herself. "Because this is his baby."

I squinted at the sun, letting the statement sink in. Lillian turned her face away, gazing out toward a big tanker making its way into the York.

"How?" I said, sounding as inarticulate as I had with my mother.

There was only the sound of the wind for so long that I thought Lillian hadn't heard me, or wasn't going to answer. Finally, she turned to me and held onto my arms again, though gently this time.

"Grace, I didn't even say goodbye to him. I don't know why I did what I did. I just left him." She let go of my arms. "I had no idea he'd come back here." She stopped and wiped at her face for a minute. Then she resolutely picked the sack up and began dragging it out into the water, heading back toward the boat. I followed her as we waded back. I tried hard to think of something to say—something that might get Lillian to tell me the rest of her story.

"That picture . . ." I said to Lillian's back.

She paused, the burlap bag swirling around her. "What picture?"

"Of Tommy . . . in the stuff you brought back." I caught up to her. The water was mid-thigh on me—it lapped against Lillian's belly.

"I took lots of pictures of Tommy," she said, squinting in the sun. "I actually sold some of them to a gallery. They were the only ones I ever got real money for."

"He looked so . . . so New York in those pictures," I said. "And the others were good, too. I could really feel the city." I was being honest. We continued silently through the water, the baby and Tommy sinking somewhere under the unsettled sparkle of the tiny waves.

After we'd climbed back onto the boat and Lillian had placed our sack of treasures on the stern, she came back to my comment about her picture-taking. "You really think so? You know, I taught myself how to take pictures. Someone told me I had a good eye for it."

I could hear Daddy snoring in the cabin, where he must have moved to get out of the sun. "You should take some shots of the Creek and the watermen," I suggested, the idea having just popped into my head.

Lillian plopped down in the deck chair and pulled her hair back. She actually seemed to consider what I was saying. "Oh, Grace," she said finally. "My cameras have been gathering dust since I got here. I guess I feel like I left all that behind in New York."

"But you brought them with you. You didn't sell them. You must've meant to use them some time or another. Just think about it," I said. "You could do the whole story of Back Creek—you know, all the watermen, and the herons and gulls, the boats. We could send them to the paper. They're always looking for good local stuff. And we could send some to Mother when we get her address ..."

Securing her hair behind her head, Lillian regained her big sister tone. "Grace, you're a fool if you think Mother's gonna come running back because she sees a few pictures of the Creek. Actually, they'll just remind her why she left."

Before I could respond, Daddy emerged from the cabin door. "Lunchtime?" he asked, rubbing his stomach and yawning.

"You get out of this sun," I said, directing him back into the cabin. "We'll fix you some lunch."

While I sifted through the brown paper bag, Lillian stood and retrieved the sack containing all our prizes. "What can we do with all this stuff?"

"Remember how Mother used to make those sculptures out of driftwood and stuff?"

In my mind, I could see the rambling pile of shells, feathers, and dried grass she spent hours shaping into art. Carting a load of what could only be described as debris, Mother would retreat into the shed outside the house and create all sorts of crazy, wonderful things. Daddy and Lillian laughed at her efforts—it was one thing they agreed on. But I loved them. I used to peek into the shed door and watch her while she worked. She didn't like to be disturbed, so I was as quiet as island grass while I watched.

She probably wouldn't have noticed me anyway. When she worked with her hands, she could always tune everything else out, whether she was creating a sculpture, painting a landscape, or even baking a pie. Sometimes, the things she created scared me a little, like when they became fierce-looking sea monsters. Once, to make a mermaid's long tail, she dyed an abandoned fishing net green.

Now that I thought about it, she hadn't been in that shed for years, maybe since Lillian left.

"Oh yeah, Mother's *art!*" Lillian hit the word with a sarcastic punch. "I bet that stuff is still sitting there in the shed," she added, grabbing up the bag of potato chips with her free hand.

She paused, a handful of chips mid-way to her mouth. "Hey, you know, I might be able to set up a kind of a darkroom in that shed. I could maybe take that old equipment Daddy stored in the attic—remember when he went through his photography phase? Anyway, maybe I could do it . . ." She stuffed the chips in her mouth and crunched them with gusto.

"Let's eat!" Daddy shouted from the cabin. "I'm starving!"

Lillian dropped the sack on the floor and moved into the cabin, asking Daddy three quick questions: "Would it be all right to clean out the old shed? Where's your old photographic equipment? And could you get the boxes down for me?"

As she talked, I sorted out the bread and peanut butter and took in a plate of sandwiches. Daddy smiled and looked like he was listening to her plans. I stood apart from the two of them, wanting to capture their picture in my mind. I didn't have any fancy equipment, so I just sat back on *Pappy*'s stern, swinging my legs and eating my sandwich, watching two old enemies conspire.

Chapter Fourteen

After lunch, Lillian crawled into the cabin for a nap. She said she found herself getting tired at the drop of a hat now—and she'd never been one to resist a physical need. Daddy pulled out two old fishing rods, and together we untangled the lines and looked around for something to use as bait. We settled on bits of bread crust, mushed together into hard balls. When I was little, I'd used the same kind of bait, though I never caught more than the occasional tiny crab.

As he unreeled his line, Daddy said he'd never known I liked to fish. After that, we watched our lines in silence, listening to the wind and the gulls who thought they spied a free meal. Every once in a while, one of us reeled in the line and checked the gradually disappearing bait, then threw the line back into the dancing water.

The thing is, I don't like to fish. I would have been happy to explain this to my father if I'd thought he was interested. I only fished because I thought he'd like it if I did. When I was ten or eleven, I could feel a hollow place in our house, a place that sometimes got filled up with shouting and emptied out with silence. The silence might go on for days, with Mother, Daddy, and Lillian all going their separate ways. I was left to figure out how to bring them back to speaking terms. The boat trips on *Pappy* struck me as the only time we laughed and enjoyed time together.

So I took to grabbing up a rod and some bread (I wasn't ready to sacrifice worms for this uncertain venture), and I sat at the end of the pier, pretending to fish. I just knew Mother or Daddy or maybe even Lillian would see me out there, right next to *Pappy*, and one of them would think about the boat rides, and remember a funny story, and soon all three would come walking out to the boat, arms full of towels and ham salad sandwiches, and climb aboard *Pappy*, forgetting whatever made them so mad at each other.

As I sat cross-legged, feeling the heat of the boards on my thighs, I sometimes closed my eyes and wished fiercely. I even wished out loud—in a whisper to the Creek. But now that I thought about it, if they had bothered to look out the window, and left their own little spheres for one minute, all they would have noticed was me, with hunched back, camped out at the end of the pier.

"Well, that's it," said Daddy. "No luck today, and it's getting dark. Better pull up anchor and head on home." We reeled in one last time and, just as we were stowing the rods, Lillian emerged from the cabin, rubbing her eyes and smoothing her tousled hair. She stopped and pointed to the left.

"Look at that sunset! Have you ever seen so many colors? It's an artist's palette!" She stood in amazement.

The horizon *was* something to behold. Clouds creeping in from the west magnified the purples and pinks and oranges that washed over the sky.

Daddy examined the horizon with a practiced eye. Finally, he turned to retrieve the anchor from the bow and pronounced, "Red sky at night, sailor's delight. Grace, take that wheel again."

"But Daddy, you can't pick up anchor now. It's too beautiful," Lillian said quietly, still standing in front of the cabin. I moved around her and into the cabin to grab hold of the steering wheel, gripping it this time with a little more assurance.

"It'll be even nicer to look at on the Creek," I said. "You just wait and see."

"If you say so," said Lillian. She moved to collect the lunch debris and the burlap sack of island treasures.

"Fire it up, Grace!" Daddy's command came floating across the bow. I turned the key, and the engine miraculously answered with a roar. We crept forward until the anchor lay safely on the deck, dripping mud. Then, with Daddy returning to take the wheel, we picked up speed as we set our sights on the Creek.

Lillian disappeared into the cabin and I stood alone at the stern, my ears barraged by the pounding engine, my eyes filled with the lowering sky. I had to grip the back of the boat tightly to remain upright; Daddy seemed in a hurry to get back and *Pappy* moved at a quick pace, bumping through the water and churning up all kinds of white. My face was fiery with what must have been sunburn, though it felt more like heat coming from the inside.

As soon as we hit the entrance to the Creek, we slowed to a crawl to limit the wake, as the big orange signs insisted. It was pretty dark, but the string of lights shining from the ends of the piers guided us. John Whythe's side of the Creek was lit up with the enormous spotlight he liked to shine on his flagpole. The huge flag at the top flapped mercilessly and, as we passed by, I noted its tattered edges. He'd have to replace the flag sometime soon. It might last the summer, but one bad storm would certainly shred it to pieces. My thoughts shifted as we slid silently past Cal's boat. I looked carefully, but I saw no light and heard no jangling radio.

"Grace, wake up back there!" Daddy shouted. "Grab that hook and get the rope!" Like a cartoon character, I shook myself, then ran around to the stern, looking for the hook and trying to rescue the stiff rope from the pilings, all while hoping that Daddy didn't notice me staring at Cal's boat. As I pulled the rope onto the boat and moved us to the next piling, I looked up toward the bow and found Lillian watching me. She stood in the door of the cabin, arms crossed, her hair now down around her shoulders and shimmering in the pier's light. I knew she had noticed.

I moved quickly to tie the ropes in the knots Daddy had taught

me as a kid. Just as I pulled the last knot tight, I spied a little aluminum skiff, nestled in the marsh grass near the shore. I saw a
figure standing there, watching us tie up *Pappy*. In an unexpected
heart pounding, I recognized the long hair and broad shoulders
and realized that Cal had come across to our side of the Creek.

"Hey, Cal!" Daddy called out, waving as he stowed stuff around
the back of the boat. "What are you doing all the way over on this
side? Come around for a little libation? . . . Hell's bells! I can't find
the cigar I brought out here. Grace! Grace! Where did you go
now? Have you seen my . . ."

The sky was a kind of steel color now. I could hardly see my
bare feet as I walked down the pier—I left Daddy and Lillian to
their own devices and went to see Cal.

Cal was leaning forward, one foot resting on the deck's bottom
railing, in the same position I had taken the day before, listening
to Daddy tell his story. Cal's white shorts glowed in the filmy
dark, and a light left on in the kitchen cast his bare back and chest
in a kind of bronze. His hair looked almost white, pulled away
from his face in a ponytail. Observing him as I walked in from
the pier, I noticed the sharpness of his features—his face seemed
chiseled right out of the heavy air around him.

I had to make these observations fast, in quick glances, because
with the first look, I realized Cal was watching me—*only* me. I
knew Daddy was still messing around on the boat behind me; I
could hear various bangs and sliding noises, punctuated by occasional blasts of language. I guessed Lillian, nowhere in sight, had
escaped to hit the shower, and probably the refrigerator after that.
I thanked God for her self-interest this time.

So Cal and I were alone in the midst of the family, such as it
was. "I found these," he announced, tossing me my glasses from
the deck. "I thought you might need them." I managed to grab
them just below the deck. Out on the boat, when thinking about
the night before, I'd convinced myself that everything between
him and me had to be different now. But here, standing with the

Creek at my back, nothing seemed to have changed. As I peered up at his now smiling face, a vision of Romeo and Juliet and the balcony scene popped into my head, along with the sudden thought that maybe I should act differently—flirt maybe, or pretend to be sexy, like the most popular York High girls.

"Oh, Cal, Cal, wherefore art thou, Cal?" I recited in a shaky voice, holding my hands up to him. It was a start. I flipped back my hair and hoped I looked older without my glasses.

"You should put your glasses on—so you can actually see who you're talking to," said Lillian, already back from the house. Shoving my frames back where they belonged, I could see her clearly as she came over to rest her elbows on the deck beside Cal.

"A crabpot by any other name would smell as sweet," she called out, laughing. "Have you come here a-courting?" She eyed Cal dramatically.

I stood silent, hands hanging down by my side—I had nothing to say. For a moment, I thought about trying to make a joke. Maybe I could turn this into something funny. But nothing clever came into my head. Lillian was the clever one.

Somewhere in the background came noises from the pier. Then Lillian screamed, "Cal, what are you doing?" and I glanced up in time to see Cal flying over the deck railing and down the eight or so feet to the ground, rolling beside me on his rear end. I could hear Lillian laughing a wild kind of laugh, shouting and clapping. I had to smile as I watched him get up and dust himself off. He headed for the marshy edge of the Creek, where he'd left his rowboat. But before he got there, he motioned to me, again saying, "I just thought you'd need your glasses."

And then he clambered into his boat, taking up the oars and pushing off from the mud. Darkness had fallen like a big blanket and I had to rely more on sound than sight. I listened to the steady banging of the oars against the aluminum, until his boat sounded a long way away. I finally unplanted my feet from the ground, feeling like a big oak tree trying to move its roots.

"Grace, you know Cal is a total whacko," Lillian said, watching me trudge up the steps. All I could see was the red glow of her cigarette. "Anyway, get someone your own age for a boyfriend—someone cute and steady, someone who'll take care of you." She waited for me, holding open the kitchen screen door. Bugs swirled toward the light and she waved her cigarette, trying to part the wave of tiny wings.

"You really don't understand much of anything, do you?" I said. I was just as surprised at my words as Lillian. I started waving my hands, too. "You really don't know how to do anything with people except fight with them and hurt them, do you? Today, I thought maybe having a baby was changing you, and that things could be like they used to. But I guess I was wrong. I guess . . ." I exhaled, but still ran out of words.

"Grace, I'm just telling you this for your own good! I'm trying to give you the benefit of my experience," she said. "Leave Cal alone. He'll just wreck things for you. He's nuts—everybody knows that. And you can't change people."

She moved herself into the light of the kitchen. I was shocked to see tears running down her face. Her tears knocked my anger right out of me. I heard Daddy's heavy footsteps coming up the deck steps, then his voice demanding dinner.

Lillian turned toward me. "Oh, let's just get some dinner and go to bed and get up and start all over tomorrow. Okay?"

With my silent concession, Lillian and I replayed the kitchen scene we had played earlier that day, except there was a quiet now—not a peace, but a quiet—that stole over our movements around the kitchen. Of course, Daddy didn't notice. He just headed straight for the refrigerator, retrieved a beer, and went to take a shower.

But we ended the day—the three of us—sitting around the table, cautiously nibbling at Hormel chili from one of Daddy's cans. The kitchen was hot and bright with light. Lillian and I were quiet and distracted, while Daddy dug in with relish. I wished we were back on the boat, with the breeze in our faces and the present at our backs.

I suppose it was in the nature of things that summer—nothing would be clear or sure. But then, when you live in a place surrounded by water, that's always the nature of things. So much depends on things you can't control—like the weather, the tides, the ebb and flow of life under the water. I had always managed to go along with this flow, never disturbing the surface of things. But something was different now. Some current had redirected its course and, as I sat under the bright light above the oak table, I could feel the new motion.

I retreated from the kitchen, leaving Lillian and Daddy to clean up the small mess. I could still feel the day's sunburn heating up my cheeks and my thoughts. As I went through all the practiced motions of getting ready for bed, I kept peeking across the Creek.

Finally, I turned out my light and peered out one of the dormer windows. I could identify a tiny pinpoint of light from inside the old Silverton's cabin—Cal must be up reading. The light didn't move and, with that comfort, I climbed into the bed my grandmother had slept in.

I lost myself in the darkness, dreaming about nothing.

Chapter Fifteen

That summer's current moved us through June, bringing us to one of the worst heat waves ever. I never minded the heat and humidity, though my hair became my nemesis and I had to invent elaborate knots to keep it off my neck and face just to survive. Lillian suffered more—in New York, she'd gotten used to the indoor life of air-conditioning, and Daddy had never entertained adding such a modern luxury to our house. She spent much of the hot part of the days setting up a dark room in the shed under the pines, the one where Mother used to work. The day after our boat trip to the little island, I'd helped her clean it up.

She bounced into my room that morning, yanking open the door and seating herself beside my head, tickling my nose with an antique feather duster that had always amused Mother. The Barnett women had probably never dusted a thing in their lives, but anything old—anything connected to family—held a sacred quality, including this ancient, molting duster.

Still deeply engaged in a dream, a confusing scene of Bay and sandy island where I'd been stranded with only an oar, I awoke sneezing. I heard her laughing and snapped my eyes open to see a zoom lens peering down at me. Before I could get my hands in front of my face, there was a click, and I was temporarily blinded by a flash that appeared out of nowhere.

"There, the first in my new series—I'll call it 'Grace in the Morning'—maybe I'll make it religious." Lillian cocked her elbows and rested her camera. Then, suddenly, she dropped the camera on the bed and grabbed her slightly bulging stomach. I pushed back the sheets and sat up in a hurry, watching her face take on a strange look. I prepared to leap out of bed, find my keys, and deliver her to the hospital again.

"Grace," Lillian said, grabbing my arm. "Grace, it moved—the baby—I could feel it. I swear!" She lifted the t-shirt she had draped over herself and pressed my hand against my stomach. "Feel!" she commanded. I waited, holding my breath. I could feel only the smoothness, the already straining flesh. Nothing moved.

Lillian exhaled. "I guess it stopped. Wow! I tell you what—there really is a baby in there. And I guess it likes taking pictures—or maybe it just likes being near you." She let go of my hand and laughed.

"Okay, come on. Let's get down to business. I need you to help me clean out that shed. I like your idea. I *should* do some work around here. I've brought out my bags and my cameras, and I'm ready to go." She bent her head and looped the neck strap of the old Pentax around her neck. The camera rested on her stomach.

"Hey, look, I've got a little shelf! Grace, get up now. Don't bother taking a shower. You're just going to get dirty. Come on."

Lillian was never so commanding as when she wanted to get something done for herself, so out we both went into the already stifling heat to sort through the mysteries of the shed, which appeared to have been closed up for some time. To get inside, we yanked on, kicked, and finally hammered at the humidity-stuck door. When at last it came open, I was holding onto the handle, and consequently was hurtled backward, landing in the scratchy brush growing wild around the shed.

Inside, we discovered the ghosts of Mother's art, carefully laid in corners and against the walls. We found canvases faithfully reproducing a tourist's Williamsburg, as well as charcoal sketches of natural areas around Back Creek. We found fantastic sculptures created from Creek debris—all manner of sea creatures, and even the mermaid I'd remembered. I wanted to stop and examine each creation, to look for some clues, or to sink into memories.

But Lillian pressed on, focusing her energies on sorting through the work and compressing its space to make room for her equipment. She worked like some kind of curator, holding the sketches at arm's length, examining them with an intense eye, then placing them in one stack or another at the shed's rear. Feeling like an intruder—Mother had never invited me to visit—I worked more furtively.

The rattle of the old station wagon and the crunch of gravel briefly interrupted our cleaning. Daddy was on his way to the office, seemingly the first time in a while he had left much before mid-morning, and I held my breath as I watched his car bump down the driveway. With relief, I watched the dust settle as Daddy turned onto the asphalt smoothness of Dandy Road.

It was still early morning, but already steaming hot. The trees lent a little shade to the shed, but there were no windows and, even with the door propped wide open, little air could enter. By late morning, we were both soaked with sweat and still had a good bit of work yet to do. Lillian's flop into a rusted metal chair signaled time to quit, at least for the time being.

I leaned against the open doorway, closing my eyes and imagining a slight breeze coming up from the Creek. The sunlight filtered through the pines, dappling the piles of needles that carpeted the dirt around the shed. Here and there, a kind of scrubby grass fought to make its way through the layers. A few bayberry bushes mingled among the pines, and I could smell the leaves' intriguing bitterness. It made me think of fall, when we used to gather up bayberry and use it to decorate the Thanksgiving table.

Thanksgiving dinners had always been held at another relative's house, never ours. While other members of the family would bring their special pies or cranberry freezes, Ken Barnett's contribution to dinner involved piles of bayberry and holly, cut in the chilly November air and arranged along the white tablecloth. I never understood who decided we shouldn't bring food—whether it stemmed from my father's relatives' basic mistrust of my mother's cooking, or whether she just plain didn't want to bother.

In the last few years, I was the one who steadfastly rose early and slipped through the cold, Mother's rose-snippers in hand, to maintain a tradition no one else seemed to care much about any more. I crumbled up some bayberry leaves in my hand and let them drop onto the pine needles.

"Grace, I'm going to get a beer. I've had it for today," said Lillian, trying to brush the spider webs off her hair and inspecting the dirt under her fingernails. "I can't get used to all this . . . dirt. New York is grimy, but down here, it's a real-dirt kind of dirty."

"The dirt here *is* natural," I assured her.

"No dirt is natural," she said. Wiping her hands on the unevenly cut-off hem of her shorts, she walked heavily from the shed toward the house.

"I'll get the mail," I announced to her disappearing back.

The quarter mile trek to the mailbox was one of the dividing points of my day, signifying the end of morning and the beginning of afternoon and all its potential laziness. It felt good to be free of the shed's closeness, even though the sun beat down on me. I strolled down the driveway, noting the way the natural world adapted to the heat. The ducks took refuge in the cooler mud by the grass. The herons rested invisibly in the branches of the tall pines lining the Creek.

Those herons were a sneaky bunch. You could never find their nests—they were up too high. You'd only see them when they made themselves seen, when they were sneaking up on some fish in the water. Even then, they blended in with the water, sky, and marsh grasses, their gray-blue color providing them the perfect camouflage.

Though it yielded mostly bills and advertisements no one wanted, the mailbox always held the promise of delivering something good. I liked being the one responsible for the mail, the one with the potential for bringing news of the outside world to our little enclave. Even the arrival of the latest *Time* magazine could be exciting.

Today, as I yanked open the rusty mailbox door, I felt a flutter in my stomach. I wasn't expecting anything, but that was usually when I got something. Among the glossy ads and newsprint flyers were two envelopes, one white and official looking, and the other smaller, also white—both addressed to me. When I turned over the smaller envelope, I discovered a tiny field of daisies painted on the back flap. I stood there, facing the mailbox, and rubbed my fingers over those daisies, a flower we didn't see much of on the Creek.

I first opened the larger one, which bore an official seal and a "Dear Student" greeting. It was from the University of Virginia. I was to fill out this form and indicate my campus housing preference. I held the letter loosely and looked back at our house, sheltered in the pines, the solid dark brick blending in with the scaly brown tree trunks.

I felt an unexpected pricking in my eyes. I wanted to think it was just the sun, but the truth was, I couldn't think about "housing" anywhere but here. I didn't finish reading the letter. I knew there would be boxes to check, and a signature to provide, by a certain deadline. Probably a check to send, too. And after that, a trunk to dig out or buy, towels to fold, sheets to pack. It was not a job I wanted to think about doing myself. Carefully, I folded the letter back into its original lines and stuck it into my back pocket. I'd look at it later.

The next letter I pried open slowly. Her typed address didn't fool me, although I couldn't imagine where she'd found a typewriter. A tiny bead of moisture dropped onto the thin yellow sheet as I opened it up. I quickly wiped the sweat away and read, my eyes running over the words with crazy speed.

"Dear Grace," the deliberate, tiny script read.

"As you can see, I'm doing fine here. I hope you all are doing as well. I decided to write you and tell you some things I couldn't explain on the telephone. I never did like the telephone, especially when you have something important to say. Which I do. Grace, I want you—only you—to know that I do not plan to come back to Back Creek, at least any time soon. I find I like it here at the farm, taking care of things. I am painting and exploring this old farm, which is more run-down than you can imagine. I have time to think here. I don't know what else to say."

I held the filmy handwriting close to my eyes.

"Of course, I miss you and Lillian, and I worry about your father. So I'm writing to ask you to keep taking care of things until the fall, when you have to go to school. I'm sure things will be settled by then and you can go off to college as planned.

"I also ask you to keep my plans between you and me, because your father may take a little longer to realize how things are. I hope you can understand someday.

"Or maybe I hope you never have to understand. Love, Mother."

With damp fingers, I carefully folded Mother's letter and shoved it in the other back pocket of my shorts. I would have to think about the news both letters had brought—sometime. The letters seemed to pull me in opposite directions, but that didn't seem to matter as much as Lillian's baby coming, Daddy up in his office, and Cal across the Creek. The summer was "here and now," and I needed—and wanted—to be, too.

Also in the mail was a postcard without a stamp—the announcement of the local July Fourth activities. The Barnetts had absented themselves from the Creek's Fourth of July celebration for the last several years. It was usually a day I spent watching things from the deck, by myself, while Daddy worked and drank in his office and Mother took off to visit Aunt Grace.

I read over the planned activities for this year's Fourth—the usual boat parade in the morning and the customary fireworks at night. But this year's festivities also included a barbeque at

John Whythe's. At the sight of that name, a vision of Cal's boat flashed into my head. With sudden determination, probably heat-induced, I decided that the Barnetts would make an appearance this year. No, we'd *actively* take part. We'd decorate *Pappy* and float along with the others in the regatta. And we'd bring our potato salad to the barbeque and be visibly patriotic.

Thinking about this made me feel better, as I began to stroll back to the house. We'd be a normal family, enjoying a holiday together, even if we were one person short. As I neared the end of the driveway, a slight, welcome breeze came off the water, cooling my hot forehead. I stood for a minute at the edge of our pier, soaking in the tiny bit of wind. I watched the water dance with the marshy tide just below the pier. I searched quickly across the Creek, and spied Cal sanding a long board stationed between two sawhorses and next to John Whythe's garage.

I don't think anyone else would have been able to find him, but my eyes were trained. I could make out his brown back, bending over the board, his arms moving back and forth in a determined rhythm. Though Lillian, Mother, and Daddy pulled my thoughts in their direction, Cal somehow entered my mind a good deal these days.

As the scallop plant's whistle blew shrilly, I felt a sudden pang of hunger and thirst. The whistle was the Creek's signal to stop, eat, and rest—and we'd all gotten used to it. When plans were announced to build a scallop plant down the Creek from John Whythe's, there were all sorts of protests. Rarely had Back Creek residents been so unified and so passionate.

However, the huge industrial-looking warehouse and rusty boats that lined the mouth of the Creek soon became a part of the scenery, just as the noon whistle became a part of our days. Every day at noon, when the whistle blew, we put down our tools and picked up our sandwiches.

From my vantage point, I could see Cal stop his scraping and reach for the cooler. I marched up the steps to the kitchen for some lunch, just as I'd been conditioned. I tapped my back pocket and thought about where, for temporary safe-keeping, I could put the letters and the dilemmas they posed for me. And I determined that I would get Lillian on board about the Fourth. Maybe we would drink a beer together to christen her dark room, and thus greet the new summer that always began officially with the Fourth of July.

So the summer took on a form and flow we had lacked since Lillian's departure. Daddy actually developed a routine of heading to the office early in the morning, visiting clients in the afternoon, and spending his evenings on the deck, sipping whiskey and, if he found a listener, telling stories. He always got to bed without anyone's assistance.

Lillian and I sat with him most nights, watching the stars and listening for the unexpected plink of a fish jumping in the water. Daddy told stories about Barnetts alive and dead—their mistakes and their triumphs. Daddy knew all the stories, and could he tell them! Lillian and I just let him talk about the past while we thought about the present. And on our side of the Creek, I constantly watched for that tiny pinpoint of light on the other side.

Lillian's present must have been a lot easier to consider than her past or her future. She was all action now, telling the stories of Back Creek in her own way, through her black and white photography. She spent her days searching for "good light," or wading knee-deep in Creek mud to get just the right angle. She was nowhere and everywhere.

One morning, she startled me by appearing lens-first under the pier. She barely avoided a barrage of buckshot when she surprised John Whythe one evening. Just as the sun was setting, she stole up on a little skiff. John had been hiding out, holding his gun in anticipation of some crab pot poachers making the rounds. He didn't have his glasses on and was pretty crocked. But, as always, Lillian ended up charming him into a "series" of pictures, kind of a waterman's expo, so to speak.

She also took a bunch of pictures of Cal at work on one of his many boat jobs. How she gained his consent, I'll never know. Most of the snapshots involved Cal sanding or painting or restoring something on the old sailboat, but a few were without the boat as background.

When Lillian wasn't around, I took time looking at one photo in particular. It was of Cal standing by the pier, reaching for something in his cooler. But he's looking for something else, something out at the end of the pier, or maybe farther out, somewhere in the Bay. Lillian focused on his face, and his eyes have this piercing quality to them. His eyes made me think of the fictional character Mr. Rochester looking and looking for someone—Jane Eyre, as it turned out. "Yearning" is the word Charlotte Bronte had for the look.

But maybe that's because I had put aside the love agonies of *Wuthering Heights* and instead was engaged in re-reading *Jane Eyre*. I couldn't help wondering what that picture revealed about Cal and what he might be yearning for. The picture fascinated me—I found myself wandering in to gaze at it whenever I knew Lillian wouldn't catch me. And I thought often about that night on Cal's boat.

In fact, that night sat in the back of my mind all summer. Though I continued to pay regular visits across the Creek, it was as if I had never touched his skin or felt his lips. Cal and I sipped on Budweisers and tossed out observations on the Creek and Creek people.

We never talked about ourselves.

Chapter Sixteen

❧

July 4, 1975 dawned red, white-hot, and blue. The droning sound of insects heralded record heat for the day. Worse, the high humidity made it feel like you were sucking air through a straw. Still, on the Fourth, the Creek held an energy and anticipation, bringing all the local people together for a giant party.

That morning, Lillian and I woke to the sound of tubas and trombones thumping. Daddy loved John Philip Sousa. He was also truly patriotic. Patriotism was a tricky thing in 1975, and July 4 was one day in the year when he could unabashedly play his scratchy Sousa marches at full blast, at least as loud as our ancient stereo could muster.

As I stumbled groggily down the stairs, still clad in my rumpled t-shirt and underwear, Daddy was already up. Directing an invisible marching band, he held an uncle's mahogany walking stick in one hand, a Bloody Mary in the other. His plaid boxer shorts were drooping dangerously, and he still sported his button-down shirt from yesterday's workday. I watched him for a few minutes, covering my ears against the noise. He looked pretty absorbed and definitely happy, so I let him be and went into the kitchen to find some cereal.

"What's with him?" said Lillian, stalking into the room like a sleepy cat.

"Oh, he likes marches," I answered, mouth full of Sugar Pops. "It *is* the Fourth, you know."

"Yeah, well, he should keep his stars and stripes to himself. Can't a person sleep around here?" She curled up in one of the straight-backed chairs pulled out from the table, her arms encircling her stomach. "Grace, stop that slurping!" she demanded.

"I'm not slurping. I'm eating." I lifted up the last bite of soggy cereal. Using the spoon as a pointer, I thought out loud, "What I can't figure out is why he's already smashed. Look at that pitcher . . ." I pointed to the cracked glass pitcher a quarter full of tomato juice and limes, an empty vodka bottle beside it. "It's only nine o'clock."

Lillian wouldn't speculate along with me. "You're giving me morning sickness with that cereal. I'm going to take a shower." Retreating upstairs, she left me to ponder Daddy's early, solitary celebration.

But it wasn't long before all three of us were drawn outside by the noise coming up the Creek. The Fourth of July Boat Parade started every year at ten o'clock, giving everyone time to get their potato salad, barbeque, plates of brownies, and coleslaw ready for afternoon picnics that would last well into the night, until the fireworks started at the Yorktown Victory Monument.

The day before, I had spent some time stringing some old crepe paper and a couple of flags across *Pappy*'s bow, anticipating we would join the noisy armada floating down the placid water. But one look at Daddy kiboshed that plan, so the three of us took our seats on the deck to watch the nautical procession.

It was quite a sight—every size of floating craft, from sleek cigarette boats on down to aluminum row boats, all of them sporting flags and ribbons and bandanas. There were working boats and pleasure boats and a few boats that floated only that one day a year. We saw red, white, and blue bikinis and tie-dyed flags.

To hark back to his dubious colonial heritage, John Whythe appeared in a gray wig and the outfit of the York High Generals mascot. The sign running alongside his Boston Whaler, "George Washington Crosses the Deleware," declared his patriotism and exposed his spelling problems.

One boat, with a pair of jungle fatigues as its only ornament, made me think about Cal, but I figured (correctly) he would avoid any sort of public display. Daddy and Lillian had a great time waving and pointing, clapping in time to the Sousa marches still blaring out from the living room.

By parade time, Daddy's Bloody Mary had been replaced by a can of Miller beer, which seemed rooted to his fingers. I knew that highball glasses half-full of Jack Daniel's would follow, and I had a feeling that before the afternoon picnic had even started, Daddy would be snoring away, passed out in his room.

It wasn't long before Lillian disappeared into the house and returned with an arsenal of cameras hanging around her neck and shoulders. She walked out onto the pier and turned every which way, picking up one camera, then another, and clicking buttons furiously.

I watched her from the deck, thinking how comfortable she seemed behind a lens. With a camera in front of her face, who could know the intense blue of her eyes, the golden glory of her hair—the beauty that had set her apart all her life? Today, on the pier, with Mother's light blue silk bathrobe billowing around her, she looked like a misplaced Madonna, searching the sky for good light and just the right angle.

I left Daddy and Lillian to their own means of escape and returned to the kitchen. Someone had to get the food ready for the picnic, and I was eager to push away the morning's forebodings by fixing coleslaw and cupcakes. I watched the last of the parade boats—a crab boat with a paper maché Statue of Liberty anchored on its bow—crawl by, honking its way past our pier.

Then I grabbed a head of cabbage still lying in the basket I'd taken to Joe's vegetable stand the day before. As I fingered its smooth outside, I thought that Mother, if she were home, would already have prepared and refrigerated a big blue ceramic bowl full of slaw, and decorated it with radishes cut in the shape of roses. I felt sad. But I took the big knife and began slicing the tough cabbage leaves, hacking away at my sadness in the pursuit of picnic fare. I turned up the radio and sang loudly as Aretha Franklin asked for a little R-E-S-P-E-C-T.

Clouds hovered on the edges of the sun's rays as I finished up the coleslaw and iced the cupcakes. The Creek was quiet again, the boats long gone around the sharp point of Dandy's peninsula, headed toward the York River and Yorktown Beach. Lillian disappeared into the shed with her film and Daddy retired to his office. Only the small sounds of the AM radio filled the silence. When I retreated to my room, I could barely hear the jangle of tunes.

I stood tiptoe at my little window, just as I had a few weeks ago to watch Tommy's boat come racing down the Creek. This time, I gazed across the water, studying the only boat tied up at John Whythe's marina. Despite all the movement behind Cal's Silverton—the many Creek people setting up for the picnic—his boat-home seemed more like a picture or a model, it was so still. But I kept on watching, not really knowing exactly what I was looking for.

There were only two times of the year when you saw all the folks living in Back Creek: the annual zoning meeting held in January at the courthouse, and the Fourth of July picnic, traditionally held at the Dandy Yacht Club's boat launch. This year, John Whythe was hosting the event, hoping to pull in contributions for a new flag, or so said Daddy. John Whythe was proud of flying the largest flag on the peninsula. His thirty-foot flagpole, with its custom-made American flag the size of a small playing field, was nothing if not attention-grabbing. Most Creek people hated its loud flapping. But John Whythe clung to the notion that it fittingly displayed his patriotism.

Sure enough, when we arrived at the picnic, we found a tall, upside down Uncle Sam's hat, labeled with a hastily printed card, "Flag Fund." Only a few dollar bills were in it, and they were probably John Whythe's.

The three of us were greeted like long-lost relatives. As I balanced my bowl of slaw to receive the cheek kisses of at least a dozen "aunts," I began to realize just how to ourselves Mother, Daddy, and I had become. Everyone crowed over how much I'd grown and how well Daddy looked. And Lillian was oohed and ahhed over, even as plates were shoved into our hands and we were led to the gingham-covered table of potato salad, barbeque, and iced tea.

Not one single question was asked about Mother's absence or Lillian's bulging stomach. This was the way of the Creek, and we understood it. They had sized up the situation immediately, but knew it was against the rules to talk about it. We were allowed only polite conversation: the depths below the surface were better left dark and murky.

I'd always known this, but today it struck me as a bad thing, especially as I watched Mrs. White, Tommy's mother, making a clearly painful effort to hold up her end of a conversation about angel food cake recipes, even while the scattered mess of her son's disaster lay in plain sight across the water. No one talked about the accident any more—all speculation about it had been buried along with Tommy.

Daddy was quick to find the beer, sitting iced in the claw-footed bathtub John Whythe had labeled an antique, and therefore felt justified leaving year-round in the yard. Year by year, the heavily cracked porcelain amenity sunk deeper into the crabgrass and dirt, until the tub had become part of the landscape. A group of men gathered around the tub, sipping beer and talking about newly proposed environmental laws limiting catches, and about tankers that wanted access to the York River. As I stood by the table helping to organize the desserts, I could hear them talking in loud voices.

They sounded as familiar as brothers. These men probably spoke with one another only a handful of times during the year, yet were bound together by life on the Creek. Daddy was always on top of the big issues of the day; his office was right next to the courthouse, and he kept up on all cases pertinent to Back Creek's livelihood and interests. Sneaking glances at Cal's boat, I realized that their talk was so limited and local that helicopter lifts off rooftops in faraway Asian cities, and even college protests of the war, had yet to enter their conversations.

Lillian proved to be quite the belle of the picnic. Any woman under the age of seventy wanted to hear about living in New York: the stores, the famous people, the clubs. Lillian had gathered a throng of listeners under the oak tree, which had challenged the sandy soil and survived since the turn of the century. Lillian sat in an old rocker and the women fanned around her, some seated on the ground, some busying themselves at the iced tea table by cutting up lemons and mixing up powdered tea and Kool-Aid.

Their voices were soft compared to the men's, and their conversation was punctuated by giggles and occasional gasps. Lillian waved her hands and rocked in the chair as she talked, her hair falling gracefully around her face as her eyes moved around the group.

The heat of the afternoon covered the picnic like a tent—it was hard to lift up a glass without sweating. We were used to the mid-summer heat and humidity, but these oppressive conditions could mean only one thing—a thunderstorm was coming. And from the looks of the bruise-colored clouds beginning to emerge from behind the sun, a doozey of a storm was brewing. As the afternoon went on, the hot brightness gave way to a duller and duller whiteness, with only an empty circle standing in the sky to remind us of the sun.

I wandered about the party, greeted by voices as familiar as the blankets on my bed. I hung about the edge of things, the only person my age in attendance. Most of the high school crowd had driven across the water to Virginia Beach to hang out with the surfers who congregated there. They would drink beer and smoke dope and get fried. If they'd thought to get tickets, maybe they'd attend an outdoor concert of local bands.

I knew all this because I'd heard about it; no one ever thought to ask me to come, and I never wanted to go. Though I'd gone to school with them since we could climb on a school bus, the high school crowd had never interested me much. I'd always felt more comfortable listening to adults than partying with teenagers.

Eventually, I ran out of desserts to organize and groups to stand on the edges of and listen to. I could feel my earlier energy leaving me, slipping out through the tiny hole created that morning by Daddy's drinking. I wandered away from the voices and activity, down to the water's edge and out onto the pier where Cal's boat lay quiet and undisturbed by the movement on shore.

I didn't really expect him to be there. He'd probably set out early that morning in his canoe, heading toward the tangled, marshy byways of the Creek, far away from the patriotic grasp of July Fourth. Sure enough, as I reached the end of the pier, I noticed loose ropes floating in the water next to the old Silverton. I don't know why I decided to do what I did next, but I was drawn to the boat. I stood beside it, one hand touching its smooth side, taking comfort in it as I always had.

Behind me was the murmur of conversations, the occasional hoot of laughter. I turned to look at the constantly moving groups, expanding and meandering like the waves of jellyfish drifting through the Creek. From far off, I heard a rumble, like the sky clearing its throat. I'd like to think I was instinctively seeking shelter when I stepped onto Cal's boat and pushed the door to the cabin, something no one except Cal had ever done.

As the door swung open, my hand automatically let go of the handle. I glanced behind me to see if anyone could notice, though I knew the Fourth of July crowd was not paying the least bit of attention to Cal's old boat or to me. The door stayed open and, almost against their will, my once-white tennis shoes shuffled across the transom. I ducked my head to enter the darkness of the cabin, then closed the door carefully behind me and breathed in the strange mix of odors that greeted me.

Sniffing, I tried to sort out the smells while my eyes tried frantically to adjust to the lack of light. From my infrequent sneak visits to Daddy's office, I recognized a stale whiskey odor. And there was some kind of oil smell—like that of the gas station in the summer. I couldn't quite recognize it, but there *was* something else. Then I knew.

It was the smell of old newspapers, like the pile constantly amassing on the old wood stove in our kitchen. No matter how often Bernice cleaned it off and threw the papers into the trash in the garage, my father was sure to remember some story he hadn't read and go fishing the pile right out of the big trash can devoted to paper stuff. I associated that smell with family times—being in the kitchen for meals and, sometimes, for arguments. That was before Mother left. Now the papers accumulated unread in the garage, bound together in their original rubber bands. I felt a small victory at recognizing that distracting, but not unwelcome, smell.

With my eyes beginning to adjust, I began to look around. I knew I should have felt like I was trespassing—Cal's handwritten sign, posted on a piling, should have reminded me of that. But I was too far in not to continue, and it was all in the service of knowing him better—or so I told myself.

I groped along the wall next to the door, discovering with my fingers a mess of objects: a plastic cup with a stiff-ended paintbrush resting in it, a tape measure, sunglasses, a half-filled beer can, and a flashlight. Who could imagine Cal having something as practical as a flashlight within such easy reach, or that it had batteries and worked?

I pressed the flashlight's stiff button, creating a tiny halo of light on the ceiling beams above me. It was just enough light to see with and not so much as to attract the attention of any stray Fourth of July picnicker who wandered down to the pier. Like an undercover agent, I sketched the outline of the cabin with the small circle of light, sweeping across the close space quickly and evenly. Then I traced again, because it took me a minute to figure out what I was seeing.

Taped and thumb-tacked on every inch of the walls were pieces of newspapers—curling, stiff, overlapping newspapers. Focusing the flashlight, I strained my eyes to read the yellowing print: "Underwater Frogmen Risk Life and Limb," "Viet Cong Body Count Rises in Delta," "Invasion of Cambodia Imminent." So many headlines, so much print—stories from the *New York Times*, the *Washington Post*, *The Daily Press*, *Stars and Stripes*—I even spied a column from the *Yorktown Crier*.

There were stories about troops in Vietnam jungles, soldiers in helicopters, pilots flying into Saigon. But up on the walls, more than any other, were stories about sailors and Marines fighting the sea war. There were fuzzy pictures of sampans and marsh grasses and military-looking vessels with uniformed boys standing at surprised attention. There were pictures of upended docks and unidentifiable debris floating alongside.

The print was faded and the articles were pinned on top of each other in haphazard fashion, but they were still readable. Using the flashlight's tiny beam, I focused in and read. I skimmed stories about defeats, stories about so-called victories, stories about soldiers coming back heroes, stories about soldiers coming back in pieces. As I made my way around the small closed space, I realized that Cal had assembled a comprehensive war chronicle, complete with pictures and maps. I kept looking closely and reading, and pretty soon I was lost in the heat and wet of Vietnam.

Until I heard a *click*.

It was a sound I had heard only in movies—in *Dirty Harry* movies, to be specific. As I slowly pulled away from the newspapers, I felt my stomach shrink and limbs melt, because I knew that somewhere in the shadows behind me was a gun barrel pointed at me.

"Identify yourself," a clipped voice commanded from the tiny closed storage space at the bow of the boat. I instinctively moved the flashlight beam to the door; it shook wildly. I had a hard time getting any voice out. "It's Grace," I whispered.

I could hear rough breathing now and the creak of hinges. The flashlight's beam drooped as I saw a shine of metal in the door's slit. I started to feel dizzy. Just as I let the flashlight drop, I felt a hand grab my shoulder tightly.

"What the hell are you doing here? Go on now!"

It was Cal. I could smell his sweat. Even in the dark that swallowed us up, I could almost see that scary, crazy look in his eyes, like the other time I'd surprised him. This time, he propelled me back to the door of the cabin, opened the door, and thrust me out. All I saw of him was his bronzed forearm. Then the door was shut tight. I stood with unsure footing on the deck. My legs wouldn't work, and the boat was now dipping and swaying with the moving water below.

Up above, a mass of pitch blackness was moving toward the Creek. A percussion beat was drifting in from the Bay, and the wind was kicking up. But I couldn't think about that. My heart was stuck way up in my throat and my knees were shaking. There was only silence from the cabin door behind me, a tomb-like calm in the coming storm. I stood there on the deck, feeling dampness on my face—the advance guard of the storm and my own tears. I felt a white cap swirl of emotion, and my heart suddenly and painfully ached.

With no other solution in sight, I sped away from Cal's boat to find Daddy and Lillian.

Chapter Seventeen

F rom behind the line of black overtaking the horizon, the sun was sending out some final long rays. They lit up the Creek with paint strokes of purple, giving everything a weird glow. I trudged up the small incline, across the crabgrass and dandelions, to the edge of the festivities. The ladies had set stones on the rippling tablecloths, and the Save-A-Flag donation jar had been anchored optimistically with some rope.

I spotted Lillian, whose audience had been reduced to one— Mrs. White, who stuck out in her mourning outfit of black skirt and blouse. Lillian's fair skin, pale hair, and white cotton dress, now billowing up in the wind, made Mrs. White seem all the sadder in her black. Because of my quick jog up from the pier, I was breathing hard. My eyes darted about the crowd looking for Daddy. He was nowhere to be seen, so, unthinkingly, I marched straight for Lillian.

"Well, it's just that he wasn't cut out for New York life, you know?" Lillian's voice rose crazy and unsure. She sounded like she was pleading with Mrs. White, who stood at attention, bobbing her head at Lillian's words. The already fierce wind was picking up, and there was a lot of commotion as women grabbed bowls and tablecloths and men grabbed chairs to head for John Whythe's porch. I was close enough to the big oak tree where Lillian and Mrs. White were standing that I could have called out to them, but they didn't seem to notice the gathering storm.

Lillian's voice grew stronger and louder as the wind increased. People shouted, "Come on, come on," and the thunder became a march beat. Way off in the York, I could see long spider legs of lightning strike the water. But the two women had practically rooted themselves by the oak, Lillian talking and talking and Mrs. White nodding and nodding.

"I didn't know he'd come back. We had a fight about something—I can't remember what—and he said he was going back, but I didn't believe him. I mean, you have to know, it wasn't my fault. Tommy was just upset about a lot of things. He didn't know what he was doing . . ."

Lillian's words were washed away by a sudden gust of wind and rain, yet Lillian and Mrs. White appeared immoveable. A sharp clap of thunder woke me to action. I ran over to them, grabbed their hands, and pulled them over to the nearby boat shed.

It was too far to get to the Whythe house, where the rest of the partyers had retreated, so I headed for the nearest thing resembling shelter. Dragging an almost catatonic woman along with one nearly six months pregnant wasn't easy. We were all soaked by the time we made it inside the big, empty shed with its concrete floor and aluminum siding. The rain made an angry rattle on the aluminum roof.

Due to some fluke of nature, John Whythe's shed remained cool even in the hottest summer heat. For the boats owned by people from Newport News, the shed provided winter storage. The owners presumed that their boats would escape the damage the winter cold could wreak on engines and wood.

The shed, however, was even colder than the water, so the boat owners always had to spend some money on their boats before embarking on their customary Bay pleasure trips during the summer. The shed was empty now. The sailboats and motorboats bobbed and rocked outside, tied to the rows of pilings.

The three of us stood in the building, which seemed cavernous. The only light entered from the outside. The shadowy dimness and cold made me feel as if I were in a forgotten cave. We hugged ourselves and stared at the ceiling. Thunder boomed and echoed around us.

Finally, I spoke, shouting to be heard above the rumble outside, "We need to get up to the house and get some towels!"

Lillian and Mrs. White both brought their eyes back down from the steel braces above them and looked at me, then at each other. Lillian shook her head, and shook her body, spewing water everywhere like a retriever coming out of the marsh. Mrs. White reached up a tentative hand and patted her soaked hair, smoothing her now flattened strands over her ears. We all stared at each other until Lillian, with a burst of laughter that echoed up and down the aluminum siding walls, said, "Well, we're some mess, aren't we?"

Mrs. White nodded in agreement, but her head had lost that mechanical motion I'd seen under the oak. I took her by the elbow, moving her toward the door, and motioned to Lillian to take her to the house, even as I was saying to her, "Now, if you just walk real fast, you'll hardly get wet at all. Let Lillian take you on up there. I'm sure they'll have some coffee to warm you up."

Lillian, shaking out the wet cotton that had cemented itself around her middle, stepped toward the older woman. "Yeah, let's go on up there. I'm sure they'll all be wondering where we went. You know how Back Creek people like to stick their noses into everyone's business." With that leap into the present, Lillian's voice took on its usual assurance—the high-pitched pleading I'd heard out by the tree was gone.

They quickly exited the shed, the rain coming in long sheets now, and the thunder receding as the storm moved on. That's one thing about thunderstorms on the Creek—they may come fast and furious, but they don't stay around long. In fact, before you know it, the wind and the thunder and the lightning give way to the sun. When it peeps out, it gives everything wet a kind of shine, like somebody up there wants to remind you there's always a calm *after* the storm.

I looked out of the shed opening and watched the gray clouds moving rapidly across the sky. The sun was already out of sight because it was getting on toward twilight. The rain, almost down to sprinkles, was easing up. I squeezed out the water from my shirt and shorts, getting ready to head up to the house and face the crowd. I was just about to leave the shed when I heard a funny sound that stopped me at the door—a sort of sobbing sound, and I immediately thought of Cal.

Though I could still feel my heart pounding from the scare and hurt he'd given me earlier, I knew I had to explain things to him. I could never *not* care about Cal. As I tried to make out the source of the sound, I thought about him sitting holed up in his boat like a prisoner of war, while the rest of the world was up the hill a little ways, having a grand time celebrating the Fourth. I figured he'd escaped from the noise and intrusions, and preferred to stay away from the crowds. But now I realized he wanted to isolate himself, as if he couldn't or wouldn't face anyone—not even me once I'd found out about him.

By sliding through that unlocked cabin door, I'd discovered his obsession with the war—and neither I nor anyone else had ever known about that before. He never talked about being over there, about coming back, or about why he came back. He stayed in the now, except for the one time he'd let slip how he'd gotten over there. The rest of his life on—from leaving high school to coming back to Back Creek—was a blank as far as I knew.

But using newspaper clippings, he had reconstructed the war, and seemed to be consumed by it. Every night he went to sleep, and every morning he woke up, he'd be reminded of it. I sighed, deciding a different Cal had kicked me out of the cabin—one I didn't know. It made me sad.

So I immediately thought of him when I heard the sobbing. Perhaps he felt bad about how he'd talked to me—bad enough to come find me and cry about it. I knew I was just imagining one of my Bronte dramas, but I definitely wasn't imagining that sound. I moved quietly down the length of the shed, listening past the plinking of the rain on the roof. The sound grew more distinguishable as I approached the back. Behind a big box full of life preservers, I found the source of the sobbing.

"Daddy?" I moved closer, barely breathing, as if I would disturb something. The light in the shed was a kind of twilight gray. I took my glasses off and tucked them in my pocket. Sometimes, it was easier to see things without them. "Daddy?" I repeated softly.

He sat on an old wooden motor box, one that must have been replaced by something newer and sturdier on one of the boats left in the shed for the winter. His legs dangled across the front of it, his worn Topsiders turned out duck-footed. He held his face in his hands, so he didn't see me at first. I don't think he would have noticed me if I hadn't hoisted myself onto the motor box beside him.

The wood was cold and slick under my bare legs. Daddy started a little when my bottom hit the box. He wiped off his face with his oxford cloth sleeve—I wondered how in the world he'd ever left the house without his ever-present handkerchief. He shook his shoulders and straightened up, so when he looked at me, he looked right into my eyes.

His eyes were red-rimmed and his cheeks bore the marks of hard-cried tears, but he gave out a great sigh and inhaled deeply, as if trying to expel the feeling that had caught him so firmly. I thought of reaching out to him, of putting my arms around his shoulders, or holding onto his hands. But he closed off into himself and placed his hands in his lap. I could feel my wet shorts gluing me to the motor box. Daddy was as dry as a bone.

"Grace," he said, his voice much too loud and echoing in that big empty space. I jumped a little. "Grace," he said, adjusting the volume this time, "I just don't know what I'm going to do." He sighed again, deeply.

I responded pretty naturally. "Daddy, you'll feel better after you've had some supper and some iced tea and washed out some of that beer you've been drinking all day. You always feel better the next day." I offered this standard line, which at one time was a sort of family joke.

He exhaled again. "No, no. It's not the drinking. It's never the drinking."

I was ready to take issue with him over this but kept quiet. Outside, I imagined the party might be breaking up and everyone getting ready to gather up their things and head down to Yorktown Beach to watch the fireworks. It had to be getting dark outside by now—there was barely any light in the shed. Daddy was observing something up along the ceiling edge, craning his neck and tilting his head back.

"It's raining," he finally said.

"Daddy, it's been thunder-storming like crazy. Where have you been?" My irritation at his typical obliviousness brought me back to the shed. "How could you miss the entire storm?" I asked, turning to him and gesturing with my hands palms up and shoulder-high.

Daddy jumped up from the box and grabbed my hands. "That's just how your mother would hold up her hands. And she'd say the same thing, with that same exasperated tone." He brought my hands together in front of me and squeezed them tightly.

"Grace," he almost shouted, "you've got to go get her." His words echoed and came back on themselves. "We just can't have her gone now." I wrested my hands free and Daddy fell down to his knees, much to my horror. He bowed his head. "I don't know what to do this time," he muttered. "I need her here. You need her here. And Lillian . . . I can't think what we're going to do with her if your mother's not here. She's got to come back."

I sat frozen to the box. This couldn't be my father speaking, kneeling like an errant knight, begging for the help of my mother. He hardly seemed to notice when she wasn't there, always pretending she was off on some kind of vacation he'd made possible.

He might tell stories about their courtship and early days, but I'd never heard him say he needed her. And I'd never known him to ask anyone for anything. He regained his feet and spoke again, calmer and softer this time.

"Grace, you've got to drive down there and bring her back. She belongs here with her family, not on some Godforsaken patch of ground with a bunch of rednecks. You tell her how things are here and she'll come back with you."

His voice took on the practiced tones of lawyerly persuasion.

"You're the only one who can bring her back."

Words, or parts of words, shot through my consciousness like so many bursts of colorful fireworks, but I couldn't get them out of my mouth.

Then, with a sudden motion, Daddy stood up and gently pulled me from my seat. I took a little leap from the motor box and landed flat-footed beside him, once again looking up at him.

Daddy seemed to change once I was beside him. He cleared his throat, rolled down his sleeves, buttoned his cuffs, and tucked his shirt into his pants. His movements made me suddenly self-conscious, and I squeezed the corner of my shorts, trying to extract a little more of the dampness. I rummaged in my pocket and found a rubber band to gather back my hair, now a heavy, tangled mess. We both straightened up—it was as if we had to return to ourselves after revealing too much to the other.

With a final smoothing of his shirt front and a last swipe over his hair, Daddy turned toward the shed door at the end opposite us. Then he turned back to me and, spotting my glasses in my t-shirt pocket, placed them gently in my hand.

"Grace, you'll get lost if you don't keep these on—or you'll trip over something and hurt yourself." I managed a smile—I'd been told this before. I pulled the wire-frames over my ears and saw a shadowed, straightened Daddy, motioning me to follow.

I shook the hem of my shirt and walked toward the shed door, feeling my tennis shoes squish sadly on the concrete floor. As we passed through the door into the gray twilight, I felt a damp coolness outside. The storm had broken the heat, at least for the evening. Daddy waved his hand and chatted with people as they packed up their plates and leftovers in the cars lining John Whythe's driveway. I paused in the shadows, checking myself, to see if that scene in the shed had really happened. Car trunks slammed and sounds of laughter hung in the air. Everyone was headed to the fireworks or home to bright kitchens and cool beds.

As my eyes hit the brightness of John Whythe's floodlights, I wasn't sure where anyone I cared about was headed. Things seemed in wild disarray, like the wet leaves and branches that littered the grass, torn away from trees by the storm's wind.

Later that night, after I'd endured a silent ride home punctuated only by Lillian's slow breathing as she slept, I found myself once again perched at my bedroom window, staring across the Creek. The water looked deep and still. All was quiet, except for the constant lapping of the water against the piers and the sad banging of the empty rope against the flag pole.

The sound drew my attention, and I zeroed in on the unlit, empty-looking ghost ship—the Silverton. I could barely see the white frame of the cabin roof.

I turned away from the window and toward my bed. My eyes looked out into the dark of my room while my mind worked hard, putting together the initial pieces of a plan.

Chapter Eighteen

The house was dead quiet, except when Daddy erupted with one of his louder snores. Even the cicadas abandoned their symphonic buzz. Maybe it was too quiet—there was nothing anchoring me to the present. My mind moved back and forth between the night's images and my visions for the future—the metallic gleam in Cal's hand, Lillian's white figure against the dark of the storm, my father's tear-streaked face, and a farm house surrounded by dormant tobacco fields. Everything was a backwards jumble. Nothing was what I had thought. The only definite I could pull from the confusion was one of abandonment—I felt completely alone.

I thought of Jane Eyre as she wandered the heath, sure there was no one for her. In fact, I turned on the light, spotted the worn paperback on my dresser, and re-read Chapter 28, finding a momentary calm in the forlornness of Jane's situation. With relief, I read of Jane's rescue. Maybe there was a chance for me after all.

I can't really explain how and why I found myself that night standing at the edge of our pier, looking intently across the Creek at Cal's boat. It was after midnight, and the clouds of the night storm had been run off by a bright moon, which cast a shadowy glow across the water. Slipping on shorts, and tiptoeing down the steps and out the door seemed like a dream, but standing out there, as close to the Creek as I could get, felt very real.

For a minute, I dangled my toes in the water, sensing a surprising warmth. I searched the water for the ghostly blobs that haunted it in such summertime abundance, but the rain and wind must have driven them out with the tide. I'm not exactly sure what I was thinking, or if I was thinking at all, when I eased myself into the water, feeling its body-temperature warmth as I pushed away from the barnacle-covered ladder. I kept my head above water as I moved slowly toward the other side of the Creek.

I kept my eyes and mind fastened on the beam of light resting on the dock right next to the old Silverton. Suspicious of Cal's potential to make trouble, John Whythe, three or so years ago, had actually paid to have a large metal light mounted on the pier Cal tied his boat to—it was the only light he left on all the time. Of course, as the years went by and nothing happened, John Whythe forgot about his initial worries, but the light remained.

Cal could have dismantled it, or casually broken the bulbs, if he'd wanted to. But he let the light continue to shine, I think as a kind of peace offering—a guarantee he wasn't there to cause problems. He just moved the boat as far forward as it would go and covered the windows in his cabin. The light provided me my direction that night—I dogpaddled toward it deliberately and calmly, trying not to think of what else might be swimming in the water with me.

When we were little, we swam in the Creek all spring, until the jellyfish problem became too bad. Mother would bundle me up in an orange, overly large lifejacket that bobbed up against my chin. Lillian was a good swimmer and Mother never seemed to worry about her in the water. She dove off the pier in a graceful arc, always entering the water shallow enough to keep from hitting her head on the bottom and to avoid any of the slimy grasses that grew there. I followed her into the water feet-first, legs churning, arms flapping.

Mother, slathering baby oil on her already brown skin and sipping from a plastic cup, watched us from her towel on the pier.

She wore movie star sunglasses and, gaping up at her with my chin pushed high by the life jacket, I thought she looked much more glamorous than Marilyn Monroe, whom I'd seen in *Life* magazine pictures. Mother wore a two-piece suit—and she looked good in it. She was the only woman in Back Creek to risk such exposure.

Until Lillian became uninterested in the Creek—about the time she was old enough to wear a bikini—she liked exploring the water and testing her physical prowess. She called for Mother to look out for boats while she swam across the channel, her strong strokes pulling her away from us until I could see only her rising and falling arms and the white wave of her kick. In those days, she always made it back across the Creek, and Mother and I always whooped and clapped as she lifted her sleek head and kicked even harder approaching home.

When I felt the water temperature chill, I knew I'd hit the channel where the Creek floor, suddenly and dramatically, drops off about twenty feet. The summer after Lillian left, my father had bought a depth finder and hooked it up to *Pappy*. Mother was already disappearing on the weekends, and so, though it was only he and I, we went out on the boat a few times, just to get the motor running. I stayed in the cabin on these trips because I was fascinated by the dips and rises revealed in the depth finder's thin blue lines. I even studied a map of the Creek's underbelly that I'd pried from Daddy's office one day when he wasn't home.

So this summer night, I had a good sense of what I was swimming across. I could see those dips and rises in my head as I reached my arms out through the water and frog-kicked my way across. The top of my hair was still dry. It wasn't until I reached the end of John Whythe's pier that I dipped my head under, grabbing onto the short ladder to hoist myself up the metal rungs. As I emerged, the only sound was the patter of drops falling into the water below. I was as quiet as the Creek itself.

I glided silently down the pier toward the unlit cabin. Because I wasn't wearing my glasses, everything had a filmy grayness to it, and I had trouble telling what was real and what was shadow. I wasn't thinking about direction, or about what I would do once I got to the cabin, or even exactly what I was doing over on this side of the Creek at this hour. I wasn't thinking at all—just moving deliberately, slowly, like the tide. Cal would have to listen to my explanation. And then he'd have to tell me the story behind all those pictures hanging by thumbtacks in the boat's cabin—and the story behind the gun.

Then I tripped. I caught my toe in a coil of hose that lay in a shadow and I went down with a thump that seemed to echo the entire length of the Creek. I managed not to cry out, though I landed right on my knee and it hurt something fierce. Struggling up, I rubbed my knee, but I knew the damage was done. That sleek swimmer was gone, and I was back to being Grace, tripping over shadows, handicapped by limited vision.

The cabin door snapped open and my eyes opened wide, trying to identify a shadow creeping around the side of the boat. I prayed that Cal had left that silver metal gleam back in the cabin somewhere, and I felt my heart pound painfully in my ears. Not a sound would leave my throat. I turned around, back and forth, trying to see past the reflection and shadow, but I couldn't focus my eyes in the gray-blackness. My knee was killing me and I was ready to turn back to the Creek and disappear into its invisible warmth.

Then I felt a hand on my shoulder, from the back, and I smelled his smell—a combination of saltwater, turpentine, Dial soap and, tonight, a hint of whiskey. The touch was gentle, and to my huge relief, he wasn't going to shoot me. I turned around, reached up to his firm shoulders, and clung to him.

"Grace," he whispered, "what the hell are you doing here? Now?" He rested his hand on my sopping back.

"I had to talk to you," I tried to whisper, but with my heart pounding and my knee throbbing, I was gasping for breath and had trouble getting any words out. "Everything is all messed up and I feel so bad and I can't stand it . . ." I relaxed my body as I felt him actually hold me.

Somewhere, a flutter of duck noises started up and Cal pulled me toward the boat. "Come on, let's get inside."

He took my hand and led me up the pier, onto the side of the boat, and into the cabin. I limped behind him, feeling like a big, dripping mess, barely able to see in front of me. Only when we passed under the dim glow of the pier's light did I realize Cal was naked.

His cabin was, if anything, even darker and danker than before the storm. My bare feet hesitated on the scratchy indoor-outdoor carpeting, but Cal drew me farther into the cabin, down the few steps and onto the bunk below. As he used a flashlight to examine my knee, I found myself amazed that sheets and a blanket actually covered the bunk.

"Lie down," he commanded, and held my leg in his hand. The skin felt pretty roughed up, but his touch was light as air, so I relaxed a little.

"But I'm all wet, and I'm messing up your bed," I said, my voice returning to me. I started to rise, but he put his arm around my shoulder and pushed me back down, his head even with mine, his long legs hanging out over the end of the bunk.

"That knee's okay, but it's gonna be plenty black and blue," he declared in a low voice. I wasn't thinking too much about the knee at that point. I was thinking about how comfortable I felt, lying on Cal's bunk in my wet clothes, his arm around my shoulders, his hand holding onto my elbow. In this stationary state, breathing in the old, stale air of the boat, I suddenly broke down. Covering my face, I began to weep silently, painfully, and completely. It was probably the third time in my life I really cried.

Cal touched my face, wiping away the tears, and drew me close to him. Then he was kissing me. And I was kissing back. My hands roved over his bare back, feeling the smooth toughness of his skin. And his hands roved gently down my stomach, across my hips, softly pushing down the waist of my shorts. At the same time, I was pulling up my wet t-shirt, until in a sudden cosmic moment, I was naked, too.

Somehow, peeling off my Creek-damp clothes freed me up. My worry and sadness sank of their own weight, as if I'd broken the surface of some deep channel. Cal moved on top of me and kissed my face, kissed all the tears away, until I was covered with his smell, his essence. I could feel my body pulling toward him with an urgency I had never felt before—me, Grace, who had never so much as kissed a boy before.

I knew this was no furtive making-out in the back of someone's car. I also knew this was not the restrained romance of Jane and Mr. Rochester. We were riding a wave of something that was neither passion nor lust—it came from somewhere deeper.

Who can explain why people become who they are in unexpected, unplanned moments? You can only tell the story and hope for understanding.

I sank into the moment, but Cal pushed himself away. He rolled over on his side, against the curved wall of the cabin. The air was heavy and I strained to breathe. Seeing the huge rise and fall of Cal's chest, I knew that he, too, was struggling to find some oxygen in the small space.

And so, for quite a while, we lay there on that now-damp bunk, barely touching in our nakedness and need. I lost all sense of time—it could have been hours, it could have been minutes. For a while, just lying there was enough—enough to give us a kind of peace, to keep at bay the looming questions and answers. The sound of our lungs working and the water lapping onto the boat's hull were all that disturbed the deep silence.

I could feel my eyes growing heavy in the humid warmth of that tiny cabin. I think I actually dozed for a while—the hint of a dream began to spin in my mind. It was a dream of wind and thunder, with strong oak branches swaying, and me stuck up in one of the boughs. In the dream, it was as if the sound were turned off and the noise had been stripped from everything. Lillian's face appeared just below me, pale and gleaming, and I reached for it, but I couldn't let go of the branch. *Why Lillian? Why now?* Unable to resolve the dream's confusion, I felt Cal as he lifted me up and out the door, into the cooler darkness outside.

At first, still caught up in the dream, I wondered what had happened to all the rain. But Cal took me by the hand and led me to the bow of the boat. So we sat, facing the west end of the Creek, where it branched off into a handful of wandering little creeks and marshes. A few pier lights blazed, and I could sense a graying of the sky, my only clues as to how late, or how early, it really was.

The uncomfortable feel of the boat's bow against my bottom made me realize that I was naked. I looked around for a stray towel or abandoned shirt, but all I could do was cover my breasts by folding my elbows and hugging my shoulders. The slight movement and fresh air felt good against my body—I felt the sweat evaporate and my nipples harden. Cal shifted beside me, drawing his knees up to his chest and wrapping his arms around himself. We sat on the top of his boat, as we had so many nights before—except everything had changed.

"What happened tonight—before?" I finally whispered, thinking about the newspapers and the gun. I turned to face his profile, outlined in the beam of the pier light.

At first, I didn't think he would answer. I listened hard, but all I heard were the Creek noises. Finally, I watched him shake his head, the damp ends of his hair curling around his shoulder. "Aw, Grace, I don't know. I was having a bad time and I . . . I needed . . . I needed . . . something, I guess." His voice dropped to barely a murmur.

Silence once again deposited itself with a heavy weight. He moved his hands in the air, as if he could catch the words he wanted. I suddenly understood he was talking about what had just happened—down in the cabin. For a second, I thought he might try to apologize—to say he respected me or something like that.

But I didn't want to hear that now. I needed to know the story before all this. I wanted him to tell me the story behind that silver gleam in the cabin door and the story of all those wall hangings. You have to take things one step at a time.

I touched his shoulder, tracing the thin, strong bones that stood out, and grabbed one of his moving hands. Then I asked him about pushing me off the boat, and about the newspaper stuff on the walls. I asked him what he was hiding, and what he was afraid of.

He took my hand and put our fingers to my lips. He stood up and I thought for a minute he would repeat his performance of another night, screaming and scaring the shit out of me. I grabbed onto his ankle, the only body part I could reach, and held on tightly.

But I was wrong. He squatted down beside me, wrapping his arms around his knees. Somewhere, far away from me, he was gathering himself, and I just had to get out of his way. So I let go of him.

Against the canopy of fading stars, his voice finally emerged in a rushing stream of words. I lost the night and myself in his story.

Chapter Nineteen

A soft gray light was just emerging over the Creek when Cal's voice finally gave out. The jungles of Vietnam disappeared, the white walls of the hospital faded, and there was just the two of us, buck naked and uncomfortable, on top of a boat. There was now enough light for us to see ourselves and realize the night was over.

What could I say to his story—which was long and detailed, yet simple enough?

After basic training, Cal had joined a Special Ops scuba unit. During what was to be his first big secret mission—the placing of mines in an enemy harbor—things got messed up, and he was lucky to get out alive. The guy he was working with wasn't so lucky. They carried Cal out of the water and flew him to a military hospital in Saigon, where they tried to fix him. Finally, because there was nothing wrong with his body, they sent him home.

If I could only be Jane Eyre and offer the right words of moral support. But I was Grace, and all I could murmur was, "I didn't know." Cal didn't seem to want or expect any response. After catching his breath, he got up and held out his hand, turning his eyes away. As we made our way back to the cabin, I wondered if he regretted giving up his story to me, and if he wished he could take it back. We dressed in silence, Cal quickly pulling on shorts and leaving me to retrieve my still-damp shirt and shorts. I kept bumping into the walls as the boat rocked gently against the pier.

I found Cal outside, preparing the canoe for another trip across the water. Everything from the night's episode seemed to vanish with the rising sun, like those vapors that make the Creek so mysterious in the morning. I squished into the canoe, taking up the paddle.

"Like I told you before," he said, "be careful sneaking back in." A moment before pushing the canoe into the Creek and letting go, he leaned down to ear level and whispered, "Amazin' Grace."

Then he was gone, retreating into the solitude of the cabin. I was alone, paddling across the flat blackness of the early morning water. I dug deep into the water, balancing the paddle painfully on my knees. A lone mallard crossed my path, his dull green head bobbing bravely in front of the canoe. The hollow plinking of the water against the aluminum sides made me think of the rain against the boat shed's roof, and of Daddy. Suddenly, July Fourth came back to me. What a mess everything seemed—maybe it was better when everyone just closed their doors and stayed away.

I dragged the canoe up the bank and laid it on its side among the grasses. Suddenly, the combined effects of no sleep and too much emotion assaulted me, and all I could think to do was to curl up beside the canoe in the soft grass and sleep.

~

"It's the only thing to do," I kept whispering to myself, "and I'm the only one who can do it." As I packed—two clean pairs of shorts, a few t-shirts, some clean underwear and, as an afterthought, a cotton sundress my mother had left in my closet the week before she left—pink streaks of dawn were just showing through the thick glass of my room's windows.

I folded each article hurriedly and stuffed everything into a small laundry bag Bernice had given me for my graduation. I made my bed, smoothing out the wrinkled sheets and using the quilt to cover over the previous night's restlessness. I thought to write a note, but couldn't find anything except notebook paper and an inkless ballpoint pen.

I tiptoed down the creaking stairs, the only noise in the silent house. At the bottom of the stairs, I turned and entered Daddy's office, pausing for a moment to appreciate the violation I was committing. But desperate times call for desperate measures. I knew there had to be a map in there, and I was sure I needed some kind of guidance to get to North Carolina. I had the name of the town nearest the farm—Hendersonville. Except for that, and my decision to go, I had nothing.

I had decided to do what Daddy had asked me to do—get to that North Carolina farmhouse and bring Mother back—all by myself. Once the coming dawn and the scratchy grass had insisted I wake up from my little nest beside the canoe, the next step seemed so clear, especially after I'd washed the Creek off in the shower and retrieved my glasses.

I dug through the drawer of a tall file cabinet Daddy had cryptically labeled "Directions," and found all kinds of stiff, water-stained maps of the Inland Waterway. Finding a roadmap turned out to be more of a challenge, especially in the dark of the office. Finally, on the back of one map, I came across an inset of Virginia and North Carolina highways, and decided it would have to do. I had to get moving before I thought too hard about what I was attempting.

I listened to the quiet of the house before I opened the front door. After yesterday's excitement, Daddy would probably go late to the office, and only hunger would get Lillian out of bed before noon. By then, I would be a long way down the road. I'd let them know where I was after I got there.

Map in hand, laundry bag slung over my back, I squeezed through the door, taking care not to let it slap shut. The sun was just beginning to appear and the insects chimed in with their own salute to the day. I heard the gulls crying after a crabber, who was baiting his pots from his boat. How often had I watched the birds dip and swerve into the water, attempting to steal a piece of old fish a crabber would jam into the crab pot's trap?

Because I had stuffed my tennis shoes somewhere deep into my bag, I walked gingerly across the driveway in my bare feet and paused in front of the two vehicles, parked side by side—our ancient boat of a station wagon, with its paneled doors and dented fenders, and Lillian's red sports car. I hesitated, but because there was so much else I was doing wrong, it took me only a minute to throw my bag into Lillian's car and pull out the keys from where they were always left—under the driver's seat.

Once seated behind the wheel, I was reminded of something I hadn't considered before making my choice—the car had a stick shift. My experience with stick shifts was limited to mowing the "lawn" (actually the sewage field) with a communally-owned riding mower. However, nothing ventured, nothing gained. So I fired up the engine, appreciating the brief roar, followed by the gentle purr. I pushed in the clutch, found reverse on the guide imprinted on the stick shift column, and quickly taught myself the basics of switching gears—an invaluable lesson, no matter how things with Mother turned out.

Lillian's car rumbled down the driveway at a snail's pace. As I struggled to keep the car moving in a straight line, I could feel a light-headedness, a kind of excitement, I hadn't expected. I always thought I'd be scared and sad when I left Back Creek behind my first time as a grown-up, but this morning, when I'd exited all the geographic bounds of my life, I felt a kind of abandon. I'd never felt this way before—I felt entirely on my own. And, despite the circumstances, it felt pretty good.

At the start, I concentrated on getting to the highway that would take me south and west, away from the water and tall pines, and toward the long fields of big-leafed plants in civilized rows, as shown in the pictures in the history books. I figured it would take me about eight hours to get to Hendersonville and the road to the

Baldwin farm. So I'd arrive before dark. That left an entire day of just me, the car, and the road—plenty of time to sift through the summer's events, including those of last night, and to try to figure out what I would say to Mother. I had a lot of thinking to do.

When I reached the end of the driveway and the road, I bumped up into second gear and then, smoother, into third. Before I knew it, I had moved well down the road, leaving Back Creek and the Barnett house far behind.

I found myself virtually alone on the road. I passed the vegetable man's old black pick-up and the newspaper deliveryman's Volkswagen van with the fading, hand-painted peace sign on the side. I waved at the men as if I belonged in that driver's seat. And they waved back. I had a tank full of gas, an accelerator awaiting my touch, and a destination I thought I could reach.

As I worked my way up Dandy Road to the big intersection where Route 17—and all its possibilities—appeared, I tried to remember the one trip we'd taken to the Baldwin farm. I must have been about eight years old then—Mother somehow got it into her head that we should "connect" with her past. I think she had a hankering to get down to the placid leafiness of tobacco farms, far away from the always-changing rise and fall of the tides.

I remember some excitement about the trip—we'd never taken a vacation trip by car before, and Mother made it sound like an adventure, with a treasure waiting at the end of the journey. Best of all, it was just us girls. Daddy stayed home, he said, to work.

Lillian was thirteen and spending her time sneaking off to parties in Yorktown, meeting high school boys. She wasn't too happy with the prospect of spending time with me and Mother in a car. She landed in the old blue station wagon only because Daddy threatened to send her to the convent school in Smithfield if she didn't come along willingly. It was the first time we'd ever done anything alone with Mother, and the last time Lillian had anything to do with the family.

As I headed down the shiny, newly-paved asphalt of Route 17, I remembered Mother and Lillian sitting in the front seat while I roamed around the back, jumping from window to window, shouting at them to look at the billboards or the fruit stands we passed. The two of them looked straight ahead, each in her own world, completely ignoring me. My mother drove fast. Peering over her shoulder, I saw the shaky speedometer jerk past eighty. I remember riding and riding, the excitement of the motion dying as I fell asleep, the pines turning to stubby fields reaching as far as I could see.

Mother and Lillian lost their stiff military carriage by the time we reached the little town of Hendersonville, North Carolina, where most of Mother's family had been born, grown up, and died. I woke up in that foggy, headachy state that sleeping in the car always induces.

I watched the small white houses behind the even picket fences disappear as we passed through the town and headed toward the family farm, which my father had once called "the little plantation." It was one of the few times I recognized sarcasm in his voice. As I gazed out the bug-speckled windshield, I saw heads turning, interest piqued by our Virginia license tag. Not too many people came to Hendersonville on purpose. There wasn't much to do or see there.

And there wasn't too much to do at the Baldwin farm, either, at least as far as I could tell. Though my mother had never described the scene, I'd come to expect a columned front porch overlooking acres of neatly planted corn, kind of like the picture of Tara I had from the movie *Gone with the Wind*. When we bumped up the potholed driveway to a small one-story wooden house, reddish paint peeling from its walls, surrounded by stationary Dodges and sporting a front porch of uneven boards, I understood for the first time the reason for my father's sarcasm, and why Mother never talked about her family.

Even to my eight-year-old eyes, the place looked and felt tired.

The farm was occupied by some cousins who'd been "looking after" things for years, since my grandmother had passed soon after my parents' marriage. It was clear that their central interest lay in having a roof over their heads. Though they seemed surprised to see us, they welcomed Mother with wide open arms, declaring, "Oh, my soul, you're a city girl now," and calling her "little Rosie," much to the horror of both Lillian and me. It was about the only thing we agreed on the entire trip.

Actually, that moment of welcome was about the only time Mother and Lillian spent on the farm. Mother spent a good deal of her time visiting relatives, especially Aunt Grace in a hospital I wasn't allowed to go to. Lillian brilliantly fought and won the brief battle to be left alone to sit by the side of the pool at the Hendersonville Motel, where we spent two uncomfortable nights sleeping in one king-sized bed under a bedspread that smelled of mildew. I was the one who spent time on the farm, because each morning I was dropped off to spend the day with my "cousins," and left pretty much to my own devices.

The three days we spent there were mostly a blur to me now, but I remembered weird things: the acrid smell of old straw in the big barn out back; a white wicker rocking chair, seatless, in the middle of the back yard; the cracked glass pitcher the cousins served lemonade from at lunch. As I drove, the taste of that sugar-laden tartness rushed back to me. It was the first, and only, time I'd ever had lemonade that came from lemons, not a can. I didn't remember much about the cousins, only softly lined faces and calloused hands.

The only other image that stayed with me was Mother's face. I stood beside her while Lillian, running the engine and listening to the radio, sat stone-faced in the car. She had the air-conditioning on full blast and I could see her hair blowing back against the seat. I watched as Mother turned to take one last look at the house and fields slightly beyond the laundry line. She drew in a deep breath and shook her head.

I didn't understand what she was looking at. Later, when we bumped back up the driveway in silence, I realized she must have been looking at the seatless rocking chair positioned in the middle of the back yard, unusable, but too good to throw away. Shortly after that visit, she moved Aunt Grace up to Williamsburg.

As I raced along, lost in my memories, my eyes caught the sign for Smithfield, and I turned off the main road, shifting in and out of gear with ease. I studied the map, zeroed in on a route number, and zoomed off, down the back roads toward the Virginia-North Carolina border.

There were no mileage markers, no indicators of which town was where and how far. I didn't pass a single car. Cornfields spread out on either side of the road, interrupted by the occasional dirt driveway leading up to a desolate farmhouse. The corn stood about my height—Fourth of July corn, ready for picking and eating. Once or twice, I passed a roadside stand, advertising fresh corn and watermelon, but actually empty of produce and people.

I tried to keep my attention on the road, looking through the dusty windshield and feeling a rush of wind blow my hair back into a completely unruly mess. But the green stalks, the mighty oak left to stretch its thick branches in the center of a field, the lone red tractor abandoned by the side of the road—those things called to me. Lillian, I thought, should be here with her camera. She could capture the life along this country road, discovering beauty that no one else would notice. But Lillian was back on the Creek, probably just heading downstairs for breakfast. I would have to capture those images myself.

The sun came out full-tilt, a throbbing mustard yellow against a faded blue. The air rushing past me lost its freshness and I felt the hot promise of a July day spent on the highway. My thoughts continued to revolve around Lillian as I tried to get comfortable in her driver's seat.

Somehow, moving fast miles away from Back Creek gave me a better perspective, like putting on my glasses to see things more clearly. I thought about how, when Lillian had left, Daddy gathered and put away all the pictures of her that lay around the house, even the charcoal sketch my mother had done of Lillian as a little girl. With all the real images gone, I had to recreate her in my imagination, stitching together scraps of memories. Before her room became a storage area for old boxes of Barnett memorabilia, I sneaked in there, closed my eyes, and tried to feel her presence. But she was gone, and had left no ghost behind.

The Lillian I created was beautiful and headstrong and artistic—of another world, really—citified and sophisticated. She hobnobbed with the rich and famous, wore stylish clothes, went to exclusive night clubs, and danced the night away. She probably lived in a fashionable loft, like one I'd seen in *Life* magazine—lots of open space and no heavy antiques, like in our house. Maybe she had no furniture at all, and nothing to hold her down. She had lovers, not boyfriends or dates. "Lovers"—it was a word I could not say out loud, but I enjoyed running it through my head.

The Lillian who showed up at Tommy's funeral still resembled the Lillian I'd created, at least in some ways. She was the kind of beautiful I had imagined—gleaming, delicate, ethereal (now *there* was a nineteenth century word). She worked to create about herself a natural-seeming mystery and distance. About her actual life in New York, I had few clues. She seemed to live in the "right now," which was just where I imagined she'd live.

She put on airs of nonchalance and independence, but her pictures gave her away. Her scenes of the Creek—the crabman repairing his pot, the black man selling vegetables from his truck, even Cal working on his boat—revealed an understanding of people that Lillian, and maybe everybody else, didn't know about. I saw it in the way she captured faces—how she managed to steal the moment of Cal's sadness while he watched the Creek; and how she found the spark of humor in an old oysterman's weathered face. I didn't think she intended any of it—it just happened.

She had stopped talking about New York. Instead, she spent

her time asking about Back Creek neighbors, exploring the small peninsula with her cameras, and egging Daddy on to tell ancient family stories. In no time at all, she had again become a part of life on the Creek, melding her new state with the ebb and flow of that defining waterway. Spinning along in her car, I marveled at how easily she'd found her new place back home. For the Lillian I'd imagined, it would have been far harder.

I shifted my sweaty legs on the hot, wet, leather seat and pushed the accelerator down farther, passing tired old towns. If I blinked, I'd miss the small white signs that announced them: Whiteville, Manor Way, Smithfield. Awkwardly at first, I shifted down and slowed to a crawl through the main streets of these towns, just as the speed limits told me to. I studied the signs of life that lined the streets. Red, white, and blue drooped from the street lights and porches.

The size and condition of the houses along the main streets varied with the town's size and affluence. Charming brick colonials surrounded by wrought iron and masses of petunias gave way to tall white clapboard monstrosities with peeling paint and rotting porches. Tiny ranch-style homes fronted by concrete donkeys and carts sat next to bigger, aluminum-sided ranchers with chain-link fences and barking dogs. Shirtless, barefoot boys and girls in their bathing suits running through the sprinkler stopped for a moment to wave and watch me pass.

Their mothers were probably out back hanging up wash or sitting in the kitchen, drinking an early afternoon cup of coffee and smoking a cigarette, trying to dream up what they might make for dinner that night. The fathers were no doubt out in the fields, or in town working at the appliance center or the bank, having returned to their jobs after the holiday but already looking forward to the weekend.

And I imagined the real life of these little landlocked towns, where things and people were constant and you knew what to expect. You didn't have to watch for speeding boats and rising water all the time.

I passed a faded sign welcoming me to North Carolina and suddenly I was starving. I hadn't eaten since the picnic, and a sudden, demanding hunger took control of me. Reaching a fork in the road, I smoothed over the wrinkled map and stopped to consider my itinerary. A hand-painted sign proclaiming "Aunt Sally's Country Kitchen" a mere three miles to the right decided things for me. I turned the wheel and hoped Aunt Sally was still cooking on the day after a holiday.

The area on either side of the road did not look too promising. The fields had given way to overgrown grasses and bushes; a few pieces of rusted farm machinery rested in their midst. Strands of barbed wire dipped along the edges and there were no signs of activity anywhere. But I continued on, even as more and more potholes forced me to slow down, and a not-so-good scraping noise came from the bottom of the car, the bumps jolting my entire body.

I considered turning around, but then, just ahead, I spied a small brick building with a flat black roof at the end of a dirt driveway. I bumped over into the driveway, which was actually in better shape than the state-maintained highway I had just left. Before me was a wooden, larger than life Aunt Sally beckoning me forward, her one-dimensional bulk promising me I wouldn't leave hungry. Up ahead, a clean white sedan rested in the small dirt area that passed for a parking lot. I pulled up beside the lone car and turned off the engine, letting hunger push any doubts aside.

As I opened the diner's glass door, an arctic blast of air-conditioning rolled over me and chilled my damp t-shirt and bare legs. I sat down in the first booth I came to and searched for some sign of human presence and a menu. A promising clanging arose from the back and, the moment I clutched my arms and prepared to head back there, a large figure in white made its way past the cash register toward my booth.

It had to be the real Aunt Sally herself, and she was truly larger than life—at least larger than her wooden representation outside. The flowered house dress beneath the white apron and her netted hair brought back a quick memory of the North Carolina cousin who'd once made me all that real lemonade.

"Well, now, what can I do for you, little lady? You're my first and only customer today. It's been awful slow. I guess everybody's staying home, out of this heat, after the holiday." She sang her greeting in an almost musical drawl. She laced together her surprisingly soft-looking white hands and held them in front of her ample bosom, smiling.

Rubbing my arms and glancing about briefly for a menu, I ordered the first thing that came to mind—a chicken salad sandwich and a lemonade. As the words came out of my mouth, I realized that was exactly what I'd eaten each afternoon in that tiny North Carolina farm house all those years ago.

"Now, honey, chicken salad is not what you want today! I got some hot barbecue in the back—just fixed it up. That'll warm you up and set you right." She cocked her head, looked me over, and affirmed, "Yep, you need some good ole North Carolina barbecue, before you say hello to those North Carolina relatives of yours. I'll be right back."

I stared at her cotton-flowered back in surprise and tried to shout, "Wait," but the rattle of the air-conditioning drowned me out. The kitchen door snapped shut and left me to my solitary wonder. I looked around at the tiny booths, at their neatly stacked sugar holders and napkin dispensers. No hint of customers—no telltale crumbs or ketchup splashes. For a minute, I imagined I was the only one who'd ever found this place—my own Shangri-La, a tiny brick coffee shop stuck on the back roads of North Carolina.

Aunt Sally came swishing back in, balancing a plate piled high with barbecue and hush puppies, a jug of tea, and a mason jar filled with ice. With surprising agility, she whipped out a paper place mat providing facts and figures about the state of North Carolina, and placed her offerings before me. The barbecue smelled heavenly and I dug in instantly.

"You eat right up," she said approvingly. "There's plenty more where that came from. I'm just glad to have someone to cook for." She shifted her weight onto one hip and rested a hand on the back of the booth across from me.

I smiled at her, my mouth full, and continued my gorging. I guess I hadn't realized how hungry I was. Aunt Sally busied herself straightening napkin holders and ketchup bottles on the tables around me, wiping everything with a white cloth she produced from an apron pocket.

I ate like a child—quickly and mechanically—thinking about how fast I could devour that tangy sweetness. Everything else disappeared and I thought about nothing for the first time since watching Tommy's boat plow into the pier.

As I was sopping up the last of the sauce with a hush puppy, Aunt Sally reappeared from the back.

"Can't let you go without a piece of our prize-winning banana cream pie," she said, placing a huge slice before me with a flourish. "First prize at the county fair last year," she added. I waved my hand in weak protest.

She interrupted me, holding up her hand. "You've got a long trip ahead of you and you'll need all the sweetness you can get," she said.

"What do you mean?" I finally got the words out, even as I picked up my fork. How could she know anything about where I was going or what I'd be needing?

She lowered her hand and smiled. "I know things about people even before they tell me—sometimes even before *they* know. I can see you're looking for someone or some place. You don't come from here, and you look like you've had a restless time lately. And you're doing something you're not quite sure about. Is that right?"

I put down the fork I was twirling. Before I remembered the Back Creek credo—keep family things to yourself—I said, "I'm down here to snatch my mother from the family farm. My sister's going to have a baby, and my father can't take care of himself, much less anyone else. It was getting bad, and somebody had to do something. I didn't get much sleep last night, and I'm not sure where I'm going."

I put the fork down, pushed back my glasses, and studied her face. Her eyes were the greenish blue of the ocean. "How could you tell?" I asked.

She reached up to push some stray hair back up into her tight gray-streaked bun and smiled, as if receiving a compliment. "Oh, it's not so hard. I saw your tags when you drove up, and nobody out of state would be down here without a good reason. You got circles under your eyes the size of saucers, and you gobbled up that barbecue like you haven't had a good meal in days. You can tell a lot about a person by the way they eat."

She paused and, as an afterthought, said, "Figuring out people's stories ain't so hard. You just have to stand back and look at them close."

Reaching over my shoulder, she took up my empty plate and cradled it in her big hands. She nodded toward the door and said, "Now, you'd better get on down to see your mother, before you get too tired. You'll find you way. All the road signs here are easy to spot."

She swished through the swinging kitchen door and I felt a new surge of energy. Maybe it was her confidence. Maybe it was the barbecue. Whatever the inspiration, I dug around in my pocket and found the wad of bills I'd taken from Mother's "Just in Case" jar in the pantry early that morning. I left a twenty and took the placemat—maybe I'd read up on all those North Carolina facts and figures someday. Or maybe I'd just keep it as a souvenir. I squeezed out of the booth and the air-conditioning to thaw in the heat outside.

I sat in the car, pondering how to get from here to there. Hendersonville was too small to rate recognition on a regular map. I turned Daddy's map this way and that, but I couldn't determine exactly where I was, according to the signs I'd passed to get here. While I was thinking about what to do, I smoothed out the wrinkles of the paper place mat. On its back was a map of North Carolina, with tiny blue veins indicating roadways and little red stars pointing out landmarks.

Bending my head close to the stiff piece of paper, I found and put my finger on the big red star marking Aunt Sally's and looked closer, finding that lo and behold, there was a tiny star for Hendersonville, down one of the little roads in blue. If I could just look closer and harder, the tiny roadways laid out on that place mat would guide me there.

I tossed Daddy's map into the back seat and fired up the engine. Getting the car into reverse took me a few tries, but finally I spun around to face the long, bumpy driveway I'd come down just a little while ago. As I retreated from the compact brick building, I glanced up in the rear view window to see Aunt Sally, apron removed, turning a key in the front door. Had she been waiting for me to leave? Or to come? Who was to say? But she did set me on the right trail, and I could still taste that tangy barbecue and sugary pie as I headed down the road.

Once I reached my point of departure and turned right, the road was straight and clear to Hendersonville. After the freezing air-conditioning of Aunt Sally's, the hot, dry wind that blew in from the road was a comfort. I drove with my eyes wide open, looking for road and highway signs.

The farmhouses moved closer to the road, and mailboxes with numbers appeared. Fields began to turn into yards surrounding neat house trailers with white curtains in the windows and red geraniums in the planters. A few white-haired women sat in aluminum lawn chairs, just watching the road and fanning themselves. Mutts rested, panting, under wide-leafed oaks. A few battered pick-ups joined me on the road, their beds filled with tools or hoses or, in one case, watermelons.

Finally, I spotted a faded Rotary sign proudly welcoming me to Hendersonville, population 1,284, followed by a sign reminding me the speed limit was 25 miles per hour. I slowed down and contemplated my next task—locating the farm and Mother. It was mid-afternoon.

I thought of finding a payphone and a telephone book and calling Mother, but quickly remembered Mother's statement that she had to "walk to the next place" to use a phone. So I figured I'd apply the Barnett circular theory of directions: if you wander around long enough, you're bound to find out where you're going. Pushing my glasses back up on my nose, I realized that this theory applied to more than driving, at least for some Barnetts I knew. But it wouldn't work for me—not this time. So I elected to do what few Barnetts had ever done before. I decided to ask someone for directions.

Noting that my gas gauge was pretty low, I pulled into Roy's Texaco station just beyond the stop sign. In fact, Roy himself emerged from underneath a car propped up in the garage. I knew it was Roy, because his name was stitched neatly on his shirt pocket, the only spot not dotted with grease. He pulled on a clean white cap with a red Texaco star on the front.

"What can I do for you, Miss?" Roy put on the not-from-around-here charm.

"I need some gas," I started. "And some directions, if possible," I added as he drew closer. Roy wiped his hands on a rag he pulled out of his pocket. "Shoot," he said with a nod.

"I'm looking for the Baldwin farm," I said, squinting up into his face.

Roy moved toward the rear of the car, unscrewed the gas cap, and inserted the metal dispenser. The pump began to hum as liquid poured into the tank.

"Well, now, let's see," he yelled over the noise of the pump. "There used to be a family name of Baldwin out the State Road." He turned to point down a tiny concrete path behind the station.

"I believe the place is pretty run-down; they don't farm there no more."

He turned back to me and smiled apologetically. "That's all I can tell you, I guess. It's funny you should ask about that place. Just the other day, my wife was filling in for the regular mailman and she delivered some big packages out that way—from Atlanta and Nashville and Maine." He returned to business. "That'll be five dollars."

While Roy washed the bug-spattered windshield, I dug into my pocket again. He offered me a Texaco salute as I pulled away in the direction he'd indicated. Sure enough, a green-lettered sign announced the appearance of the State Road. Following the rows of cornfields lining either side, I drove slowly, in second gear, searching for another sign—I figured I had to be close now. A dull red ball of a sun began to sink in front of me.

It was only by chance that I spotted the mailbox at the head of a dirt road leading off the State Road, almost hidden by tall grass and wild growing shrubs. The mailbox was newly painted—a mallard green, with a bold silver "B" on the side. Without thinking too much, I turned into the dirt driveway beside the mailbox and toward the vaguely familiar white frame house that appeared before me.

I reached the end of the driveway in a cloud of dust, pulling up next to an ancient brown Nova that seemed rusted to the spot. I heard the squeak of a screen door and turned my head to see a figure moving toward me. The hair and the clothes were loose and floating, and the feet were bare.

But it *was* Mother.

Chapter Twenty

I sat in silence, watching her walk gingerly down the once-bricked walkway, now given over to tufts of tough grass. My eyes shifted to the house behind her, which looked less tired, more recently painted than I remembered. Pink and purple petunias grew around the porch, a contained riot of color against the already browning grass. The house looked tended, as did my mother.

"Grace," she said, sounding happy. She brushed back her hair with a simple gesture as I hooked the tangle behind my ears, wishing desperately for a rubber band and waiting for a comment from my mother. But there were no such comments forthcoming as we reached the end of the walkway and she threw her arms around me. I hadn't thought about what I'd do when I actually saw her, but I found myself squeezing her tight, as she did me—just like families do. I could feel the graceful slant of her shoulders and realized that, without her heels, I stood almost a head taller than her.

She pulled back from me and, her hands on my shoulders, examined my face with her hazel eyes—the same eyes that had stared back at me from my dresser mirror. One hand moved up to stroke my cheek and hair.

"I'm so glad to see you, Grace. I've thought about you and Lillian and your father all summer. Somehow, I just knew you'd get down here." Her words had a new length to them—just a trace of a revived accent. She hooked elbows with me and drew me toward the house.

"Let's go in and have a Coke. You've got to be hot and tired—and probably hungry, too, after that long drive."

Not a word had come out of my mouth since I'd driven down that driveway. All those stored-up questions and speeches vanished like the morning mist. All that mattered, suddenly, was that I was here and not there. I felt like someone who'd washed up on a tropical island, greeted by a beautiful native instead of the expected head hunter.

We walked around to the side of the house, Mother holding the screen door open for me so we could enter the kitchen. The ancient linoleum floor was cracked but scrubbed. The white muslin curtains with the ball fringe looked new, or freshly washed and ironed. The long plank table in the middle of the room held dozens of old pickling jars, laid out on tea cloths and catching the last rays of the sun as it streamed in through the windows over the sink. A bucket of cucumbers sat on the floor by the table, and several watermelons took up a good deal of the counter. There was a life and comfort to the room and, despite my better judgment, I instantly felt at home.

Mother directed me to a ladder-back chair pulled up to the table. "I was just taking a break from my painting, looking for some of those old pickling recipes," she said. "I was going to put up some bread and butters and maybe some watermelon pickle—you can help me with all that tomorrow." She turned from the refrigerator, two long green Coke bottles in her hands.

"That is, depending on how long you plan to stay." She snapped off the bottle tops like punctuation marks.

As I sipped my Coke, I contemplated what she was asking. What I'd come down here to do suddenly seemed a lot more complicated.

"Yes, I'll be here through tomorrow," I said.

"Good. We'll do some pickling then." Mother took a long drink from her Coke. In the chair across from mine, she sat in a comfortable slouch, her elbows on the table. I'd never seen her in anything but lady-perfect posture. She was always admonishing me to keep my back straight and to cross my legs at the ankles—postures I never could get right.

For a minute, I continued to drink the cold brown fizz and study her face. I'd never really noticed how much the shape of our faces nearly matched. Somehow, I'd gotten it into my head that she and Lillian were closer in looks, maybe because I knew how beautiful Lillian was and how often I'd been told what a beauty my mother was. I talked myself into thinking that I was a throwback to the hardy Barnett women. But as I sat across the table from this new mother of mine, I realized we looked at the world through much the same face.

Mother took another long sip and set her bottle in front of her, playing with the watery residue making its way down the glass. For a minute or two, there was only the sound of the heat-pestered insects outside, a steady hum that rose and fell for no apparent reason. I waited, tracing the wet ring the bottle left on the table. I was trying to think hard about what I should, or could, say—trying to grab onto a rehearsed speech I'd spent time composing on the hot drive down.

Somehow, though, my mind fastened onto a suddenly sharp memory rising up from the Creek. I was on Cal's pier, feeling the water dripping off me, and my clothes clinging to me. I traced that ring over and over, trying to clear my head. Mother's voice, describing her efforts to plant a garden, brought me back to the kitchen table and the last rays of sunlight drifting lazily through the windows.

"So, why are you still here?" I asked, interrupting the blurring stream of her chatter. "When are you coming back? And where's Aunt Grace?" The words just popped out of me.

A deep silence washed over the kitchen. If you'd told me twenty years had passed, I would have believed you. Mother just sat, holding on to the Coke bottle for dear life, looking hard at the table.

"You asked about Aunt Grace," she said. "Well, this is a hard thing to say, but it's the truth, and I've promised myself to tell only the truth from now on. Aunt Grace isn't the reason I left Back Creek to come down here. The truth is . . . well, the truth is that your Aunt Grace has been gone these past six years. She just up and died in her sleep one night. The nurses said she got hold of some pills and must not have realized what she took."

For a minute, I sat in stunned silence, then said, "But . . . all those years, you went every Sunday. Where'd you go? Why didn't you tell us she died? I don't get it."

"Grace, that's the part no one'll understand. I guess I was more than a little crazy . . . I just couldn't let go of my sister. For me, she was my last piece of home. So, even after they buried her in that sad little cemetery by the hospital, I kept going up to visit, at least at first. I'd sit with the other women there and listen to their stories. Eventually, I started to bring up my sketchpad and draw them while they talked. I really liked doing that. I don't know why I never told anyone. It was my secret, my pain. I didn't want to share it.

"Anyway, I kept traveling up there every Sunday, just like always. I started sketching around the hospital and then around Williamsburg. I tried to draw the people I found and the stories I imagined for them."

After she stopped talking, she reached over to touch me. Her fingers were cold from holding onto the bottle, and I shivered when I felt them. I raised my head and looked into her clear eyes. She'd made peace with some things—I wished she could pass that same peace to me.

"Oh, Grace, there's so much I should tell you—should've told you. But there's so much you need to tell me, too. You've let me go on and it's nearly dinner time." She rose and faced the sink. "I'll fix something for us," she said mechanically.

A confusion of words rose to my surface. "But . . . I came down here on my own . . . to see about you, to find out . . ." The words struck my tongue like so many fragile bubbles. I stood up quickly, overturning the thick green bottle. I instinctively looked around for something to wipe up the spreading brown puddle while Mother calmly and deliberately opened a drawer, pulled out a red-checked cloth, and soaked up the spilled soda.

And that was when I fell back into the chair and broke down crying for the second time in twenty-four hours, realizing that the mess I'd left back home would not be as easily sopped up as I had foolishly imagined.

Mother pulled me toward her, hugging me tightly while I shook with silent sobs. She let me cry out the fear, the worry, the sadness, the confusion. For the first time in a long while, she mothered me.

Once the tears finally dried up and I sat there, wiping my nose on a napkin she handed me, Mother began moving around the kitchen, gathering up tomatoes ripening on the windowsill, pulling eggs from the refrigerator, and peeling potatoes retrieved from under the sink.

While she worked, I started to talk like a tidal wave, telling her all that had happened on the Creek since her departure. Mother just listened. By the time she was pulling a delicious-smelling casserole out of the oven, I had caught her up to the night before. I kept to myself the story of crossing the Creek. But it was the first time I'd ever really talked to her.

As we ate and talked, the night drew over us like a cool summer blanket. Still sitting at the table, I looked past my mother's back as she washed the dishes. The clouds raced past a full moon that tried to stake its claim on the night. Cooler air seeped through the window. I could feel the weather changing.

Outside the kitchen lay a quiet I'd never experienced. On the Creek, there was always noise—the lapping of water against the shore, ducks and geese talking to each other, the muted knocking of the boats against their docks, the flapping of John Whythe's flag. Here, in this brown, flat place, there was no such noise. There were no radios or telephones or boat engines or gravel-crunching car wheels to distract the ear and mind. There was just the land and the house and the sound of running water as Mother washed dishes.

She showed me to her old room, which, she told me, still looked pretty much like she'd left it as an eighteen-year-old girl. Still on the walls was the same tiny rosebud wallpaper she'd selected. The brass bed she'd shared with her sister was covered with the quilt her mother—my grandmother—had made. I ran my hand over the worn material, with its wedding ring pattern. Mother was sleeping in her parents' old bedroom, she told me, and I could stay in this room as long as I liked—the sheets were clean and the room dusted.

I thought I could never fall asleep in an unfamiliar room, but after pulling off my clothes, putting on the nightgown she gave me, and inhaling the dried-on-the-line freshness of the soft sheets, it was maybe ten minutes before I closed my eyes for the night, and I didn't open them again until late the next morning.

It was well after eleven when the smell of bacon forced me from my dreamless sleep. My eyes caught my reflection as I passed the bureau mirror on the way to the bathroom. The sight of me in Mother's pink-checked nightgown, ruffles forming an embarrassingly low-cut V right between my small, barely visible breasts, was enough to wake me up completely. I shrugged it off and headed for the kitchen, suddenly feeling ravenous and nearly clear-headed. The floors creaked as I walked down the hall and Mother called out to me from the kitchen.

A mess of pickling was apparently in its early stages. Large clouds of steam rose up from the stove, where vats of water boiled. Bushels of cucumbers were strewn around the area and piles of cut-up vegetables covered the counters. The watermelons had been sliced and some of their bright red juiciness had dripped onto the floor.

Mother steered me toward the table, hidden beneath the army of different-sized jars. She brandished a cleaver and warned me that we'd be eating watermelon all day, until we got down to the rinds. To prove her point, she chopped through a slice and motioned me toward it, indicating, "Here's some breakfast." So I plunked myself down in a chair and began working on the watermelon. Mother glanced over at me and said, "Well, Grace, that nightgown fits you nice. You look like a grown-up, instead of a tomboy in your t-shirts and shorts." Then she turned back to her chopping and boiling. I decided to keep the nightgown on.

Following her instructions, I joined her in the chopping and mixing. The magical smell of pickling spices wound around us, and it wasn't long before we were in another world—far away from boats splintering piers, far away from siren sisters, far away from scuba divers planting underwater mines. Here, I was suddenly immersed in the hand-written recipes Mother resurrected from the back of the Hoosier cabinet—in the cheesecloth filled with mustard seed and pungent dill.

As we followed the recipes her mother had followed and her mother before that, we talked in an abstract way. As the afternoon wore on and Mother kept talking, I was listening to preserve the stories in my mind.

"I can remember watching my grandmother and mother rushing around this same old kitchen, putting up all kinds of vegetables—their own hand-sown, hand-picked crops—for the winter. The kitchen would get so hot. At the end of the day, with the shiny jars all lined up, they'd come out on the front porch and rock on those chairs.

"My grandmother would tell her stories about growing up right here, on this piece of land. I'd sit up so straight, with my bare feet just touching the porch—we never wore shoes in the summer. I loved listening to her; Mama Grace knew so many stories about the family—some were hilarious and some were tragic. People would tell her their happenings and she stored up all these lives in her head. Anyway, I'd listen while we all shucked corn or shelled peas. I wish I'd asked more questions, but in those days we were taught to listen, not to speak."

When she paused and indicated we were taking a break, I shifted in my chair, gazing out toward the stubbly fields that circled the house, trying to imagine the neat rows of green tobacco leaves that must have been there once. There was no breeze, as there almost always was on the Creek—only the waves of noise the bugs made, and they washed over us like a light wind. Mother turned her gaze outward, too. Together, we sat at the kitchen table, ordered lines of filled-up jars between us.

Pots still steamed on the stove, but Mother's attention seemed directed backwards as she began to speak about the past. She spoke with a slow cadence, a rhythm punctuated (or maybe inspired) by the natural symphony around us.

Chapter Twenty-One

❧

"It was nice growing up on the farm," she began. "We never had any money, but we had the Baldwin land. You never met your grandfather, but you've seen his picture on my bureau. He was always trying different things—new crops, new farming methods, new equipment. Eventually, he started trying new businesses—selling vacuum cleaners, chinchillas, mail-order Jesus figures. There wasn't much of anything he didn't try."

Hours later, Mother paused in her story telling, staring out at the darkening sky. We had moved out onto the porch and the cooling air. I sat in one of the big old wicker chairs, slowly rocking in time to her story. Her voice had lulled me out of my present and into her past.

She had fallen into the lilting North Carolina accent I had only heard her use when she'd drunk too many whiskey sours. Here, on this porch, watching some stray clouds roam across the lowering sun, her slurred syllables and soft vowels seemed as natural as the weepy calls of the mourning doves from the ancient oak in front of our house at the Creek. And it occurred to me for the first time that she must've worked hard to get rid of that accent—her natural way of saying things must have been something she had to keep to herself.

"I've talked enough about the past for one day," she said finally. "You can't dwell on what's happened. You can only get on with things best you can. That's what I'm learning, anyway. And right now, we need to dwell on some more jars that need filling." She pulled me back into the kitchen. I turned to glance at our chairs, still rocking slowly on the abandoned porch.

Later that night, I drove into Hendersonville, found a pay phone, and made a call back home. It was strange to hear Lillian's voice on the other end of the line—she finally picked up after ten rings. At first, she sounded distant and confused.

But during our brief conversation (I was running out of dimes), she let me know that Daddy was okay and she was okay. She said she didn't care about the car—she was too big now to fit behind the wheel, and, besides, she didn't feel like driving any more. She was going over her photographs of the Creek and finding "interesting textures," she said.

And finally, she asked about Mother and when we were coming back, as if it were a foregone conclusion Mother would return. I could almost hear the empty seconds marking time inside the long black phone lines. "I guess pretty soon" was the best I could come up with. Then there wasn't much more to say, and I had to go, having pushed the last dime I could dig out of the little change purse Mother had given me. Lillian's "Well, Grace—" was cut off in mid-exasperation, and I hung up the pay phone, fingering the empty coin return.

For the two weeks I stayed, Mother and I fell into something of a routine. Time got lost and the rhythm of the farm took over, though there was no harvest to reap, just the crop of memories we preserved, along with a ten year supply of pickles. Mother told me her stories as we worked, and I gathered them in. I listened to her realities, and tried to let go of mine. I think we both came to understand things we hadn't before. I had to be willing to listen to find out what I needed to know. And I guess that's what I drove all the way to North Carolina to find out.

After hours of listening, I finally heard the story I'd been waiting for—how and why she came to marry Daddy.

Before she left the farm, she said, she could sense, from a

number of snide remarks she'd overheard, the resentment or envy of practically everyone in Hendersonville—her classmates, the town folk, even her own family members—for thinking she was so special she could only find something befitting her talents someplace other than Hendersonville. She had won a scholarship to the Virginia Commonwealth University School of Art, and she wasn't about to give that up, for anyone or anything. It was a long, miserable summer before she left, which convinced her even more she should go.

Her mother never said a word—just washed, pressed, and packed Mother's small wardrobe, and stood with her in the fierce September sun, out by the highway, waiting for the Greyhound bus that would drop her in Richmond on its way to New York. She stood with lips pursed, eyes searching the road. For the first time, Mother noticed that her mother's back was a little hunched over and her hands looked old.

The bus arrived in a swirl of dust and fumes. Mother gathered up her battered suitcase and bag of food for the trip. Just as she placed one foot on the metal step, her mother handed her a book of stamps and told her to write. "It was the only thing she ever asked of me." Once she settled herself in the sticky vinyl bus seat, she looked straight ahead, not turning to watch the tobacco leaves shimmering in the sun.

She really hadn't any idea what the city and the school might be like; she couldn't have imagined the gray blur of landscape interrupted by the most exciting colors, noises, and smells. She had to squelch her fears of the men wandering the street. She kept her gaze straight and blocked out their "Hey, baby" catcalls.

She had to learn not to stare at the beautiful women who shopped the fancy department store windows, dressed in clothes she might have gotten married in if she'd been in Hendersonville. And, oh, the smells of coffee and fried eggs in the morning drifting out of fashionable diners, and hot dogs and barbecue at lunchtime coming from the little stands pulled by shaggy ponies.

Plus the noises! The rumble of trains always in the background (the school was situated near Richmond's central station), promising all sorts of exotic places, from New York City to Pensacola, Florida. The bustle of traffic, horns honking, policemen whistling, hawkers selling newspapers and cigarettes. Richmond was built on tobacco, and everywhere you went, huge towering billboards reminded you of Lucky Stripe's good taste and Salem's smoothness. It was hard to believe those flat green leaves, so hard to grow, could bring such life.

Mother loved art school. To spend all day just listening to people talk about art and artists and colors and lines was more heaven than she could ever have imagined. Her head had to make room for all the names and forms she didn't know—she hadn't realized how little Hendersonville High School had taught her.

She couldn't understand why some of the other girls never went to class, and started their weekends on Wednesday nights, taking the bus to Charlottesville or Lexington, and not returning until late Sunday night, just in time to give their parents a call and report on which boy they were close to snagging.

She lived in a pathetic student apartment on the third floor of a studio building—the rent was actually free as long as she swept up the studio each night and emptied the trash. She kept to herself, knowing she had only to open her mouth to confirm what everyone else on campus knew—she was a hick straight off the farm.

But within that first month, she became so totally filled with art and the city that she almost forgot where she came from and who she'd left behind. The seasons changed and she changed. She could almost imagine herself growing a new exterior; she even looked different, she decided. She was shedding her past and taking on a future; she wasn't looking back, either. And she put all memories of the farm and planting time right out of her head.

All was well until she got a letter from her mother, mailed care of the "Virginia School of Art." She didn't even have the name right. Mother's daddy hadn't changed much since she'd left;

he was still spending too much time staying up late sipping on Horace-up-the-road's latest batch of moonshine and having too much trouble getting out of bed the next morning. Her mother was managing, with the help of the Baldwin cousins, who probably had an eye toward getting the place eventually (which they did, my mother reminded me).

But it was her sister Grace whom her mother was most worried about. She was running around wild and people were saying things about her—right to her face. What should she do about her sister? she asked Mother in the letter. In those days, and especially on farms, children were supposed to pull their own weight.

Mother read the letter over and over one bright spring day. She knew she should go back home and at least talk to her sister. She stayed up one night sipping coffee heated on a hot plate and watched the tree shadows on the pockmarked sidewalk just below her apartment's one window.

But in the morning, to her eternal shame and guilt, she threw the letter away, crumpling it into a tiny ball and finding a trashcan in a classroom she never visited again—somewhere she wouldn't be tempted to return, to retrieve and unravel the note, to reconsider. She knew if she went home, she would be planted forever right on that flat patch of used-up ground. And the image of chickens in the front yard and stained long johns hanging on the line was unthinkable to her, at least at that point in her life. So she pretended she never got the letter.

As she headed into May and the end of her first year, the worm of guilt began to eat away at her heart. All her sketches of women, she belatedly discovered, had Grace's pug nose, instead of the long elegant lines of the models posing in the drawing class studio. She had trouble sleeping at night, something she'd never experienced before. She took a trip to the five-and-dime on the corner and spent a long time choosing notepaper, finally spending more than she could afford on pale pink sheets bordered with tiny rosebuds. Though she had to go without lunch for two days to pay for the stationery, she still couldn't sit down and write.

Finally, one Sunday afternoon—the kind of Sunday afternoon that brings a stampede of families and lovers out to the city park—she woke up, threw a few things into her broken down suitcase, collected all the spare change she'd stashed in drawers and pockets, and headed for the train, which was the fastest way she could think of to get home.

On her way out, she did a crazy thing. She had been working on a huge canvas, painting the figure of a tall, Greek model whose family owned the bakery down the street from school. For reasons she couldn't know, or maybe for no reason at all, she grabbed that canvas, with the face and torso sketched out, and carried it with her—as if it would tie her to the school and make sure she returned. With the canvas bumping against her knees, she ran down a Richmond street, hightailing it back to North Carolina, promising herself she wouldn't even unpack once she got there.

Though I knew the rest of the story, I waited for Mother to tell it. We were again seated on the porch, which was now our nightly ritual. This time, we were shelling peas from the garden Mother had resurrected. The last light of the sun crept out from behind some menacing black clouds—thunder and lightning threatened later.

Each time I leaned over to put the pea pods into the little bucket next to Mother, I glanced up into her face, looking for changes. I had gotten used to her loose hair and overalls. I couldn't even conjure up a picture of her in the Creek outfit I'd known so well—her hair pinned and hairsprayed, the coral fingernails, the navy pumps, the navy suit. Here on the farm, she was this barefoot, dirt-under-the-broken-fingernails, no-makeup person.

As I rocked, my fingers turning a pale green with the pea pods, I marveled again at how quickly change can become reality. Mother took off with Daddy, leaving the train, leaving the canvas, and leaving Grace far behind. "Sometimes people . . . life . . . it pulls you away, and sets you off in another direction," was the only explanation she offered—as if she couldn't come up with something better.

Chapter Twenty-Two

🕊

The day Mother and I heard about the coming hurricane, I woke up knowing for the first time where I was since crossing the VA-NC state line. Even before a rooster's crow could rouse my senses, I was awakened by something I had not experienced my entire time on the farm—a breeze, enough to ruffle the muslin curtains in my little bedroom. It was still too early to tell if the sky would take on shades of blue or gray, but anyone who lives on the water knows weather, and as I took in the slight movement of the heavy white curtains, I knew something was changing in the atmosphere. I got out of bed and dressed, wondering which way the wind would blow and what to expect.

In the hallway, the same eyes stared at me from their grim faces. Mother had taken on the task of preserving the few Baldwin family pictures the cousins had stowed carelessly in the barn after taking over the farm. She cleaned them up and made frames for them herself, noting on the warped backs who the stiff figures were, guessing at the dates and some of the names.

Oddly interspersed among the collection of grave-looking farmers and their big-boned wives were fantastically surreal landscapes in cacophonies of purple and pink—Aunt Grace's artwork that Mother had also found and hung. This bizarre juxtaposition never failed to give me the creeps, and I tried to walk down the hall with my eyes closed. The strategy presented its own set of problems, including the one I encountered that day—stubbing my toes on the uneven pine floor and collecting enough splinters that I hollered out in pain.

Mother, who'd probably been up since before dawn, responded to my yelps with bandages and ointments, finally soaking the wounded foot in a pan of warm water while she scrambled eggs and made toast. As I watched her work, I thought about the cold cereal, with or without milk, I usually gobbled down while rushing out the door at home. Here, the smell of butter and eggs frying in the pan and the comforting feel of the warm water on my foot made me feel young and cared for. Outside, what had seemed a breeze was turning into a minor wind. I could see the oak's branches in the front yard waving and shaking out some dead brown leaves, which came to rest unceremoniously atop the surface roots.

"There's a storm coming," Mother announced. "I heard about it on the radio this morning." For the past two weeks, the sounds of music and radio chatter had been missing from my daily activities. I didn't even know she had a radio, or any sort of electrical device that could keep us in touch with the outside world.

"Radio?" I pulled up my foot and dried it gingerly with one of the red-checked tea towels Mother had strewn around the kitchen.

"Yes," she said. "I keep a little alarm clock radio in my bedroom." She scraped the frying pan vigorously. "Your eggs are just about perfect," she concluded with satisfaction, and dumped the entire steaming heap onto a plate, which she presented to me with the command to "dig in." When she moved to the sink to wash up, a huge cloud of steam rose around her as she ran hot water over the dirty pans. I ate, thinking.

"Actually," she said, her voice rising over the sounds of the running water, "there was some news of a hurricane behind this storm. But it's not going to get this far inland, so we really don't have to worry."

I stopped chewing and swallowed hard. She might as well have sounded an alarm, because to anyone who lives near serious water, like the Chesapeake Bay, the word "hurricane" pushes some major panic buttons. While I'd never actually experienced a hurricane in my lifetime, I'd heard too many stories about Hazel and Eunice and the one in the '30s that flooded the entire peninsula our house rested on, wiping out everything on or under the water.

According to rumor, a great-uncle, hard-hit by a hurricane, lost a huge stash of Depression-era gold bullion somewhere in the marsh muck. Such stories were always followed with the direst warnings that the "big one" would undoubtedly come some time between mid-July and October. Every year, all of us waited for a sign that the next one would be the big one.

"Hurricane?" I said. "Is it headed for the Creek? Shouldn't we call? I'll have to get back . . ."

"Grace, what's wrong with you? You'd think I'd announced the end of the world. Sit down and eat those eggs before they get cold. I'm sure whatever weather is coming will turn before it gets up to the Creek. It always does. Now, if the weather isn't too bad, I thought we'd go into town and pick up some groceries and some more paint."

I watched her continue her dish-doing as if there was nothing to worry about. And I thought about how something had been created during these past two weeks—an imitation family, consisting of only my mother and myself, operated strictly on her terms. I'd come down here to bring her back, and to make things right. Instead, in the midst of these flat, still fields, I'd forgotten that *I* would have to go back. I'd been lulled into forgetting about the Creek.

"But, Mother, don't you think we need to at least call? Make sure everything's okay? You know Daddy. He'll wait until the last minute to put anything away . . ." I moved over to the screen door at the side of the kitchen, watching the wind move like a small wave through the patches of pink and white impatiens.

Mother set down the dripping frying pan, turned off the water, and wiped her hands. It took her a deliberate moment or two to respond. I stared at the tiny flowers as they bobbed back and forth.

"I'm going to tell you something, Grace. You've got to learn to let people fend for themselves. God knows it took me long enough to learn that. All those years, all that time . . . and finally, well . . . I ended up back where I started."

My mother had always made statements as if they should be clear to everyone. But I didn't know what she meant. I'd only seen the front door closing, and heard the tires on the driveway as she took off to visit Aunt Grace or whatever the hell she did when she left. And I'd only remembered her telling me to always look after my father.

"Mother," I said, shifting in my chair to face her, "are you talking about Daddy? Or Lillian? Or Aunt Grace? Because I know you pretty well left me to my own devices, except for nagging me to keep my glasses on and to talk to more boys. Who exactly did *you* fend for?" I could hear the last words catch in my throat, but they came out. I ducked my head and studied the floor for a second, breathing hard. Perhaps the wind had blown in a new Grace.

I was surprised by her cool touch on my arms, which were resting on the table. I looked up, saw pain in her eyes, and was suddenly aware of the tiny, shining streaks of silver laced in with her dark auburn.

"Oh, Grace, I took care of your father. You don't realize how much care I thought he needed. He's not as strong as you think he is. Then I figured out that everything I was doing—the Women's Club teas, the Sunday family dinners, the cocktail parties—was for him." She stopped talking and turned back to the sink and the window.

Outside the window, a host of gray clouds bore down on the stubby fields. She watched those clouds while I watched her. Her back straightened and I saw she was deciding something. I knew she resisted going back home, but I realized she thought about him—and Lillian. For two weeks, we'd avoided the near present, living on the farm or dwelling in her past. Taking the path of least resistance, I'd let her talk, enjoying the peaceful distance. But it was time to scratch below the surface of the stories she'd told me, to get back to the Creek.

"But you were always leaving . . ." I said.

Mother turned away from the approaching storm, back into the humid kitchen. As I waited for her to speak, my mind absently compared the humid, broken heat of the Creek with the drier, relentless heat of the flat land. Mother moved to the table and sat down across from me.

"When my mother died, I had to take care of Grace—she was my sister. At the time of my mother's funeral, Lillian was about ten and you were little. I got down here and found things a mess. Grace was acting . . . well, not right. I didn't know how bad she'd gotten—her emotions were totally, wildly different from one day to the next, and sometimes in the same day—but the cousins filled me in real quick, and I could see there were big problems.

"She wouldn't or couldn't take care of herself, and she shouldn't be allowed to live by herself—that much was clear. I tried to imagine how my mother alone had managed Grace all those years, but it was too painful to think about. I couldn't take Grace home with me—I had a family. And what would your father have done, with Grace and her wild behavior for everyone to witness and worry about? I couldn't even tell him the worst of it, until a lot later, when I had to.

"For a while, she lived on the farm, with the cousins looking out for her. Of course, Grace didn't know they were looking out for her. And she tried to run away so many times. Run to where, I don't know. But she'd always call them, from some truck stop on the highway, like she'd woken up from a dream, or, more likely, because she'd run out of money, men, or time. After a while, the cousins couldn't handle the middle-of-the-night phone calls, not to mention everything else, so they got the papers drawn up and sent her to the local institution down in Whiteville.

"Well, I couldn't let Grace wind up like those zombies there. The time I came down to visit—do you remember taking a long car ride with me and Lillian?—I realized I had to do something. So I worked desperately to find her a nicer place, close enough that I could at least try to take care of her.

"I had to ask you father to pay for it, which he did. The idea of his wife having a crazy sister running around was not to be considered, so he paid for a pretty nice room at Eastern State, where they could keep watch over her. That way, I could still visit, at least on the weekends—and feel like I was taking care of her.

"At first, I hated to visit. Grace was so unpredictable—she was sullen and silent, or yammering away at something, or crying for no particular reason—and I didn't know what to do for her. At home, I'd always fix myself up nice—make-up, hair, heels—and try to repair the damage I thought 'wild Grace' had done to the family.

"Once they started giving her the medicine, she got lost—in time, that is. She thought I was visiting her from art school, and she insisted on seeing my latest paintings. So I had to invent some, to satisfy her and to keep her quiet. I started bringing canvas and paint up with me, so we both could have something to do, because I couldn't bear talking to her.

"This went on for a year or so—me coming up to Eastern State. At first, it was every two weeks, then every week. After that, I was surprised to find that what had originally been an awful burden for me had become my release. You just never know how life's going to work out, Grace."

Mother paused and grabbed up her breath. This part of her story had come out in a rush of air, like the wind now rattling the bird feeder outside the kitchen window. Every time she said the word, "Grace," I felt my heart twitch, like you do when you think someone's talking about you. But Mother said my aunt's name in a different way—all soft and stretched, like she was back in her gingham jumper and pigtails, waiting for the school bus along a dusty stretch of North Carolina highway.

"I think your father preferred not to know about those visits," she said. "By then, he'd taken to hiding in his study when he was at home, and I guess I'd moved into my bedroom, because I needed more closet space, I decided.

"I did take you and Lillian up to see Grace one time. Do you remember? I guess not. You were too young to know much of anything, and Lillian always knew more than was good for her." She lightly ran her hand over the table's edge.

"No," I said, having to clear my throat to make a sound. "I don't remember."

"It was easy for us to drift apart. I felt less and less anchored to the house. I doubt I even thought about it. One fall, after she'd been there almost three years, Grace up and did what she'd probably been trying to do all along. She got friendly with the male nurse who handed out the medicine, and accumulated enough to put her to sleep forever. I'd like to think it was an accident, like they wanted to at the hospital. But one look at her room—she'd taken down and stacked all her paintings in a neat pile—and I knew she meant to do it.

"I remember walking into that room, the bed already stripped, her pitiful stack of clothes and what they call 'personal effects' thrown in a cardboard box, next to the canvases with their bright colors and crazy lines. I'm sure I was in shock. I didn't know what to do with any of it.

"They sent me to the basement to identify her body. I guess they used it as a kind of morgue. All I could do was follow the man in the white jacket—everyone there had white jackets except the patients. He kept switching on lights until we opened a heavy door to a stark white room on fire with light. There was a long makeshift table—like the kind they put up for church potlucks— in the middle of the room. And on this table, all wrapped up in a sheet, was Grace, or what was supposed to be Grace.

"The man in the white jacket marched over to the table and waved me forward. I saw that the covers were tucked in around her, like someone was afraid she'd get cold down there in that room, so far away from the sun.

"Somehow or another, I got over to the table. He grabbed hold of the sheet and lifted it, where her face should have been. I pretended to look, but I really kept my eyes shut. I didn't have to look at her to know it was her. I nodded, and we marched back upstairs to fill out a few papers.

"Grace was cremated, and I kept her ashes in the metal box they gave me, way in the back of my closet. I never told anyone. I brought them in one of my suitcases when I came down here this time."

Mother paused again, but her voice had already dwindled to a whisper. I could feel my heart constrict in pain—for her. How terrible, I thought, to feel that soul-sinking kind of regret, sorrow, and guilt. But she did what she could. When I thought objectively about Mother's comings and goings, and not as the one she was leaving behind, I could see how much it had cost her to do what she did.

"But Mother," I asked her directly, "all those Sunday afternoon visits, all those overnight trips, after Aunt Grace died—where did you go? What were you doing? Was there somebody else?"

Mother's face lost its tragic appearance. Outside, the wind died down for a moment and an actual bit of sun, a last burst straining from behind the threatening clouds, lit up the kitchen floor and warmed my back.

"There was only ever me, Grace," my mother said, smiling sadly. "That's what took me so long to figure out."

We spent the rest of the day washing clothes, marking and sorting the jars of pickles and vegetables we had put up, and choosing some paintings and old photographs for me to take back home with me in the car. The radio, retrieved from Mother's bedroom, jangled all day with weather news and country music, and I tried not to let my worry about the hurricane make me dash to the car and roar off before we were finished.

I managed to survive what seemed like a leaving ritual, as if I were going off to college instead of returning home. I sensed that Mother needed to do this—needed to go through the motions of sending me off. I understood, without asking, that she wasn't coming back with me now. And I guessed she wasn't ever coming back, except to visit.

It took most of the day to get my things together, and I was shocked to find the little sports car jammed with stuff by the time we finished loading it up—cardboard boxes piled with jars, their contents sloshing in the glass; brown paper bags filled with neatly folded clothes; and jumbles of those home-made frames. Here and there an unframed, rolled-up canvas jutted out, crazy colors mingling with conservative renderings of the farmhouse. Mother had included some of her artwork along with pictures painted by Aunt Grace. I thought I'd frame these canvases and hang them in my room, creating my own family art gallery.

When I finally squeezed myself into the cracked leather seat, I noticed an envelope on the dashboard. "For your father," Mother said. At least I could bring him her words. Somehow my entire mission in coming down here had been transformed.

But right now, a new mission called to me. With this storm coming on, Daddy and Lillian might need my help. The Creek was where I needed to be, and so, with a final clasp of our hands, a hug, and a wave, I started up the car and jerked down the driveway, picking up speed.

I thought hard about Mother and her stories as I sped down the highway, as if I could outrun the heavy gray clouds that spread out across the sky. At the farm, it had made some sense, but the black asphalt and the slap of the tires were less forgiving.

The farther I traveled from the farm, the clearer I saw my mother's weakness, and her words, "There was only ever me," came to mean something different than I had first understood. She and Lillian had a lot more in common than they knew. People can kill you with disappointment when you find out who they really are.

But I kept driving. I knew my way back.

Chapter Twenty-Three

❧

I drove east with a vengeance—I passed by fields of waving corn, the tiny lanes leading off to the once proud farmhouses and vacant front porch stoops. The occasional fruit stand stood empty and tractors waited, idle, in the fields. I drove fast, imagining Lillian's car as a spot of angry color on the steely landscape. The car's top was down and all the stuff I carried from the farm shifted with the wind and the car's motion. But I didn't lose anything.

I twisted the radio dial whenever I could spare a hand, trying to find a weather report. The world was not as concerned with the coming storm as I thought it should be; Aretha Franklin still demanded respect, and Seals and Croft sang about summer breezes. I listened to baseball scores and farm market reports and ads telling me I had "come a long way, baby." It wasn't until I hit an actual crossroads, moving from North Carolina Route 58 to Virginia Route 64, that I finally heard the voice of a weather man. He cheerfully predicted flooding and wind damage, all because of the historically early arrival of Hurricane Amie.

He even spelled out the hurricane's name, so listeners wouldn't confuse it with the familiar spelling of Amy. Trying to understand what he was saying about the storm's path, I pulled off the road and thought, *I don't know anyone named Amy. I certainly don't know anyone named Amie.*

Then I remembered the word from fifth grade French, when I was given a ditto with instructions to fill in the blank: "Mon amie est ___." I scribbled the name of the girl sitting next to me, not wanting to give the exercise the significance the other girls might. When the radio voice changed back to a man hawking used cars, I returned to the road, making a turn and thinking that whoever named hurricanes must have a peculiar sense of humor.

The farther east I got, the more cars joined me on the road, including a wood-paneled Vista Cruiser with bikes and beach chairs tied to the top, and a Volkswagen Beetle with surfboards somehow hitched to it. Clearly, the beach was emptying out the more pessimistic vacationers.

Seeing the traffic increase gave me a worse feeling about the weather, despite the fact that the farther east I traveled, the stiller the atmosphere became. When I was able to look at something besides the black asphalt and white lines in front of me, I noticed the solidness of the sky—a dark gray, almost green, mass was forming a kind of wall. I felt sweat gathering on my forehead and my legs sticking to the seat—the humidity was deceptively dense. It got stiller and stiller the closer to home I drove.

The *clackety-clack* of Lillian's worn-down tires provided background noise to the reel-to-reel tape recorder operating in my head, replaying scenes and dialogue from my two weeks at the farm. I had quickly gotten used to Mother, with her hair down around her shoulders and her feet bare. I tried, but I couldn't see the pictures I knew rested on her dresser back home, testimony to her once-real life on the Creek.

Instead, I could only see Mother peeling cucumbers in the kitchen, or weeding the little patch of garden in the side yard, her hands crusty brown with dirt, or rocking on the front porch, mixing paint on a palette, or telling stories, digging into the past—her past. As I collected her stories, I saw that she—and Lillian and I—were inexorably connected to the farm's dry, dusty soil.

But it was to the water that I raced now, feeling the powerful call of the Creek. I came to the end of the reel at the farm, with Mother standing on the porch, both hands raised, like she was giving me some kind of blessing. The image repeated over and over: the wind whipping through her white, loose-fitting, flannel nightgown, and her hair billowing around her head, as if it had a life of its own. She was smiling serenely, and now that I thought about it, she had never looked so beautiful to me, even in those well-posed wedding pictures. She was where she was supposed to be.

I turned my attention and imagination to what I was heading toward. I wondered if Lillian and Daddy were paying the least bit of attention to Amie and what needed to be done to get ready for her. Living in artificial New York had surely dulled Lillian to the improbabilities of the atmosphere.

I could see her resting languidly on the deck, watching the swirling clouds and lifting up her face to the wet breezes blowing in from the south. She might decide to take a few pictures, screwing on the right lens to capture the high water and the changes it brought to the landscape.

And who could predict what Daddy might be doing in the face of a storm like this? Would he think to store the deck furniture and secure the boat? Would he listen to the radio for evacuation warnings? Would he leave before the water got too high?

My mind whirled with the possibilities, and my thoughts grew darker with the sky. The rows of corn stalks and the occasional spreading oak gave way to swaying pines and scrubby brown grass. I turned off the highway, parting from the pack of speeding cars and panicky vacationers.

I pressed down on the accelerator and shifted into high gear, only to slam on the brakes at the sight of a deer bounding out of a marshy area by the road. I was close enough to see the flaring nostrils and hear the startled hooves, and I could have reached out to touch the smooth fur. The deer, a yearling, didn't even flinch or turn an eye. It headed straight across the road, leaping with abandon into a grove of bent and tired apple trees. With a flash of its white tail, it was gone.

I waited uneasily for the rest of the pack to cross—you could usually count on three or four traveling together. The car idled noisily while I watched the overgrown marsh. I felt the sting of wet in the air, but so far, not one drop of rain had fallen. In between the impatient engine's rumblings, I heard the air rush through the reeds in the marsh. It made an eerie, lonely noise. At its sound, I took off, the tires squealing as I shifted into too high a gear. The deer must have been a loner, or maybe left behind by the pack. All by myself on this last stretch, I raced down the road, intently looking for any other highway signs.

I paused at the top of our lane. I had been the only car on the road since turning off the highway, and I wondered if that meant no one was evacuating, or if everyone had already left. The deep ditches beside our street were filled to the top with rippling water. I noticed one of the neighborhood's fat white ducks swimming pointlessly in a ditch. Even before it hit, the hurricane was turning nature around.

I turned onto the gravel slowly and began the long curve that led to the Barnett house, aware that the water was rising as I drove. I tried to swallow the panic that was rising with it: I'd never seen water like this at our house. The hurricane was on its way up the coast—this was just its calling card. The little car kept moving, creating two wakes behind the rear tires.

But as I neared the bridge that allowed access over the marsh surrounding our peninsula, I realized I couldn't see the bridge. With a violent stab at the brakes, I barely managed to stop in time—just ahead were the heavy timbers that had once been the bridge. After closing the car windows and pulling up the convertible top, I swung my feet out the car door and into the water. Shockingly, it was as warm as my skin. I sunk in and out of marsh grass as the water rose above my knees, but I plowed on.

Finally, I reached the edge of the driveway and the thinner veneer of water that covered the gravel. The stones hurt my feet, which had lost their summer toughness at the farm, but I paid little attention.

My eyes scanned the lane ahead, only to find the old station wagon parked haphazardly, water reaching the bottom of its dinged hubcaps. Farther on, I saw a slapping screen door, and beyond that, a flooded marsh, with the shocking sight of an upturned boat hull. All of it carried an air of abandonment, but I yelled out Daddy's and Lillian's names anyway. The noise was yanked out of my mouth by the wind, and I listened hard to the silence that followed.

I sloshed across the driveway to the front steps. Thin rain began to fall. By the time I reached the front door, I was dripping. Opening the unlocked door, I felt heavy with the wetness, and suddenly all I wanted to do was to lie down in my own bed and go to sleep and not wake up until the storm had passed.

Inside the house, everything was dark. I flipped a switch—nothing happened. We never had a flashlight, and I knew better than to look for one. I did find some matches and a pack of Lillian's cigarettes, left behind on the stairs. I pocketed the matches and padded around the house, looking for signs of life.

There was just enough light for me to see the shadowy outlines of furniture. Outside, the gray of the sky appeared to meld with the gray inside, and there seemed no break, except for the raindrops marking the windows.

In the dimness, I called out again, but clearly the place was deserted. They must have evacuated, and in a hurry. The possibility that Daddy and Lillian were somewhere else simply hadn't occurred to me. With no one to rescue, I sat down at the kitchen table and wondered what I should do now.

I was wet, I was tired, and I could feel the sharp pricking of tears at the back of my eyes. I willed myself not to cry and add to the pool of water I'd already created on the kitchen floor. The wind was now making an insistent whine through the screens and I could almost feel the Creek water rising. I rose from my damp seat and went over to the bay window to check the water level.

In the time I'd been searching the house, the water had risen to cover the pier. I strained my eyes, searching for the white outline of Cal's boat across the Creek, but oddly, the dock was empty, with only the ropes whipping in the wind.

My eyes moved across the marina. John Whythe's new flag flapped furiously, already ripping at the seams. The sailboats jumped and bucked at their restraints. The masts rocked back and forth threateningly. There must not have been time to pull them all up onto land. Dangerous as it was, they would have to wait out the storm floating on the Creek.

As my eyes took everything in, I realized I'd seen no vestige of human life, nor any sign of Cal's Silverton. I knew the boat hadn't been moved in the three years I'd been watching from across the Creek. I didn't know if it even had an engine. Where could it possibly have gotten to?

I would have puzzled over this longer, but the hurricane decided to demand my full attention, trumpeting its arrival with now gale-force winds. As I watched, the roof of John Whythe's boat house began uprooting its shingles—they flew off like a flock of gulls startled by the roar of an engine. I couldn't take my eyes off the disaster happening so nearby. One of the sailboats tore loose from its bindings and pitched its way out into the Creek, and down the channel toward the Bay, as if it had an invisible sail. I watched until black clouds enveloped the ghost mast.

But my attention was jerked back to the house by the sudden sound of glass shattering. I jumped back from the bay window, only to realize that the sound was coming from below me, from the garage, where water and debris must have been rising high enough to bump against the garage windows, which meant the garage would soon be flooded.

I had to do something to protect the house, but what? I'd seen pictures of people nailing boards across windows and piling up jugs of water, but these seemed like things that should have been done hours or days ago. Without further thinking, I began running impulsively from window to window, downstairs and then upstairs, uselessly closing and locking them against the wind, rain, and flying debris.

I finally slid into my room, and in the deepening darkness, I found myself barely able to recognize it. I knew by feel where the bed, dresser, vanity, and bench were; these objects had kept their places. But just from my frantic glance around, the room looked different—as if someone had tidied things up. My paperback copies of *Jane Eyre* and *Wuthering Heights* rested neatly on the nightstand, their curling pages rebelling against removal from underneath the bed.

I grabbed them both and breathed in their old library smell, taking refuge in them yet one more time. My room felt like a guest room, the same way Lillian's had after she left but before Daddy began to use it as a storage room. The shadows of the neatly made bed, quilts folded and tucked, made my heart clench for a second.

But the sound of a loud crack and ominous rattle made me toss the books onto the bed and move quickly over to the bank of dormer windows, where I'd watched Tommy White's disaster. Of course, I'd never taken the time to close the window I'd popped open that day, and now the wind had blown it off its hinges—or was about to. The thick-paned frame beat wildly against the side of the house, and I pulled the bench over so I could reach out, pull it back into place, and close it.

The wind was roaring now. The tall pines surrounding the house swayed back and forth, nodding their heads and saying "told you so." I stuck my head out and grasped the side of the window, pulling it toward me, against the wind. Rain pelted my skin. Before I could bring the window to its latch, my eye caught sight of something white coming up the Creek.

I struggled to get it in focus, suddenly aware that, in my haste, I'd left my glasses in the car. I strained my eyes, just as I strained my arm to keep hold of the window frame. The white object was weaving like a water skier working his way in and out of a wake. I could measure its progress as it crashed against the white caps, the first I'd ever seen on the Creek. Suddenly, I knew what the object was—Cal's Silverton. Then the window snapped shut, producing a sudden quiet in the room.

But where could that old boat possibly be going in this mess? I felt goose bumps rise up on my arms. *Where was Daddy? Where was Lillian?* I clung to the edge of the little window, mesmerized by the erratic but purposeful movement of the white boat against the solid black of the water. I strained my eyes for a human figure—an assurance that someone was driving the boat.

Suddenly, a tiny figure emerged from the back of the cabin and took hold of the engine box in the back. The figure wrestled with the box and the wind, which was fiercely blowing every which way. I could make out a chunk of blond hair, and I knew it had to be Cal. The boat must have stalled, and Cal was working desperately to get the engine operating again. Without some propulsion, the wind would blow that boat right into the marsh and sink it.

But that had to mean that someone else was at the steering wheel—someone who knew how to drive a boat. I could only think of Daddy. As flashes of lightning began illuminating the sky, it hit me—both Daddy and Lillian must be on the boat with Cal.

Deciding I had to get to them, I slip-slided down the stairs to the front hall, then sailed around the corner to the kitchen. It seemed contrary to primal human nature, to the very concept of self-preservation, to leave a dry, safe house to venture out into the wild wetness, but with my family in jeopardy, I pushed away any thoughts of sitting back in relative safety and waiting to see what happened. I pushed the kitchen door open and raced out onto the deck, the rain actually coming sideways at me now.

The water below completely covered any sign of land, and the pier was nowhere to be found. Only the pilings were visible, and the ropes that once held our boat in place were now flapping wildly. With the rain pelting every inch of my body and the wind forcing me to grab onto the deck's railing just to remain upright, I hesitated. I couldn't quite see the steps that would lead me to the ground, but I knew they had to be there. I could just see the whiteness of the boat on its weaving pathway. It seemed headed for the end of the Creek, and would have to pass by, or over, our submerged pier to get there.

I couldn't think. But I had to do something right away or I would be blown off the deck. Pulling myself hand over hand along the railing, I made it to the steps. Still grasping the railing, I forced myself to find first one step, then the next. The rain blinded me. I could focus only on the railing and the white skin of my hand clasping onto it.

As I stepped down toward the ground, the water seemed to be rising to meet me. Finally, I held my breath and launched myself away from the railing. I felt the goo of what was once solid ground, gravel and mud squishing between my toes, but I leaned against the wind and plowed toward those pilings. I moved in slow motion, grabbing onto whatever branch or marsh grass was available. I looked up long enough to see the boat moving forward again, heading, like me, straight for the pier.

By the time my feet felt the firm smoothness of a pier board, the water was up over my knees. Thunder crackled everywhere around me. I panicked—every waterman shrinks in fear when thunder announces the arrival of lightning. I spun my head back crazily, looking for strikes of lightning in the wall of rain.

The whiteness of the boat drifting closer to the pier was the only relief against the darkness. I could just make out the mass of the boat—the wind and the rain stung my eyes. I moved forward by fixing my sights on the water streaming in toward the house. There wasn't much time—I had to move fast if I had any hope of reaching Cal and the end of the pier.

The waves of rising water kept pushing me back and threatened to knock me off the pier entirely. The boat was just yards from the pier and I doubted that anyone could even see me. I would have to take a plunge, then use the pier boards to pull myself along. So I dove forward and worked myself along the pier, board by board.

Salty water pounded my face as I tried to keep my head up. Overhead, the thunder continued, sounding like the sonic booms we used to hear when jets made their way back to Langley Air Force Base. Whenever I could spit water out of my mouth, I found myself hollering to the boat with no people in sight.

Soon, I felt myself running out of gas. Just as I reached the first set of pilings, which was about the halfway point, it occurred to me that I might drown out here, swept away from the moorings, just like old *Pappy*, which sat hull-side up in the marsh. What had I been thinking? *Why had I come out here in this disaster, when I should have sat out the storm inside our house? It might sink, but it wouldn't be blown away. What, or whom, did I hope to save?*

In the kind of epiphany that comes like an electric shock, I suddenly realized I would have to save myself first if I was to save anyone on the boat.

I tried to hold myself up on one of the piling tops, wrapping one arm around its slick perimeter and waving my other arm. Now I could actually detect the cabin windows, and I had at least a small chance that someone would be able to spot my white t-shirt. The boat was almost moving forward now. In another few moments, unless some contrary wind blew in from the west, the old Silverton would move even with the pier.

"See me!" I heard myself shout. "Come get me!" The boat kept moving. My arm began to slip from the piling and I felt the wind push me back into the water. "Help me! I need you!" One last yell before fear choked me. The boat was nearly parallel with the pier. I felt I would sink into the Creek—sink right to the bottom. A random picture of Jane Eyre on the moors—homeless, starving, and betrayed—flooded my senses. I knew I would have to give up, just as she had tried to.

But then the boat became a bow and the white moved nearer.

I grabbed the piling with both arms and shook the water from my eyes. There was no mistaking it. The Silverton was headed toward me. The wind argued with its change in course, but the boat stayed steady.

As the Silverton drew even with the side of the pier, the figure I'd briefly seen turned into Cal. He was covered in a yellow slicker, the hood flapping back to reveal his long blond hair, loose and wild. An absolute wave of relief passed through my body when I heard his voice over the wind and rain. I almost let go of my grip on the pier boards.

The next thing I knew, Cal's strong arms were pulling me over the side of the boat. Then he draped a life jacket over my head and shoulders and pushed me toward the cabin. He turned back to the motor box just as I entered the cabin and the wind slammed the door shut. I heard a loud hoot and the engine grinding, then the motor box lid drop onto the deck with a thud.

Daddy, seated at the wheel, was turned, I guess, to watch for signals from Cal. When I entered the cabin, Daddy looked like he was seeing a ghost. He stared and let go of the wheel, holding out his hands to touch me and make sure I was real. Then the motor started up and he had to grab the wheel and work to get us away from the marsh we were drifting toward. The boat was rocking something fierce the whole time and I had to hold onto the side walls just to keep my balance.

All of a sudden, Daddy and Cal started to shout directions at each other. Daddy turned the wheel frantically, and Cal squatted down at the stern, turning by hand the outboard engines at the back of the boat. I wanted to get out there and help him, but I floundered around, looking for a rope or something I could tie myself to the boat with, just as they did in the movies.

But I heard a low moan, then a crazy call for help coming from inside the sleeping area of the cabin. The voice was all too familiar, and I yanked open the door to find Lillian sprawled out on Cal's bunk, grabbing her stomach and rocking back and forth.

With the boat knocking me back and forth, I made my way over to her, yelling at the top of my lungs, "What's the matter?" I spied a brownish red seeping into Cal's wadded-up blanket, and I just managed to sink to my knees before I threw up.

Lillian couldn't talk, except to command me to hold her hand. Her short nails dug into my palms, but I held onto her with all my might. As I desperately tried to imagine some way of stopping Lillian's bleeding and pain, I felt powerless. Only my holding onto her seemed to calm her. So we sat, jolted together by the boat battling the storm, both of us with our eyes closed. Water ripped across the small portholes on the walls above our heads, but we hunkered down in Cal's bed and tried to block out the wet around us.

Finally, I felt Cal's arms draw me up into the cabin and I watched him carry Lillian from down below. Covering her with his own slicker as best he could, he took her out to the stern, where he handed her over to the waiting Coast Guard men reaching with outstretched arms to receive her.

Daddy held the heavy ropes tying their boat to the Silverton as it pitched and bucked like a young colt, resisting the control of the wind. An unexpected, momentary break in the wind allowed Cal to get Lillian across the stern without incident.

Mercifully, Lillian passed out as soon as he'd picked her up. The wind picked up again and Daddy and Cal worked together to launch the Coast Guard skiff, which then moved swiftly toward the bank of swaying pines in the distance, toward the flashing lights of an ambulance, which pulsed under the grayness like the thin arteries under my skin.

The Coast Guard moved out, promising to return, but it took only another hour for Cal's boat to finally wreck itself on this same, now deserted, bank. The three of us then took on the job of heading for dry land with a sense of relief, having only our own lives to worry about now.

Chapter Twenty-Four

The harsh white silence of the hospital room seemed as deafening as the wind and thunder still pounding in my head. I woke to find myself, still damp, sitting in one of those green plastic chairs, with a hospital-issued blanket wrapped around me. It took me more than a minute to figure out where I was. I had moved so fast that day—from flat field, to flooded marsh, to wild boat ride, to serene hospital room.

But as my eyes adjusted to the bright fluorescent light, I could see a figure on the bed beside me. With my eyes, I traced my arm to that figure and realized I was holding onto Lillian's hand through the bars of the bed, and had probably been holding onto it all night. Suddenly, I knew we had all survived the hurricane.

As I watched her sleep, her face remained angelic, seemingly untouched by the recent turmoil. But hadn't that always been the way with Lillian? She was always there to stir things up, then able to lift herself out and away, sweeping back all others in her wake.

Lillian stirred, removing her hand from mine and placing it over her stomach, which rose like a furrow from under the thin white flannel. When she awoke and took in her surroundings, she turned her head toward me and, for once, I saw slightly dark circles under her clear blue eyes. She whispered, "Grace, is the baby . . ?" and grabbed my hand again.

"Everything's okay," I assured her, as it all came back to me. "It's a miracle, though. You had a lot of doctors and nurses running around here last night." I watched relief flood her face and knew my face mirrored hers.

"Where's everyone—else?" she asked, her face pursed in concentration. "I remember being in such pain, something going wrong down there, and then Daddy wrapping me up in an old quilt and carrying me out in the rain, and then . . . It was Cal—wasn't it? How did he do it? The Creek was so wild, like the ocean. And we were on a boat, weren't we? How did I get off? And how did I get here?

"Grace," she continued, "I was so scared—for the baby, not for me. I forgot about me. But where were you? When did you get back? And where's Mother?" She looked past the door, as if expecting Mother to be standing just outside, consulting with doctors and instructing nurses.

I tried to muster up an answer, but it all seemed so far away now, like a dream—the little white farm house, and Mother with her hair down and her feet bare. I was saved by a nurse bustling in, obviously distressed by a patient who had the temerity to wake up on her own and not need the help of nurses. We fell to silence as she measured Lillian's blood pressure, checked the IV, and took her temperature. I released Lillian's hand, moving away from all the activity.

Another nurse entered with a tray of tiny cups and a plastic pitcher of water. Before either of us could protest, Lillian was ordered to take this and that pill and told that under no circumstances should she try to get up—she needed complete bed rest. Before Lillian could even ask about the baby, she nodded off, lulled to sleep by the little red pills the nurse had held to her lips a few minutes earlier.

I guess it was all for the best, because I was worn out and felt a gut urge to get home. I had to see Daddy, Cal, and the house, to make sure they were still there—to make sure this wasn't some kind of dream. I would return to the hospital soon, and tell Lillian my stories of North Carolina, and hear her stories about the Creek during the time I'd been gone.

I took one last look at Lillian's baby-doll face, framed by a spray of still-tangled yellow hair. I wanted to comb that hair, put it right again, but I knew I had to tend to my own first. I was sure my hair looked just like that mess of marsh where we had junked Cal's boat. I tiptoed out of the room, hugging the hospital blanket around me, and leaving damp footprints behind.

Lifting the blanket hem like a queen's robe, I walked down the hall and into the waiting room to get a phone or a ride or whatever I'd need to get home. The sight of Daddy and Cal in the waiting room nearly knocked me over. Clearly exhausted, they must have waited out the night there in their wet clothes, wanting to be near Lillian if she needed them.

As I hugged Daddy and reached out to touch Cal, I couldn't help but think how small they suddenly felt and looked—some of their bigness had been swallowed up in the hurricane's fury. Here, in the bright antiseptic whiteness of the waiting room, they seemed like anxious first-time fathers, unsure what to do or say—just knowing how important it was to be there.

We three sat alone in the waiting room. After I let them know that Lillian was sleeping peacefully and everything was all right, Daddy began talking about the hurricane. At our house, Daddy had seen the water getting higher and higher and Lillian feeling worse and worse. He tried to get the station wagon out, but couldn't get the thing started in all the wetness. Daddy knew he'd have to get help, and figured Cal was the only one still around and able. So he wheeled the cannon under the roof overhang and shot it off, hoping to get Cal's attention and his boat over to our side of the Creek.

Cal knew at once he had to get over there, and somehow managed to get the Silverton's engine revved up and working. The Creek was like a wild thing, running this way and that, making a simple ride nearly impossible. Then came a dramatic docking at our pier, when Daddy carried Lillian out to Cal's boat, the water lapping at his feet as he made his way out. Soon after he got the Silverton underway, Cal spotted me and determined he'd have to return to the pier to get me, despite the very real risk of crashing his boat.

Their voices got louder and more animated as they interrupted each other. They got so it sounded a whole lot like one of their late night discussions of Civil War battles—except, for once, they agreed on the bad guy and on the heroes.

I folded myself up in the blanket, letting them talk and talk. Their voices rushed over me until I finally fell asleep, thinking I was once again in my third floor room, listening to their words floating up from the deck below. I barely noticed when Cal lifted me up and carried me out of the hospital to the waiting ambulance, which carefully transported us home.

By the time we arrived, the water had receded into the Creek and then into the Bay, sweeping clean the marshes and piers and leaving bare the big brick house. "Barnett's folly" had withstood "the big one."

Chapter Twenty-Five

The mess left by Hurricane Amie was unlike anything Back Creek had seen in a long time. Electrical wires were down all along Dandy Road, and that kept the VEPCO people busy for weeks. Roof shingles, gutters, windows, screen doors, and, in at least one case, an entire front porch were missing from expensive waterfront homes as well as neighborhood shacks. So many cars and trucks were swept into the marsh by the high water that Mr. Owens from the Sunoco station was able to afford a late summer vacation after towing all the stranded vehicles out of the muck.

Actually, lots of people made money off the storm. Bob Ewell, Back Creek's deck and pier man, had to scrounge around for teen-age boys to help him repair and replace pier boards and railings before school started. Charlie Folks, everyone's yard man, who usually looked forward to long August afternoons spent fishing, had to bring his brother-in-law in to help him haul away all the debris left by the high water. Only two places in Back Creek remained solid and intact—the concrete statuary in front of the old house belonging to Tommy White's mother, and the Barnetts' brick monstrosity.

That's not to say we emerged unscathed. In fact, we had quite a bit of cleaning and repairing to do. Almost as soon as we got home from the hospital, Daddy and Cal went in search of the Silverton while I took a shower and, with a towel still draped around me, fell asleep in my familiar old bed. By that afternoon, they had managed to have the boat hauled back to our yard, where it was mounted on blocks and the deep gash in its side examined and repaired.

Cal was lucky. Most of the boats at John Whythe's place had wrecked themselves, and either lay at the bottom of the Creek or were a tangle of wood on the shore. Even Cal's sailboat, the one he'd been restoring, was knocked off its sawhorses and tossed around the yard. It was a sad sight. But Cal was pretty good about it. He gathered together what was left of the hull and put everything away in John Whythe's dry storage shed. After that, he kept mostly to our side of the Creek, helping Daddy and me pick up the pieces.

I was lucky, too. Somehow, all of Mother's and Aunt Grace's artwork stayed dry and intact—I'd had the presence of mind to put the convertible top up.

It had been a long time since I'd seen Daddy so galvanized, so energetic. He got up early and stayed outside late, repairing the pier, hauling out the branches and bushes, working on our cars and the Silverton. When I think about it, I don't remember him disappearing into his study a single time, nor do I recollect seeing him with anything stronger than a Budweiser in his hand. Somehow, the disaster had washed up some part of him that had been sunk for a long time—at least since Mother had started leaving on her weekend trips.

When I could finally get myself in order—back in my cut-off khakis and t-shirt—I told Daddy about Mother and about my stay at the farm. It was the evening of the first day we'd returned and Daddy and I were sitting at the kitchen table, waiting for Cal to get back with some fried chicken from Pop's. Daddy was sweaty and dirty from his work outside, his arms a mess from little scratches. He looked like he worked in a garage, with grease under his nails despite repeated hand-washings. But his face was relaxed and alert.

Telling him was hard for me. I squirmed around in the hard

ladder-back chair while he turned the pages of the *Yorktown Crier.* I folded my legs under me until I sat cross-legged. The chair moaned in protest and Daddy looked up at me.

"Grace, what the hell are you doing to that chair?" He noticed my face. "You're going to hurt yourself," he added lamely, making his own noise rattling the paper.

"Daddy, you haven't asked me about my trip," I said. "To the farm," I added, in case he didn't know which trip I meant.

He folded the newspaper carefully and sat up a little, giving me his full attention. We all had bad posture at the kitchen table, unless Mother was there to tell us to sit up. It was almost as if mentioning the farm brought her posture reminder to the table.

"No, I haven't," he finally said. I waited a few long moments. Somehow, I'd expected more from him. I uncrossed my legs and touched my feet to the braided rug below.

So I described my trip down to the farm, where he'd insisted I go. I paused, holding in my mind the picture of Mother coming out that front door in her overalls. Then I pressed on.

"She looked different because she was . . . different. She was painting and fixing up the garden and even making pickles. She was . . . happy." There, I'd said it, to him and to myself.

Daddy slumped a little at the word. I watched his face. It was hard for me to keep my eyes trained on it; while talking to him, it was always so much easier to look out the window at the Creek, or down at my feet. But this time, I had to see him thinking. His face didn't crumple the way I'd expected; his eyes sort of softened. He was the one to look out the window. Then I saw him wipe the back of his hand across his nose. Once again, I realized with surprise that my father didn't have a handkerchief with him. So I handed him a paper napkin and followed his eyes to the Creek while he collected his thoughts.

As he did, I focused on a lone blue heron, rising suddenly from the marsh. Flying gracefully over our pier, he came to rest in the high branches of a tall pine that had survived the hurricane. It

was the trees' ability to bend with high winds that determined
their survival. Lots of them had crashed into the marsh, and one
had fallen in pieces across our deck. But enough of the trees made
it intact that the landscape stayed familiar and the herons had
plenty of places to nest and keep safe from the foxes.

Daddy cleared his throat. "I guess I always knew she wasn't
entirely happy here," he began. "Well, hell, who would've known?
Still, I hoped. Having a baby—I thought that would be enough.
Then I thought having her sister nearby would be enough—she'd
have the taste of home she needed. Then I thought she'd come to
realize how wonderful life on the Creek is—how wonderful living
with me, and you girls, could be." He was looking steadily at me
now and I was looking back.

"But Daddy, it was never about us," I said.

I could tell Daddy had some trouble with this idea, though he
looked like he was working hard to understand. His eyes were as
intent as I'd ever seen them, as intent as the day he kicked Lillian
out. He sat with his hands together between his legs, almost like
he was praying. He covered up his dirty nails by folding his fingers
in together. I wondered briefly if I'd said too much, if I should've
just told him she was there with Aunt Grace and kept up the lie.

The deep silence was punctuated by the roar of an engine out
on the Creek. Our eyes traveled to the window, where we could
see some joy riders in a big cigarette boat steaming down the
Creek, completely disregarding the "No Wake" edict. Daddy rose
from his seat and strode purposefully to the screen door and out
onto the deck. Shaking his fists at the passing boat, he shouted,
"Slow down!" But his words were lost in the roar of the engine.
The bikinied girls waved and the bronzed boy held up his beer
can in a toast-like gesture. "Damn kids," Daddy mumbled as he
returned to the kitchen.

I could tell something had let go in him, or maybe something
had come back to him. "Grace, if I ever catch you out there on a
boat like that . . ." Then he stopped, remembering something. He

disappeared and I heard him open the door of his study.

Now I really felt bad. Had my words sent Daddy back to the study and his old friend Jack Daniel's? Should I have kept quiet? I wrapped my arms tightly around my knees and rocked in the chair, thinking hard. I watched the sun dance on the little waves the boat had created and listened for the sounds of the car and Cal heading up the driveway. Maybe he could save us.

I heard the study door slam and Daddy walking purposefully back into the kitchen. His face looked clear, the way the water lies calm and deep after a storm. He had an envelope and papers in his hands, which he tossed on the table before me.

"Grace, you did what you could. It'll just take some time until we all get used to . . ." I heard his voice fade and almost crack. But he bent with the wind and came back upright, just like those surviving pines.

"Anyway, you need to know you did the right thing, even though I was mad as hell at you for leaving without telling me or Lillian, and driving that broken-down little car, and then waiting a day to call me. What were you thinking?" He stopped again, gathering himself up. "Water under the bridge now, I guess . . . It'll take time to sort all this out. But we have a lot of cleaning up to do here, so I'll have some time. And Lillian will be coming home soon and she'll need taking care of."

I knew he wanted me to be here to take care of her. And I would be, because he needed me. I opened my mouth, ready to tell him I thought Lillian should stay in his study on the first floor, but Daddy held up his hand and continued. "And I'll have to get a nurse in here or see if Bernice will help out."

I opened my mouth again, to protest. He kept his hand up.

"Because you're not going to be here. I received this notice of fees due to the University of Virginia, for matriculation of one Grace Baldwin Barnett in the fall of 1975. So I paid them, and I wrote a letter explaining that you'll sign up for classes when you get there. And you're due there in three weeks, for 'orientation,' whatever that is. I never needed any orientation, but then . . ."

I stared at the papers in front of me. I saw a fancy seal at the top of one page—the seal of the University of Virginia. I remembered the day I'd taken the letter with that seal out of the mailbox and stuck it in my back pocket, certain it had no immediate relevance to my life. But the seal, the letters, the idea of going to college—suddenly, they all took on a larger meaning, of new possibilities. I squinted a little behind my glasses, trying to see myself as a college student. I could only visualize the edges of a picture.

"So," Daddy continued, "you've got to get yourself ready for school. I can write a check, but I can't begin to imagine what you'll need or want to take with you." He stopped and cocked his head. "Thank God that boy is finally coming with our meal. I could eat a horse." He pulled open the refrigerator and grabbed a beer for each of us. "Course, if he went to Pop's, we could actually be eating horse."

"Well, Daddy, at least it'll be hot." I popped open the top of my beer and let the foam slide down my throat. It was good to be back on familiar, well-trod territory.

From the driveway came the sound of a car door slamming and Cal's holler, "You should have seen the line at Pop's. All those VEPCO men—they've taken over the damn place, with their hard hats and all kinds of crap hanging off their belts. I had to wait . . ." His voice trailed off, probably as he stuck his head in the car to fish out the rest of our meal.

And so it was decided—I would be off to college in three weeks. The matter had been settled in the usual Barnett way, with a beer and a short conversation. We would talk more about the University of Virginia that summer, late at night on the deck. And I would hear all about where to live and where to drink and where not to get caught drinking.

Even Cal would join in the conversation, casting grim warnings about the laxity of college life and having all those books to read, and what might happen to someone who leaves the water to live next to a bunch of mountains. We worked during the day, putting things back together and cleaning them up.

All the while, we waited for Lillian to come home.

Chapter Twenty-Six

She rested, quiet and immobilized, in a hospital room over-looking a concrete parking lot, where she watched cars pull in and out, unloading doctors, or visitors, or soon-to-be-patients—people facing death, perhaps, or maybe new life.

Poised by a window that would not open, I, too, watched the flow of life below as Lillian asked about the Creek. I came to visit late in the afternoons, when the heat of the day chased Daddy into his bedroom for a nap and Cal inside the garage to work on the Silverton's engine.

Daddy came to visit her most every morning, as early as they'd let him in. I actually looked forward to the break in the day, the respite from the sweltering house and the contemplation of pre-paring to leave for college.

"Leave for college!" The words still sounded funny to me. When I told Lillian about Daddy's talk and my new plans, she pushed her hair back from her face, narrowed her eyes, and looked hard at me, like a subject for one of her pictures. I couldn't quite discern what she was thinking, but the moment was over quickly when yet another nurse entered to take her temperature. The doc-tors and nurses never stopped coming—Lillian, I suppose, had worked her magic on them, too.

I returned to the window and imagined the heat shimmering up from the asphalt, listening to the faraway thump of a jackham-mer somewhere, and appreciating the cool peace of the hospital.

Inside Lillian's room, it was all quiet talk and soft white shoes scooting across shiny floors—a little oasis of cool white calm, with Lillian at the center, where she was always most comfortable.

We stayed mostly in the present when we talked those afternoons. I reported on Daddy's and Cal's progress that day, something funny Cal had said, and what we'd had for lunch or dinner. She listened with eyes turned toward the window, her hands resting on the mound that was the baby. I knew she was usually listening, because she asked questions and laughed in the right places, but I also knew her mind wasn't always with me.

As she said to me the afternoon I stopped telling her stories, the hospital gave her time to think. She had no camera lenses to hide behind, no grainy black and gray shadows to color things. But by telling me the story of her leaving Back Creek and her coming back, which she did that afternoon, she was giving me her own series of pictures.

I don't know what got her started on that story. I felt as if I'd been doing all the talking, trying to take her mind off where she was and why. The doctors had indicated she might be able to go home soon, but only if she rested and stayed quiet. This should have been good news, but Lillian seemed slightly disturbed by it. She moved herself around in her confined position, restless, as she listened to me recount how Cal had tied himself to the chimney while replacing some shingles.

"At first," I said, "he looked like some kind of big bird, there on the roof—like that pelican that appeared, out of nowhere, and sat on the roof for days, waiting for the rest of his crew. Do you remember? You must have been about twelve, I guess, because I was pretty little. I can barely remember—I can just see Mother hanging out the window, trying to get a good look at him, so she could sketch him." I stopped for a few seconds, merging the picture of Cal squatting on the roof line and the picture of the patient, misplaced pelican.

"There's a lot I barely remember," she said. "Mostly stuff I should, too." I glanced at Lillian's face. It was not like her to regret anything. But her tone definitely suggested some sadness.

"What do you mean?" I said.

"Oh, Grace, you know. I've had nothing to do but sit here and think. I've tried to make my mind stop working, but it keeps running through the past. Now that I know the baby will be okay, I have to worry about me . . . being okay, that is."

"Lillian," I said, reaching out to touch the starched edge of the sheets, "what the hell are you talking about?" Why should she be sad today? Only this morning, the doctor said she might be allowed to return home over the weekend. She had been cracking jokes with the nurses just a few minutes ago.

She turned her face away from me, toward the window, where light struggled to penetrate the thick Venetian blinds the nurse had closed. Outside, where the parking lot baked in the relentless late afternoon sun, a siren sounded—dim at first, then louder. Our attention was caught by the sound, and I wondered if it marked the beginning or the end of disaster.

She used both arms to push herself into something resembling a sitting position. The size of her stomach and her general weakness made that difficult. With anyone in the room, she was usually content to rest in place, against the extra pillows the nurses had found for her. But today, she struggled to lift herself up just a little more. I wanted to help her, and rose out of my chair, but she waved her hand like she was swatting a fly. Even this little movement left her breathing harder, and I watched while she gathered some air from the air-conditioned coolness.

"In New York," she began when she was again in control, "I used to hear sirens nonstop, night and day. I lived down by the river, right near a hospital, and the ambulance and police sirens were loud and constant. I couldn't get used to it—other people just got numb to the noise.

"But I always felt like they were coming for me, like I'd done something wrong and was about to get caught. Or that something terrible was about to happen to me and the hospital was waiting for me. I felt jumpy all the time.

"I had this great view of the river—that was the only virtue of what was a pretty crappy apartment. I would look out at the river to try to find some peace—the Creek used to make me feel like everything was all right. But the East River was so dirty and filled with stuff—I never got used to that, either." She drifted back to the light that lingered just beyond the dusty metal blinds.

I left my chair and lifted myself so I could sit on the edge of the hospital bed. "Lillian, you never told me much about Tommy. Tell me now."

I had issued the invitation before, and while Lillian was happy to talk about most anything to do with her pictures, or growing up, or what I should do, or New York life in general, she'd been silent on this last part of her last five years.

Hugging her stomach, she sat silent.

"Please, Lillian," I persisted, "you said he was the baby's father. I'd like to know more about him."

After a long pause, Lillian began speaking in almost a whisper, watching the door as if she were making a confession.

"I found Tommy working in a bar down in Greenwich Village—I just happened in there one afternoon, when someone I was supposed to meet nearby didn't show up. Actually, it was the guy who lived in that crappy apartment I told you about. When he didn't post, I knew I'd be gathering up my stuff and moving on, and I was furious both at him and at life for dumping me that way.

"I remember it so well. It was a cold day in December, and New York was gray and freezing. You can't find that kind of cold around here. It was ten o'clock in the morning and, of course, everyone was at work or asleep, but the door to this place was open, so I marched in and sat myself down at the bar.

"I didn't even take off my coat—I just yelled out into the emptiness: 'I want a Bloody Mary.' No, I think I said: 'I *need* a Bloody

Mary.' When I heard my words echo, I sounded like a real New York bitch, except this Tidewater twang crept in, holding the words in the air. And all of a sudden, I wasn't mad anymore—I was just sad. So I jumped off the barstool, grabbed up my pocketbook, and turned to leave.

"Just then, a voice came out of the back: 'Lillian Barnett, how the hell are you?' I was mystified—most people I knew in New York didn't know my last name. So I turned back to the bar and, to my utter amazement, there was good ol' Tommy White, with long hair and a smile that was like the sun shining, even in New York, in cold and dreary December."

As she paused, I thought I saw a ghost of a smile cross her face. Maybe she saw Tommy again in the darkened bar, wearing a white apron, muscular forearms crossed like he was hugging himself, grinning like a Cheshire cat at finding the mysterious Lillian Barnett, a Back Creek escapee, sitting right there in his New York City bar.

"It was like coming home—seeing Tommy. I thought I'd left the Creek behind for good, but I can't tell you the relief, the happiness, that came over me when I heard his drawl. Tommy had taken all sorts of acting lessons to get rid of his accent, but it never took the way he hoped. But that day, seeing him was like finding a light at the end of a pier on a foggy night.

"He took his apron off and brought out some coffee, and we sat at a little corner table just talking. He told me about coming to New York to be an actor, his mother pulling out change and crumpled-up dollar bills from an old sock to help him pay the bus fare. But it was harder than he thought and he wasn't getting any breaks, and he was too embarrassed to go back to the Creek, so he was tending bar for a while.

"I told him about my pictures, and about people I'd met, and about parties I'd gone to. It was so easy to impress him; I guess I laid it on pretty thick—like I can. I didn't talk about why I'd come to New York in the first place, only about how great it was being there. Before we knew it, lunch had come and gone, and we'd talked the day away. Finally, about four o'clock, the little Italian bar manager came out and fired Tommy. So we left together and walked seven blocks to this tiny room he rented above a Chinese restaurant. Somehow, I ended up staying there . . . for a while."

As she talked, I tried to reconcile the picture of Tommy she'd painted with the picture my mind continued to carry of him: a tall figure, standing ramrod straight, rushing along the water toward that pier, blond hair blown back around his head like a kind of crown.

"I didn't mean for it to happen the way it did. I tried to tell him that, but he wouldn't—or couldn't—listen. I was happy living with him those couple of months. I got some breaks—I sold some of my photos, and I was talking to people at a magazine to do more. It was nice to have someone to share the good stuff with. And good to come home and feel like I'd done just that—come home. And Tommy . . . well, he liked taking care of me. And I needed taking care of . . .

"When I first ran into him at the bar, Tommy had been all set to leave New York. He was going to come back here and do something else—get a job on the water, I guess, and take care of his mother. He was giving up on being an actor in New York—that 'cold concrete island' is what he called it.

"And I gotta tell you, he never had a chance. He was too honest and too innocent to ever do what you have to do to get acting jobs like the ones he wanted. Tommy wanted to be someone else. He wasn't in New York for the money or to see his name in some theater program. He thought he liked trying to get into someone else's skin. But he could never get away from being Tommy White, from Back Creek, Virginia. I could tell that right away. But I never told him.

"And I could also tell that having me with him made him a different Tommy White. Being with Lillian Barnett made him feel special, like realizing a high school fantasy or something. I let it happen, though. I needed a place to stay and he needed a part to play.

"Then, just as I was starting to do something with my camera, I got pregnant again, but I never told him. This time I could take the subway and walk right into a clinic, and get the procedure done legally. Or so I thought. But something happened to me after I took my seat in one of those metal folding chairs. I looked around at the cinder block walls. Somebody had painted big pink flowers every couple of feet to cheer people up, I guess. Those flowers seemed like they were reaching out to get me, or something crazy like that. I started to sweat, even though the air-conditioning was already on and it was an unnatural kind of cold.

"I looked at the other two girls in there with me. One looked like she was about fourteen and the other about forty. The young one looked scared out of her mind—she had some poor baby of a boy with her, and they held onto each other like it was the end of the world. The other woman looked tired and sad. She was reading some scandal magazine, like she was waiting to get her nails done or something.

"I kept looking back and forth between them and then, all of a sudden, I had to get out of there. I couldn't go through with it—not this time. I still can't explain why. At least in my mind, the baby didn't become a baby until I got back here to Back Creek. But I bolted out of that clinic. And I made up my mind to leave Tommy and New York. There was only one place I knew to go.

"I never knew Tommy would take my leaving him so hard. I swear. I think he tried to find me for a while, but I hid out with someone I knew while I sold off apartment stuff and used the money to buy a car. When I left New York, all I could think to do was come back here. I had no idea Tommy had already come back here . . . or that he would end up like he did."

She stopped abruptly, her voice going out of her like a deflated balloon. She hung her head, her golden halo of hair hiding her face. For a minute, I thought she might be crying, and I held my breath and listened hard.

"Did you love him?" I whispered.

"Love him?" She repeated the words, as if she was having trouble understanding English. "Did I love him?" she repeated again, as if it didn't have anything to do with anything.

Just then, we were interrupted by a soft knocking at the door. Lillian lifted up her head, and her face was washed free of everything, just like the bare beaches of those Bay islands after the big storm.

A smile lit up her face as the doctor hurriedly entered the room, brandishing a chart. In the most normal voice I'd ever heard, she asked him, "Looks like it's time for me to go on home, right, Dr. Jim?" He smiled in return.

I still couldn't believe it. Lillian had lived with Tommy for months, mostly as a convenience to her. Then, without explanation, she left him, avoided him, and never told him about his baby. I remembered Mother's words.

I stood up and gently pushed my chair back against the wall. Then I walked out the door the doctor had left open. Outside the room, a world of nurses and doctors in green scrubs busied themselves caring for the sick. For a moment, I stood there in the hallway while the world moved past, carrying trays and charts and medicines to relieve patients' suffering.

But no one could bring me relief. Forgiveness and redemption require patience and faith, and I was completely out of both.

All I knew was that I had to get back to the Creek, back to that mirror of water to see what to do.

I walked right through the hallway and out of the hospital, ignoring Lillian's faint calls from her room.

The old brown station wagon had been miraculously resurrected after its brush with deep water, and so, as I guided it home that steamy afternoon, I thought about my summer. I had come to see, if nothing else, that to know someone—yes, to love someone—you had to be willing to dive under the surface and risk hitting your head on the bottom. Love had its risks.

And I was also coming to see that for most people, Lillian included, floating along the surface was enough. Not for me, though.

I bumped down the driveway, still full of holes left by the storm, and pulled in beside Lillian's now permanently parked car. Daddy and Cal were probably stationed on the deck, already sipping on something and discussing the day's work, or maybe the gossip a waterman had passed on. Or maybe they were talking about tomorrow, because tomorrow had become an option for them both.

I would join them later. But first, I turned to the house, to my little room on the third floor. Here I hoped to find some solace, and maybe some understanding about the nature of humanity—maybe even a hint or two about the nature of sisters who look like angels but have hearts of stone. In the stories of Charlotte and Emily, surely there had to be a few clues—a few insights.

Outside, the final red fingers of the sun were overtaking the silver of the water. As I began packing for school, I found myself looking forward—genuinely looking forward—to college, to the new world it presented. I looked forward to moving away—not moving on.

My story was beginning to emerge through the individual streams of everyone else's, melding together into one body, one creek. I wanted to write the story down, make the leap from Catherine to Bronte, but I found it hard to capture its realness—it was hazy and surreal, flowing just beyond my grasp.

So I tried to start with what is real and always there: the Creek. The Creek reflects the life above it, but it also hides so much life below the surface. I would never leave it, and it could never leave me.

Somewhere, in all that water, flowing as far along as I could ever see, is my story.

I'll fish it out—eventually.

Acknowledgements

This novel is the product of much doubt and labor and, consequently, of many fits and starts. Without the encouragement and determination of my writing and teaching friends, I am quite sure I would still be rewriting the opening, if I hadn't already abandoned the project long ago.

I must express my great gratitude to my original writing group friends: Lavinia Edmunds, Lauren Small, and Brucie Jacobs, whose spirited discussions of our work made us all more committed and better writers and readers. I must also thank Anne Heuisler, Joyce Brown, and Ellen Abbott, who generously committed their time and support to this endeavor, especially in the early stages.

Back Creek has been read by lots of people. I thank David Chestnut, who provided the first editing of the work, for his insightful comments.

I owe a great deal to my agent and subsequent publisher, Bruce Bortz, and his assistant Harrison Demchick. I thank them for their belief in this book, and for their extensive help in making it what it became, as well as for their advice and encouragement.

Several institutions have lent support to my writing efforts. The Maryland Council on the Humanities awarded a generous prize in fiction for an excerpt from the novel, providing not only some financial incentive, but a tremendous motivation to complete the novel. Roland Park Country School, where I have taught for more than a quarter century, has supported my writing work from the beginning, and I am so grateful for the kind encouragement of my colleagues and friends there.

Finally, I thank my family: my husband, Scott; my daughter, Emily; my son, Ben; and my brothers and sisters, for giving me space, time, and their support. I thank my father, Hunter Creech, for having the vision to visualize a house and a life on a marshy peninsula on a deep creek, and for providing the frame for my story. And I thank my mother, Betty Alford, for her part in it all.

English Department Chair at Roland Park Country School, an independent girls' school in Baltimore, since the year 2000, Leslie Goetsch twice has been awarded the school's prestigious Anne Healy English Faculty Prize. Since 2000, she's also served on the faculty of the Student Writers' Workshop, a part of the Maryland Writing Project.

She has twice won grants to further her writing. She won one from the Maryland State Arts Council for the development of this novel. She was awarded a similar grant by the National Endowment for the Humanities.

Before beginning her teaching career in 1982, Goetsch earned an undergraduate degree from Duke University and a graduate degree (MLA) from Johns Hopkins University.

Although she currently lives in Baltimore with her husband and two children, she's a native of Virginia, having grown up in an area much like Back Creek, one of the many deep tributaries that cut through the state. Baltimore has been her residence for more than twenty years now, but like Grace Barnett, the protagonist and narrator of *Back Creek*, Goetsch's heart remains in a smaller community just south of her adopted home town.

She's currently at work on a second novel—this one a coming-of-middle-age-story.

"With a sure hand and a generous heart, Leslie Goetsch lovingly depicts the land, the water, and the inhabitants of Back Creek, a fictional town on Virginia's Eastern Shore, in the summer of 1975. Finely wrought prose, keen observation, and a compellingly authentic voice make this a thoroughly memorable, engaging, and enjoyable read."—**Margaret Meacham, Author of** *Oyster Moon* **and** *A Mid-Semester Night's Dream*

"Starting on line one, the characters burst to life with a vibrancy and truth that are nothing short of compelling. When I finished the book, I felt as if I had lost a friend—I wasn't ready to lose touch with Grace—and I continue to wonder how she's doing."—**Carla Spawn-Van Berkum, Author,** *Children Hungering for Justice*

"Teenage girls will identify with Grace, *Back Creek's* down-to-earth protagonist, as she struggles with family secrets, a boy's mixed signals, and her own uncertainties. Grace's perceptive yet innocent personality makes her a believable and endearing character who will engage readers and have them hoping she can find her way amidst the confusion of growing up."—**Peale Iglehart, 17, Baltimore, MD**

"The journey to Back Creek, a small enclave in Tidewater Virginia where families have lived for generation upon generation, is told by Grace Barnett, the youngest and only functional member of her otherwise dysfunctional family. Her mother disappears from

time to time, ostensibly to care for an ailing aunt, while her father is often at home in a semi-drunken or totally drunken state. Cal, their closest neighbor and Grace's only real friend, is a Vietnam veteran haunted by the war. Except for a mysterious suicide, all seems to be going along as usual until her sister Lillian turns up with unsettling news. The stories of Back Creek will hold your interest from the first sentence to the last and make clear why Grace must ultimately leave the creek she loves. 'Floating along the surface' might be okay for others, but it is not okay for her."
—**Janice Moore, Director of Libraries, Roland Park Country School**

"I loved *Back Creek*! The author beautifully captured the easy rhythm of life in a Tidewater tributary community. The natural setting, combined with a story of self-discovery, kept me reading late into the night. I couldn't stop until I finished."—**Kathy Richardson, Teacher, Prince William County, Virginia**

"A Chesapeake coming of age story whose spunky, bookish heroine, Grace, over one dramatic summer, arrives at a new understanding of her unruly family and a new awareness of her own possibilities." —**Rachel Eisler, former chair, The English Department, The Bryn Mawr School**

"With *Back Creek*, first-time author Leslie Goetsch instantly proves herself to be a writer to watch. In a seductive and assured narrative voice, Goetsch weaves a rich tapestry about a Tidewater Virginia family that, like other equally memorable Southern generational sagas, finds its lifesource in the inexplicability of tragedy and the profound mysteries of the human heart. Carefully observed and deeply felt, *Back Creek* calls to mind the early work of Pat Conroy, as well as Beth Henley's Southern-sisters classic,

Crimes of the Heart, yet manages to stand out all on its own. An accomplished and impressive debut."—**John Rowell, author of** *The Music of Your Life*

"Who is Grace? A daughter, a sister, a friend; a confidante, an acquaintance; a young woman on the brink of everything, and somehow connected to everyone and no one at the same time. Over the summer before college, she learns a valuable life lesson—that no matter how much we love, we can ultimately only control (or even truly understand) ourselves. 'It's not about you, Grace,' . . . but it is."—**Ruth Miller, Mathematics Department Head, Roland Park Country School**

"Grace's voice is realistic, authentic, and dear. She reminded me of myself as a kid, so I found it effortless to slip into her story. Grace's mother (and her mother's family) are intriguingly mysterious (I assume Grace's aunt is meant to echo Bertha in *Jane Eyre*), particularly in the scenes at the farm, which I loved . . . I found myself completely understanding Grace's mom's preference for the stability of the earthbound farmhouse to the tempestuous humidity (and jellyfish!) of the bay . . . I like that Grace is myopic. It contributes to her lack of confidence and creates questions about her self-image. Her myopia also symbolizes so much about Grace—her excessive, even unhealthy (anti-social) reading habits; her naiveté about her family and all its hidden skeletons; the small, sheltered, trapped-in-the-past landscape that limits her vision of the big picture, etc. Of course, there's the added notion of family stories, and how the perspective shifts depending on the speaker's POV. It's important that the father's version of the train meeting is SO vastly different than the mother's . . . This is a lovely, thought-provoking, very readable young adult novel that I think girls will really, really enjoy." —**Aeric Treska, Former High School English Teacher, Lake Placid, NY**

"The setting is as real and vivid as the characters, which is saying a lot. Main character Grace comes alive on the first page, and as she proceeds to grapple with her unique family, she quickly grows up, developing wisdom beyond her years. All of this makes *Back Creek* a compelling 'coming of age' novel for girls and women—and one that I truly loved."—**Jean Waller Brune, Head of Roland Park Country Day School, and District IV Regional Director, The Cum Laude Society**